BOOKS

Simply Learning, Simply Best!

Simply Learning, Simply Best!

伍羚芝 ◎ 中文
倍斯特編輯部 ◎ 譯

倍斯特出版事業有限公司
Best Publishing Ltd.

跟著

偶像劇

的腳步學

生活

英語

會話

Let's Talk in Love

陶行知：

愛情之酒甜而苦。
兩人喝，是甘露；
三人喝，是酸醋；
隨便喝，要中毒。

愛總是引領著生命的前進，
這次就讓偶戲劇裡的愛成就英文學習力吧！

什麼是 *toxic bachelor*?
什麼又是 *metrosexual*??
同性結婚是 *same-sex marriage*???
而我只想 *TV home shopping*!!!
**80** 個愛情偶像劇情境 帶你從愛裡來，英文裡去!!!

# 作者序
Preface

　　你是否和我一樣，都曾在電視機前面守著當紅偶像劇，為一段段淒美動人的戀曲感動到流下淚水；被一句句幽默風趣的台詞逗樂到捧腹大笑呢？

　　還記得那些耳熟能詳、朗朗上口的經典台詞嗎？我們不但能藉由這些台詞得到人生的體悟、學到更圓滑的應對進退方式，現在，我們更可以從英文學習的角度來重溫戀人們在日常生活中的對話和浪漫的枕邊絮語。

　　在偶像劇所帶來的美好時光裡，我們嘗盡戀愛中的酸甜苦辣、陪伴劇中戀人們度過情路上遭遇到的各種阻礙，就像自己身歷其境一樣隨之又哭又笑、談了一場又一場的戀愛。在本書中，我將自己對完美戀情的想望和理想情人的投射編寫成共 80 個情境，藉由出場人物的個性塑造和人際關係連結，交織成連我自己都十足入戲無法自拔的「紙上偶像劇場」。

　　在撰寫本書的三個月內，每當我正在構思哪一段情境要由哪幾位人物出場？出場後又要交給他們甚麼樣的任務時，我筆下的人物就越顯得像是真有其人似地，在我心中出現清晰可見的形象。他們每個人都有自己的個性和適合的崗位；每個人都各有所長、心有所屬。有時我甚至覺得不是我在編寫他們的故事；而是他們在耳邊催促著我幫忙記錄下他們的人生。

　　因此，我可以大言不慚地說自己完成的是一本小說嗎？（笑）我希望能讓讀者在翻開書頁後驚訝於這不只是一本英文學習書，細細閱讀之後更能隨著書中人物的情緒而起伏。能讓你／妳在入戲的同時淺移默化地連帶學習到相關英文知識，我就心滿意足了。

伍羚芝

# 編者序

　　轉開電視頻道，不難發現眾多電視台正同時播送著中日韓台等國的電視偶像劇，也許沒有 24 小時全日候播送，但觀眾幾乎隨時想看都看的到，足見其受歡迎之熱烈程度。

　　偶像劇裡的部分劇情對很多人來說，過於天馬行空，但卻是這樣的劇情叫人心神嚮往，讓人願意每日守在電視機前，享受如癡如醉的片晌一刻。

　　拜全球化之賜，台灣觀眾打開電視便能輕易的接收到各國的電視偶像劇，這更加地凸顯語言的在這個各國大量且迅速交流的時代的重要性，此外，我們也經常聽到語言學習者常問偶像劇中，哪句經典話語的英文如何表達，總怕自己說出口的過於生硬，或者落入台式英文的窘境。如能同時滿足學習者對於偶像劇的興趣，與英文學習之需要，學習各種生活情境中使用到的道地英文，則是皆大歡喜、事半功倍！

　　鑑於此，倍斯特編輯部於本書精心規劃 80 英文會話單元，讓主角們在浪漫卻又實際的情境中的對話，帶領讀者在又笑又哭之餘學習英文，對話內容生動活潑，語言也力求精準道地，在此與各位讀者分享！

倍斯特編輯部

# Part 1

# 經典浪漫橋段

# Part 2

## 超芭樂的誤會…冰釋

# Part 3

# 情轉淡？小三出場？

# Part 4

## 誰都要來參一腳

# Part 5

# 夢想熱血在我心

Part **1**

# 經典浪漫橋段

# 情境 1    同學，可以跟妳一起看課本嗎？

## ⭐ Let's Talk in Love

John, a college **freshman**, is now getting used to the busy yet enriched college life.  As he gets to the classroom today, he finds that he forgot to bring the **textbook** for the course.  It's only ten minutes left for the bell to ring.  It's definitely too late to rush back to the **dormitory** for it.  It would be, he thinks, a pity to **skip the class** for not bring the textbook... So, he summons up his courage, walking toward the girl who has been drawing his attention ever since the very beginning of the **semester**.

大學新鮮人 John 漸漸習慣了上大學後忙碌卻充實的生活，今天他到了課堂上卻發現自已忘了帶上課所需的課本，眼看距離上課鐘響只剩十分鐘，趕回宿舍拿勢必來不及；因為沒帶課本就翹課也很可惜……於是他鼓起勇氣走向他從剛開學就注意到的女同學——Linda…

| | | |
|---|---|---|
| John | Hi, I'm John Miller.  We take the same course. | 嗨！妳好，我是跟妳一樣修這一門課的 John Miller。 |
| Linda | Oh, hi, John.  I know you.  What's wrong? | 喔，嗨，約翰。我知道你，怎麼了嗎？ |
| John | Well, the thing is...I forgot to bring the book with me.  I'm wondering if it's all right for you that we use yours together? | 其實是這樣的……我忘了帶課本，請問這堂課方便跟妳一起共用課本嗎？ |
| Linda | OK, no problem.  You can sit next to me. | 好啊，沒問題，你可以坐在我旁邊的空位。 |

| | | |
|---|---|---|
| John | Thank you so much!  You are a lifesaver! | 真是太感謝妳了，妳救了我一命！ |
| Linda | Come on!  The **professor** won't bite you. | 沒那麼誇張吧！沒帶課本教授又不會咬人。 |
| John | But it would be hard to understand what he talks about without the book. It would be like wasting time sitting here in the classroom. | 可是沒有課本，上起課來便難以理解教授所說的內容，感覺白白浪費了這一堂課的時間。 |
| Linda | Surprisingly you are hardworking than your **appearance**.  Can't really judge a book by its cover. | 沒想到你比外表看起來還要認真耶，看來果真不能以貌取人。 |
| John | I would take that as a **compliment**. May I buy you a cup of coffee, if it's not too sudden? | 我就把這句話當作稱讚囉。如果不會太過突然的話，待會下課後是否可以讓我請妳喝杯咖啡當作謝禮呢？ |
| Linda | You don't really have to do that.  But, I really want to know more about you. That's a deal. | 這就不必客氣了，不過我倒是很想多瞭解你這個人，就這麼說定囉。 |

## ⭐ Some Words to Know

**❶ freshman** **n.** 新鮮人
They met when they were freshmen and married soon after they graduated.
他們倆還是新鮮人時就相見，且一畢業後就結婚。

**❷ textbook** **n.** 課本　字彙連結站　course book
The textbook is as thick as a dictionary. It's really heavy.
這本課本像字典一樣厚。真的很重。

**❸ dormitory** **n.** 宿舍
The dormitory at the university is like my second home.
大學宿舍就像是我的第二個家。

**❹ skip the class** **v.** **phr.** 翹課
You will be flunked if you go on skipping the class.
你再繼續翹課下去遲早被當掉。

**❺ summon** **v.** 鼓起（勇氣）；召喚、傳喚
He finally summoned up his courage to ask for a pay raise.
他終於鼓起勇氣要求加薪。

**❻ semester** **n.** 學期
The new semester will start in two weeks and I have not finished my summer assignments yet.
新學期再兩個禮拜就要開始了，我的暑假作業還沒有完成。

**❼ professor** **n.** 教授　字彙連結站　assistant, assistant professor
That professor likes my final term paper a lot.
那教授非常喜歡我所交的期末報告。

**❽ appearance** **n.** 外表；外觀
We can't judge a person by his appearance.
＝Don't judge a book by its cover.
我們不能以貌取人。

**❾ compliment** **n.** 稱讚、恭維
Are you fishing for compliments?
你正試著得到別人的讚許嗎？

## ⭐ 30 秒會話教室

在課業上有受同學或是學長姐幫忙時，除了真心感謝之外，有機會也
可以買杯咖啡或是飲料表達謝意，這樣除了讓幫助你的人知道你很有
禮貌、會做人，也會拉近你們之間的距離哦！

Q：我可以請你喝杯咖啡嗎？　May I buy you <u>a cup of coffee</u>?

## 情境 2　滾球情緣

 **Let's Talk in Love**

When Helen, as usual, is walking past the **soccer** field to the classroom, a soccer ball is **rolling** from the **players** to her.  One of them seems to **shout** at her but she can't hear him clearly.  She picks up the ball and walks to the player...

Helen 像平日一樣，走過大學的足球場旁準備前往教室上課。這時一顆球從正在練習的球員們腳上滾了過來。其中一位球員似乎對 Helen 大喊了些甚麼話，Helen 聽不清楚，便拿起球走向那位球員…

| | | |
|---|---|---|
| Helen | Here's your ball. | 這是你們的足球。 |
| Raymond | Thank you for taking it **all the way** here.  I was asking you to kick it back to me. | 謝謝妳還親自拿著球走過來。本來是想請妳把球踢過來就好了。 |
| Helen | That's what you were shouting?  The **distance** is too far.  I can't hear you clearly. | 原來你剛剛是要跟我說這個啊？距離太遠了，我聽不清楚。 |
| Raymond | You walk through here to the Fine Arts Building every day.  You are a student of the Department of Fine Arts, aren't you? | 妳每天都會經過這裡前往美術大樓，應該是美術系的學生對吧？ |
| Helen | How do you know that?  I'm Helen, a freshman here. | 你怎麼知道？我是一年級的學生 Helen。 |

| | | |
|---|---|---|
| Raymond | Because I see you every day carrying the heavy **paraphernalia** and walking to the Building. | 因為看妳每天都背著沉重的畫具走向美術大樓。 |
| Helen | You always check out passers-by when you **practice**？ No wonder the ball was out of the field. | 你練球的時間都在注意來往行人嗎，難怪球會踢歪。 |
| Raymond | Actually I was just trying to catch your **attention**. I never thought that I could talk to you like this. | 其實我把球踢過去只是想吸引妳的注意，沒想到竟然有機會能像這樣跟妳對話。 |
| Helen | Seriously, if you want to know me, just walk to me. Don't keep your teammates waiting for too long. | 下次想認識我就直接走過來吧，別讓你的隊友們等那麼久。 |
| Raymond | Oh, you're right. I have to go back for practice. I will formally **introduce** myself to you next time. | 喔，妳說得對，我先回去練球了。下次我會主動向妳自我介紹的。 |

## ⭐ Some Words to Know

**❶ soccer　n.　足球**
The quadrennial World Cup is a very big event for soccer fans.
四年一度的世界杯足球賽對球迷來說是一大盛事。

❷ roll **v.** 滾
A rolling stone gathers no moss.
滾石不長苔。

❸ player **n.** 球員
The teamwork of the players is the major reason for the team to win the champion.
球員之間的團隊默契是這支球隊贏得冠軍的主因。

❹ shout **v.** 大喊
The policeman shouted "Freeze."
警察大喊：「站住。」

❺ all the way **adv.** **phr.** 一路；完全
We went all the way to Kenting by scooter.
我們一路騎機車到墾丁。

❻ distance **n.** 距離
It is a long distance from Taipei to Melbourne.
從台北到墨爾本有很長的一段距離。

❼ paraphernalia **n.** 隨身用具
These are paraphernalia necessary for a painter.
這些是畫家必備的畫具。

❽ practice **n.** 練習
Practice makes perfect.
熟能生巧。

❾ attention **n.** 注意
Please pay attention to what teachers say during the class.
上課請注意聽老師講話。

❿ introduce **v.** 介紹
The host solemnly introduced the guest who was going to make a speech.
主詞人鄭重介紹上台致詞的佳賓。

## 30 秒會話教室

當你在遠處聽不清楚對方所講的話時,可以說 Sorry, I can't hear you. 或是請對方說大聲 Could you speak a little louder? 相反地,如果要確認對方是否聽的到自己的聲音,可以問 Can you hear me?

## Soccer

四年一度的世界盃足球簡直是足球的奧林匹克殿堂,總讓全球足球迷陷入瘋狂,也造就很多如黑珍珠比利、馬拉度納、足球金童貝克漢等傳奇球星。但卻常常有人搞不清楚足球到底叫 soccer 還是 football,尤其是後者從字面上看上去,就一副該叫做足球的意思,事實上這答案既是也不是。此話怎說呢?這就要看你是從哪國人的口中聽到的這個字才能決定它真正的意思。大體上美國、加拿大、或澳洲等美式足球盛行的地方,football 會被拿來指作橄欖球;而英國、歐洲等地稱足球為 football。因此促進世界盃舉辦的世界足球協會的正式名稱(法文):Fédération Internationale de Football Association(簡稱 FIFA),總部設在瑞士蘇黎世,名稱上當然使用 football。有趣的是,據說 soccer 這字是英國人想出來的,但自己卻用 football 指足球。

# 情境 3　畢業舞會

 **Let's Talk in Love**

Raymond is going to **graduate** from the Business School of the college.  He asks Helen to be his date in the **promenade**.  As they, dressed formally, arrive at the prom, the **band** is playing a very romantic song...

Raymond 即將從大學的商學院畢業，他邀請 Helen 當他今晚的畢業舞會舞伴。當身穿正式服裝的兩人抵達非常有情調的舞會會場，現場的樂隊正演奏著浪漫的舞曲…

| | | |
|---|---|---|
| Raymond | May I have an honor of danãng with you? | 我有這個榮幸可以請妳跳一支舞嗎？ |
| Helen | **Certainly**. | 當然可以。 |
| Raymond | You look so beautiful in the **evening dress**. | 妳穿晚禮服的樣子真是漂亮。 |
| Helen | You look great in the **tuxedo**, too. But I think you look better on the soccer field. | 這套燕尾服穿在你身上也很好看，但我還是覺得足球場上的你最帥氣。 |
| Raymond | Remember the first time we talked beside the field?  I was so **clumsy**. | 還記得我們第一次交談的時候就是在球場旁，那個時候的我真是笨拙。 |
| Helen | Actually, I was glad that you talked to me.  It's just a pity that you're going to graduate. | 其實聽到那些話我很高興，只可惜你就要畢業了…。 |

| Raymond | I've **decided** to stay in this ãty for working and playing soccer.　Will you be there and always **back** me **up**? | 畢業後我決定留在這個城市裡一邊工作一邊練球，妳願意一直為我加油嗎？ |

Raymond　I've **decided** to stay in this ãty for working and playing soccer.　Will you be there and always **back** me **up**?

畢業後我決定留在這個城市裡一邊工作一邊練球，妳願意一直為我加油嗎？

Helen　Why don't you just say "Will you be my girlfriend?"

你為何不直說『請妳當我的女朋友』呢？

Raymond　Well, will you?

那…妳願意嗎？

Helen　Would you, dear, please get me a **cocktail** to celebrate our first day being together?

親愛的，可以請你幫我拿杯雞尾酒慶祝我們交往的第一天嗎？

## ⭐ Some Words to Know

❶ graduate **v.** 畢業
President Roosevelt graduated from Harvard University in the United States.
羅斯福總統從美國哈佛大學畢業。

❷ promenade **n.** （高中或大學畢業前夕舉辦的正式）舞會（簡稱 prom）
The promenade is an important ceremony for students to end their school days.
畢業舞會是學生們告別學生時代的重要儀式。

❸ band **n.** 樂隊
It costs a lot for this band to play for a whole night.
這支樂隊一晚演奏下來要價不菲。

**❹ certainly** adv. （回答時）當然；沒問題

"Can you lend me one million dollars?" "Certainly!"

『你可以借我 1 百萬嗎？』『沒問題！』

**❺ evening dress** n. 晚禮服

Every girl wears the most beautiful evening dress for the prom.

每位女孩都穿上最漂亮的晚禮服參加畢業舞會。

**❻ tuxedo** n. 燕尾服

The gentleman wears a becoming tuxedo.

那位紳士穿著一套合身筆挺的燕尾服。

**❼ clumsy** a. 笨拙的、不得體的

Her clumsy refusal hurt that boy's heart.

她笨拙的回絕反而傷害了那個男孩的心

**❽ decide** v. 決定

They decided to move the whole family to Vancouver.

他們決定舉家搬到溫哥華。

**❾ back up** v. phr. 支持

Parents always back their children up.

父母親永遠都是孩子的強力後盾。

**❿ cocktail** n. 雞尾酒

She got drunk over just one cocktail.

她只喝了一杯雞尾酒就醉了。

**30 秒會話教室**

有這個榮幸請你跳支舞嗎？共有以下兩種說法：

1. Do/May I have a pleasure of dancing with you?
2. Do/May I have an honor of dancing with you?

若你已經在跳舞的場合中，那麼只要伸出手對對方說
May I? 就可以了。

##  Prom

在美加地區，高中生的畢業舞會（senior prom）是校園生活一大盛事，許多青少年電影都會將此場景作為其中一幕，如 80 年代的回到未來、90 年代的美國派、2008 年的暮光之城等電影裡，prom 都是相當重要的場景，可以是展現男子自信氣概、搞笑、更重要的是浪漫氣氛。當然，邀請對象不一定得是男女朋友或是曖昧對象，有時也可以只是異性好友。雖然參加舞會的畢業生穿著正式服裝的用意是展現自己成熟變大人的一面，但慢慢的在某些地區，國中也開始辦起畢業舞會（junior prom），相對於高中會選出 Prom King 和 Prom Queen，國中則選出 Prom Prince 和 Prom Prinecess。

# 情境 **4**　忘了帶傘怎麼辦？

 ## Let's Talk in Love

Off work, Tracy takes the **subway** home. It's raining cats and dogs when she **gets out of** the **station**. She, forgetting to take an umbrella with her and not knowing what to do, is planning to raise the bag over her head. Just right at that moment....

Tracy 下班後搭地鐵回家，出了車站才發現外面突然下起了傾盆大雨。忘記帶傘的她看著雨勢不知該如何是好，正準備拿起包包擋在頭上往外跑時…

| | |
|---|---|
| Phil | Miss, hold on a second! Did you **forget** to take an **umbrella** with you? |
| | 小姐，請等一下，請問妳忘了帶傘嗎？ |
| Tracy | Uh, yes. It was quite sunny when I left home this morning. It just keeps raining **all of a sudden**...I was planning to **head** home in the rain. |
| | 嗯…對啊。早上出門時看天氣還很晴朗，沒想到突然就下起雨來…我正準備這樣冒雨回家。 |
| Phil | You will catch a cold. How far is your place from this station? |
| | 妳這樣會感冒的，妳家距離車站大約多遠呢？ |
| Tracy | It's probably a 15-minute **walk** away. |
| | 用走的大約 15 分鐘吧。 |
| Phil | Well, then. I can't let you go home in a rain like this. Here, take my umbrella. |
| | 那我更不能讓妳在這樣的大雨下跑回家了，來，用我的傘吧！ |

| | | |
|---|---|---|
| Tracy | What about you? | 那你該怎麼辦呢？ |
| Phil | That's Okay.  Phil Collins is the name.  I've just left my office **nearby**.  I take the subway from this station.  My place is just somewhere near another station. | 沒關係的，我叫做 Phil Collins，剛從附近的公司下班，從這裡搭地鐵出站後就到家了。 |
| Tracy | You are really doing me a big favor!  I'm Tracy Spark.  How can I return it, please? | 你真是幫了我一個大忙。我叫 Tracy Spark，請問我之後該如何把傘還給你呢？ |
| Phil | I leave the office around this time every day.  I will **await** you right here tomorrow. | 我每天下班差不多都是這個時間，明天我一樣在這裡等妳吧。 |
| Tracy | OK.  Thank you, Phil. | 沒問題，謝謝你，Phil。 |

 **Some Words to Know**

❶ subway 地鐵　字彙連結站　metro
The subway provides the mass a simple and fast alternative for transportation.
地鐵給了人們一種方便又迅速的交通選擇。

❷ get out of [v.] [phr.] 離開
We've worked for 16 hours.  That's enough for today and let's get out of the office.
我們已經工作了 16 個小時，今天這樣夠了，我們離開辦公室吧。

❸ station 車站
Every day Hachiko waited for its owner outside the station.
忠犬小八每天都在車站外等待牠的主人。

❹ forget [v.] 忘記
Don't forget to send out the invitations.
別忘了把邀請函寄出去。

❺ all of a sudden [adv.] [phr.] 突然地
The flowers seem to blossom all of a sudden as the spring comes.
春天來時，花彷彿突然開。

❻ head [v.] 朝；往…出發
He headed straight for the fridge.
他朝著冰箱的方向直直走過去。

❼ walk [n.] 步行距離；步行路程
The station is a 5-miute walk from here.
那車站離這是 5 分鐘的走路路程。

❽ nearby [a.] [adv.] 附近
The supermarket nearby is having sales.
附近的超市正在特價。

❿ await [v.] 等待
The long awaited sequel is now available on TV.
那讓人等待已久的續集現在在電視上看的到。

## 30 秒會話教室

表達<u>雨頭雨勢很大</u>可以說 It's raining <u>heavily</u> outside, please don't go out.（外頭正下著大雨，不要出門。）或是 It's raining <u>hard</u>. You have to take the umbrella.（現在正下大雨，你必須帶傘。）以及經常被誤會外頭正在下貓下狗的 It's raining <u>cats and dogs</u>.（現在正下著傾盆大雨。）

##  MRT, Underground, subway, & metro

世界上多數的大城市多有自己的地下鐵運輸系統，如台北就有所謂的MRT（Mass Rapid Transit，大眾捷運系統），雖然台北捷運並不是全然都地底下，很多重要交通路線和捷運站卻都設在地面以下。不過比起世界第一條真正地下鐵的興建，台北捷運時間上可是晚了133年、最終在各界市民殷殷期待下才建好的。世界上第一條地下鐵是1863年的倫敦地鐵（London Underground），在當地人們稱之為Underground，暱稱為the tube（或the Tube），因為圓圓的地鐵隧道就有如管子，因此我們捷運站稱作MRT station，他們就稱作tube station。美國則稱地下鐵為subway，而這個字在英國反而是地下道的意思。此外，不知你是否有注意到台北捷運公司的標誌上寫著『metro』等字樣？這字其實也是有地下鐵的意思，雖然英美人士也會使用，但多是法國人在用，因為它來自法文的地下鐵Chemin de Fer Métropolitain（直譯意思為大都會的地下鐵，英文metropolis就是大都會的意思），後來簡稱為métro，字母e上頭多了一撇是法文，而metro則是英文寫法。

**Let's Talk in Love**

Rebecca goes **alone** to a restaurant near her company during the **lunch hour**. After she finishes lunch, she is ready to go back and continue her work in the afternoon. When she walks to the **counter** for paying the **check**, she **searches** here and there but just can't find her **purse**...

Rebecca 在公司午休時間獨自到附近的餐廳吃午餐。吃完午餐的她準備回公司繼續下午的工作,到櫃檯結帳時,她在全身上下東摸西找,就是找不到自己的錢包…

| | | |
|---|---|---|
| Cashier | Hello, it is $380 altogether. | 您好,您的餐點一共是 380 元。 |
| Rebecca | Where's my purse? Excuse me. A second, please. | 咦,我的錢包呢?不好意思,請再等我一下。 |
| Cashier | No problem. | 好的。 |
| Rebecca | (To herself) Oops. I seems to come here without bring anything with me. It's almost the time to clock in, and I don't even have a cellphone to call my colleague to bring my purse here... | (對自己)糟糕,我好像甚麼東西都沒帶就出來了,下午的打卡時間快到了,又沒有手機可以請同事幫我送錢包過來…。 |
| Joseph | Let me pick up the lady's tab as well as mine. Here's my **credit card**, please. | 我先幫這位小姐結帳吧,連同我的帳單一起算。麻煩妳,這是我的信用卡。 |

| Cashier | Ok. Sir, please sign your name right here. | 好的，收您信用卡。請在這裡簽名。 |
|---|---|---|
| Rebecca | Thank you, mister. I am so grateful. I'm Rebecca, and you are? | 這位先生真是太感謝你了，我是 Rebecca，請問該怎麼稱呼？ |
| Joseph | Joseph Anderson. Here's my **business card**. | 我叫 Joseph Anderson，這是我的名片。 |
| Rebecca | Thank you. My purse and cellphone are left in the office. I will call you and return the money back to you right after leaving the office. | 謝謝。我的錢包和手機就放在公司裡，等我下班後馬上跟你聯絡並把錢還給你。 |
| Joseph | No hurry. It's no sweat at all. Why don't we meet here tomorrow noon and you pay for the lunch? | 不急，只是舉手之勞而已。不如明天中午換我在這裡等妳請客吧。 |

## ⭐ Some Words to Know

**❶ alone** adv. 單獨
She stayed alone and worked overtime in the office.
她獨自一人留在辦公室加班。

❷ lunch hour  n.  phr.  午餐時間
The company's lunch hour is only 30 minutes.
這間公司的午餐時間只有短短的 30 分鐘。

❸ counter  櫃檯
Mary stands behind the counter and takes orders from customers.
Mary 站在櫃檯後面為客人點餐。

❹ check  n.  （餐廳的）帳單  字彙連結站  tab
May I have the check, please?
我要買單，謝謝。

❺ search  v.  搜尋、尋找
The police sent out 95 men to search for the missing child.
警方派出 95 人去找尋那位失蹤孩童。

❻ purse  n.  錢包（通常指女用）  字彙連結站  wallet
My purse was stolen last night.
我的錢包昨晚被偷了。

❼ clock in/out  v.  phr.  打卡
She clocks in at 9 every morning.
她每天準時早上 9 點打卡進公司。

❽ credit card  n.  phr.  信用卡
Credit cards can be very convenient tools while they can also put you in deficit.
信用卡可以是方便的工具，也可以害人消費透支。

❾ business card  n.  phr.  名片
Businessmen always carry business cards with them.
商務人士總是隨身攜帶名片。

## 30 秒會話教室

在英國餐廳裡的帳單會用 bill 這個字，但美國人與加拿大人則用 check。因此要結帳的時候可以說 Can I have the check, please? 或是 I'd like the check, please. 最簡短的則是說 Check, please. 就可以了。此外，tab 也有餐廳帳單的意思哦。

## Business card

中國老祖先擅發明，據說連名片的發明都早了西洋一千多年。中國至少在秦朝末年，那時漢高祖劉邦還沒揭竿起義，仍只是個亭長（類似今日的派出所所長），接見各路人士，就會用到名片，當時叫做謁（音同葉），即將名字等基本資料寫再竹片上遞出去；而西方據說是在十五世紀才出現，當時稱作 visiting card，用來唱名，宣告到訪目的，也會被放在貴族宅邸門前作為求見的請函，當然宅邸主人可以依上面書寫的頭銜與求見目的來決定是否接見。名片的交換則在 17 世紀開始，但此時名片還是一種身分地位的象徵，只有貴族或顯貴人士才擁有。現在名片則是全民皆有，就連樣式設計、材料都很新穎，甚至還有立體名片和透明名片！

# 情境 **6**　計程車等等我

 **Let's Talk in Love**

Gill takes a cab to the **client's** company.  After she gets out of the taxi, she finds that her **laptop** is left on the seat.  She needs it to present her **proposal** to her client.  But the taxi drives away without any stop.  She, in such a hurry, asks a favor from a man who's parking at the **roadside**.

Gill 搭乘計程車抵達客戶的公司，一下車就發現自己要向客戶做提案用的筆記型電腦還放在坐位上，可是計程車正頭也不回地開走，她連忙請前方一位正在路邊停車的男子幫忙…

| | | |
|---|---|---|
| Gill | Mister!  Please stop that taxi!  Now! | 先生！請你幫我叫住那輛計程車！快！ |
| Owen | Too late.  It has turned left into the **boulevard**.  What's wrong with it, miss? | 來不及了，車子已經左轉到大馬路上了，小姐怎麼了嗎？ |
| Gill | I left my stuff in the taxi!  What should I do? | 我的東西忘在車上了！怎麼辦？ |
| Owen | That's simple.  Just make a call to the taxi company and ask them to **assist** you. | 很簡單啊，只要打電話到計程車行，請他們幫妳留意就行了。 |
| Gill | But I don't remember the taxi's **plate** number.  What if it's taken by other passengers? | 可是我完全沒注意那輛計程車的車號，要是途中被其他乘客拿走怎麼辦？ |

| | | |
|---|---|---|
| Owen | Is it something important that you miss? | 妳忘的是很重要的東西嗎？ |
| Gill | I'll have to present my proposal to a very important client in this building after 30 minutes, but all the files are in the laptop that I forgot! | 我 30 分鐘後要在這棟大樓裡跟重要客戶做提案簡報，可是資料都在我忘了拿的筆記型電腦裡了！ |
| Owen | That's really **awful**. We might be able to **catch up with** it if we start chasing now. But can you **recognize** the taxi among other cars? | 那真的挺糟糕的！現在追過去或許還來的及，但是妳有把握能在車陣中認出那輛計程車嗎？ |
| Gill | I remember how the driver looks and the car model. | 我還記得司機的長相和車款。 |
| Owen | Get in my car then! | 那妳快上我的車吧！ |

## ⭐ Some Words to Know

**❶ client** **n.** 客戶
Insurance agents have to go out and visit clients every day.
保險業務員每天都要外出拜訪客戶。

**❷ laptop** **n.** 筆記型電腦 (字彙連結站) notebook
This is the latest laptop. And it's pink!
這是最新型的筆電，而且是粉紅色的！

❸ proposal **n.** 提案
Her proposal was turned down by the company.
她向公司提出的提案不被採納。

❹ roadside **n.** 路邊
We stopped at a roadside café for coffee.
我們停在路邊的咖啡廳喝咖啡。

❺ boulevard **n.** 林蔭大道、大馬路
We strolled along the boulevard.
我們沿著林蔭大道漫步。

❻ assist **v.** 協助、幫助
My job is to assist you in designing the museum.
我的工作就是要協助你設計這間博物館。

❼ plate **n.** 車牌
The car sped off so quickly that I didn't get a good look at its plate number.
那輛車開得太快，我來不及看清楚車牌號碼。

❽ awful **a.** 極糟的
His handwriting is awful.
他的字寫的糟透了。

❾ catch up with **v.** **phr.** 趕上
I finally caught up with the last train of today.
我總算趕上了今天的最後一班火車。

❿ recognize **v.** 認出、識別
It has been years that we haven't met each other. I almost cannot recognize you.
好幾年不見，我幾乎快認不出你來了。

## 30 秒會話教室

當我們對他人的遭遇感到遺憾時，可說 Oh, that's too bad. 或是 How awful! 以及 It's terrible to hear that you didn't pass the exam.（你沒通過考試真是太可惜了。）

## Taxi & Cab

現在英文中，taxi 與 cab 都可以用來指計程車，因為這兩個字都源於計程車 taxicab，後來大家慢慢多只用 taxi 或是 cab；而 taxi 從 taximeter 而來，意指車資指示器；cab 原意則為駕駛室或座位空間。計程車司機除了叫 taxi driver 外，還有個不正式的說法：cabbie（或 cabby）。在美國電影中我們常看到司機與乘客之間會隔著透明板子或是鐵網，中間開個遞車資的小窗口，這一方面讓乘客保有隱私，一方面也可避免司機載到圖謀不軌、欲搶劫的歹徒時，可保護自己。此外，並不是所有國家的計程車都像美國、台灣隨招隨停，很多東亞國家地區如日本、新加坡、香港都還像台灣一樣採街道巡迴攬客的方式，但很多歐洲國家如英國、德國、法國都採招呼站的方式，也就是乘客得先到招呼站，司機才願意載你。此外，國情不同，在英國計程車駕駛的收入可是屬中上，很有意思吧！

# 情境 7　迷路小孩不要怕

## ⭐ Let's Talk in Love

Matt is taking his time enjoying his holiday by himself in a famous **sightseeing spot**.  When he **gets to** an area where there are more **tourists**, he finds a little boy sitting alone on a bench crying.  Looking around, Matt doesn't find his family; he **approaches** the boy...

Matt 到一處知名風景區享受一個人的休假時光。當他來到人潮較多的區域時，發現有一位小男孩獨自坐在長椅上哭泣，四周看起來並沒有小男孩的家人，於是他趨前關心⋯

| | |
|---|---|
| **Matt** | Got lost, boy?  Why are you crying alone here? |
| **Boy** | Boohoo!  I want Daddy and Mommy. |
| **Grace** | Excuse me.  What have you done to this boy? |
| **Matt** | Oh, I saw that he **seems** to **separate** from his parents, so I came to see if I could do something about it.  Do I look like a bad guy? |
| **Grace** | I'm really sorry.  I might **get you wrong**.  Let me try.  Where's your daddy and mommy, little boy? |

小弟弟，你迷路了嗎？怎麼一個人在這裡哭？

嗚嗚～我要我的爸比跟媽咪。

不好意思，請問你要對這個小男孩做甚麼！？

喔，我看他好像跟父母走散了，所以就過來問問能否幫上忙。我看起來這麼像壞人嗎？

真對不起，可能是我誤會了。讓我來試試看吧。小弟弟，你的爸爸媽媽呢？

| | | |
|---|---|---|
| Boy | Boohoo! I ran here to see the **fountain**. When I turned around, Daddy and Mommy are just gone. | 嗚嗚～我剛剛跑過來這裡看噴水池，一回頭爸比跟媽咪就不見了。 |
| Grace | Don't cry. Let's go looking for your daddy and mommy, OK? | 不要哭，讓我帶你去找爸爸媽媽好不好？ |
| Boy | Boohoo! OK. | 嗚嗚～好。 |
| Matt | **Impressive**! My name is Matt Hughes. You girls are good at lulling kids. | 佩服！我叫 Matt Hughes，果然還是女生比較會哄小孩。 |
| Grace | That's not true. Men can do this quite well, too. You just don't spend enough time with kids. | 才不是這樣，男生也可以做得很好，你們只是沒有花足夠的時間陪伴小孩。 |
| Matt | At least in this case, you are way better than me. | 至少現在這情況，妳比我厲害多了。 |
| Grace | In for one penny, in for one pound. You come and help. Let's go to the visitor center first. | 好人做到底，你也跟過來幫忙吧。我們先到遊客中心去問問。 |

## ⭐ Some Words to Know

**❶ sightseeing** 🄝 觀光
We had not time to go sightseeing in Prague.
我們沒時間在布拉格觀光。

❷ spot **n.** 旅遊勝地
Every spot in Taiwan is so packed with tourists on every holiday.
每到假日，全台灣的各大旅遊勝地都擠滿了出遊的人潮。

❸ get to **v.** **phr.** 抵達；到
Call me when you get to Kyoto.
你到京都時打電話給我。

❹ tourist **n.** 觀光客
The famous sightseeing spot is full of tourists every day.
那著名的觀光景點每天充滿了觀光客。

❺ approach **v.** 接近；靠近
If you look out of the window on the left of the bus, you'll see we are approaching the Notre Dame.
如果您現在從巴士左手邊的川窗戶往外看，你會看到我們正慢慢接近聖母院。

❻ seem **v.** 似乎
She seems not content with the gift from her boyfriend.
她似乎對男朋友送的生日禮物不太滿意。

❼ separate **v.** 分開
The teacher always tries to separate the two infamous troublemakers.
老師總是試著將那兩個惡名昭彰的麻煩製造者分開。

❽ get someone wrong **v.** **phr.** 誤會某人
I am sorry that I got you wrong.
我很抱歉我誤會你了。

❾ fountain **n.** 噴水池
People throw coins into the fountain for making a wish.
人們將零錢投進這座噴水池許願。

❿ impressive **a.** 令人欽佩的；讓人印象深刻的
The speech given by the president is impressive.
總統的這場演講給人留下深刻的印象。

## 30 秒會話教室

In for a penny, in for a pound. 就是我們中文所謂的「一不做,二不休」,也可引申為乾脆好人做到底的意思。

# Fountain

情境中,小男孩為了看 fountain,因而和家人走失;fountain 有時真讓人覺得不可思議,看著水不斷對抗地心引力,往上噴出,彷彿充滿的生命力與自由意志,不甘受困作一攤死水,極欲掙脫一樣。噴泉的起源有人說早在西元前 6 世紀左右的巴比倫(Babylon)空中花園就有使用,也有人說是希臘時代開始,但確定的是文藝復興時代(西元 14~16 世紀)後,噴泉結合藝術與科技獲得重大發展,而 17、18 世紀時達到巔峰時期,然而並非所有噴泉都打造得美輪美奐,也有紀念意義深遠的小噴泉,如比利時首都布魯塞爾(Brussel)有個相當著名的尿尿小童噴泉(Mannekin Pis,建於 1619 年),據說是紀念一名小男孩用尿尿的方式將當時法國侵略軍炸城的引信澆熄而建造,這噴泉還曾受到法王路易十五的加封成為貴族,路過士兵還得向他行禮;至今仍相當受歡迎,雖在小巷弄間,卻是旅客必到景點,每到節慶小童就會穿上應景的衣服,附近商家販賣很多尿尿小童的周邊商品,如巧克力、糖果、鬆餅等,甚至還依他的造型做出裝飲料的容器,而飲料出口的水龍頭就是他尿尿的地方!

英文中的 fountain 不僅指的是人工噴泉,也可指自然的湧泉,此外美國黃石公園的老忠實(Old Fathful)因為噴出的水和蒸氣是熱,這種噴泉則稱作 geyser,不可不辯哦。

# 情境 8   誰是樹上小貓的英雄？

 **Let's Talk in Love**

While Stella is walking on a street decorated with rows of green trees, a few **weak** sound s of meows come to her ears suddenly.  Looking up, she finds a kitten **stuck** on the tree and might fall at any minute.  A **passerby** walks near when she doesn't know what to do.

Stella 走在綠樹林蔭的街道上，突然有一陣陣微弱的貓叫聲傳進她的耳裡。Stella 四處張望，抬頭一看發現，原來有一隻小貓卡在樹枝上，看起來隨時有可能掉下來。她正不知該如何是好，此時有一位路人走近…

| | | |
|---|---|---|
| Gordon | Miss, you've been walking around under the tree.  What's going on here? | 小姐，妳從剛剛就一直在樹下轉來轉去，怎麼了嗎？ |
| Stella | Oh, mister.  You've just come at the right time.  There's a kitten stuck on the tree and can't get down. | 喔，這位先生，你來的正好。有一隻小貓卡在樹上下不來。 |
| Gordon | Let me see.  Yeah.  It looks **terrified**. | 我看看，真的耶。牠看起來嚇壞了。 |
| Stella | Is there any way to get it down.  It may be too late to get the firefighters. | 不知道有沒有方法可以救牠下來，叫消防隊怕會來不及。 |
| Gordon | This tree is not tall and has lots of **branches**.  I'll **climb** up to save it. | 這棵樹不高，樹枝又很多，我爬上去救牠吧。 |

| Stella | Really? Isn't that too **risky**? | 真的嗎?這樣會不會太危險了? |
| Gordon | I was good at climbing trees when I was little. You have to catch it when I hand it to you. | 我小時候可是爬樹高手呢！等我抓到牠的時候妳可要在樹下接好喔。 |
| Stella | OK. I got it. Mister, you are a hero. | 好。我接到了！先生你真是位英雄！ |
| Gordon | Much **obliged**, thank you. How's the kitten? | 實在不敢當，謝謝妳。倒是小貓沒事吧？ |
| Stella | I'm taking it to the **vet** for **examination**. | 我這就帶牠去獸醫那裡檢查看看。 |

## ⭐ Some Words to Know

**❶ weak** `a.` 虛弱的
Women who have just delivered a baby are weak.
剛生產完的婦女身體都很虛弱。

**❷ stick** `v.` 被⋯困住（stick, stuck, stuck）
He's got stuck in his old thinking and can't get out of the box.
他被困在自己的舊有觀念裡，無法跳脫框架思考。

**❸ passerby** `n.` 行人（注意：複數為 passersby）
There are many passerby walking on streets in Taipei.
台北街頭有許多行人來來往往。

**❹ branch　n.　樹枝**
The typhoon broke the branches of trees at the roadsides.
颱風將路樹的樹枝都吹斷了。

**❺ climb　v.　攀爬**
The team has decided to climb Mount. Jade next week.
登山隊決定下周去攀登玉山。

**❻ terrified　a.　受到驚嚇的**
The little girl was terrified by the ghosts on TV.
小女孩被電視上的鬼怪嚇壞了。

**❼ risky　a.　冒險的**
It's very risky to drive in a heavy rain.
在大雨中開車很危險。

**❽ obliged　a.　感激的**
Much obliged for your assistance.
您的幫忙讓我感激不盡。

**❾ vet　n.　獸醫（veterinarian 的簡寫）**
The farmer called the vet out to treat his sick cows.
農夫叫獸醫治療他生病的牛隻。

**❿ examination　n.　檢查；考試**
The evidence is still under examination.
證據還在受檢查當中。

## 30 秒會話教室

當受到別人的稱讚與感謝時，可以用以下說法來表達「不敢當」「過獎了」等謙虛之意。如 Much obliged, thank you.（實在不敢當，謝謝。）Much obliged. It's no big deal.（不敢當，這不算甚麼。）或是 I don't deserve your praise.（我不值得你的讚美。）

## Cats

貓兒時而冷漠、時而撒嬌、時而兇猛、時而優雅、時而穩重、時而可愛，既讓人憐，也讓人三不五時肝火大動！貓多樣性的個性和可愛逗趣模樣讓牠在世界各地總能擄獲一票死忠貓奴，貓不但是家裡的寵物或是重要的陪伴，也是很多作家的靈感來源，20世紀英國重要詩人艾略特(T. S. Eliot)就很喜愛把貓的形象寫進他的詩中，近期我們也會三不五時看到書坊、報章雜誌出版關於貓題材的書籍文章，這些主人總是一邊抱怨著貓的任性和國王皇后脾氣、卻又同時展現愛到深處無怨尤。而貓跟人類的關係是從甚麼時候開始的呢？專家們相信貓與人類發展關係最早的時間可追朔西元1萬年的肥沃月灣，也就是今天波斯灣到地中海東岸一帶的兩河流域，而真正成為家裡的成員的時間點恐怕未有定論，多數認為是西元前3600年的埃及，但最新考古證據顯示西元前9500年的地中海小島賽普勒斯就有人將八月大的小貓放在牠專屬小墳墓中，一同與旁邊人類朝西邊安放，因為貓有著終其一生守護單一地域的特性，且更不地中海多數島嶼的原生物種，所以證明此時人類與貓之間已經有一定特殊且親密的關係，極有可能是豢養的開始。

# 情境 9　PUB 遇上美女

 **Let's Talk in Love**

Ivan and several good friends go to a pub on a weekend night for some drink. He finds a woman that is just his type. **Urged** by the friends, he takes the **courage** and walks to the girl...

Ivan 跟幾位哥兒們在周末的夜晚到 pub 去喝酒。不久他就發現 pub 裡有一位女孩正是他所喜歡的類型。在朋友的慫恿下，他決定鼓起勇氣向那位女孩搭訕…

| | | |
|---|---|---|
| Ivan | Hey, how's it going? It's really hot here tonight. | 哈囉，妳好！今晚這裡真熱啊！ |
| Jessica | I don't think so. | 我不這麼覺得耶。 |
| Ivan | Well, are you alone? With friends? | 嗯…妳一個人嗎？還是跟朋友一起來的？ |
| Jessica | I just **broke up** with my boyfriend, or **ex-boyfriend**, so I'm here for **drinking**. | 我剛跟男友分手，或說是前男友，於是來這裡喝幾杯酒。 |
| Ivan | Whatever it is, he didn't know to **treasure** you. Here! **Cheers** to you. | 無論如何，一定是他不懂得珍惜。來，我敬妳。 |
| Jessica | Why do you think so? | 你為什麼會這樣想呢？ |
| Ivan | If I were he, I would definitely treasure a beautiful girl like you. | 像妳這麼漂亮的女生，如果是我一定會好好珍惜。 |

| Jessica | You might say this to every girl, but I am in a better **mood**.  Thanks. | 雖然你可能對每個女生都這麼說，不過聽完我的心情確實有比較好了，謝謝你。 |
| Ivan | It's not quite healthy to drink **sorrow** down.  Maybe we can go jogging or have breakfast in the morning sometime.  That will make you feel better. | 藉酒澆愁不太健康，有機會的話我還可以帶妳去晨跑或是吃頓早餐，讓妳心情更好。 |
| Jessica | Haha!  You are really good at **comforting** girls. | 呵呵，你真是個很會安慰人的男生。 |

## ★ Some Words to Know

**❶ urge** [v.] 慫恿
His friends urge him to join the navy.
朋友慫恿他去加入海軍。

**❷ drink** [v.] 喝（酒） [n.] (U) 酒
He never drinks before driving.
他在開車上路前從不喝酒。

**❸ courage** [n.] (U) 勇氣
It requires great courage to admit one's mistake.
承認自己犯了錯需要很大的勇氣。

❹ ex-boyfriend **n.** 前男友
They broke up because her ex-boyfriend beat her.
因為她的前男友對她動粗，所以兩人才分手。

❺ break up **v.** **phr.** 分離
The admirable screen couple broke up in a flash last week.
那對令人稱羨的銀色情侶竟然在上周閃電分手了。

❻ cheers **int.** 乾杯
Merry Christmas!  Cheers!
聖誕節快樂！大家乾杯！

❼ treasure **v.** 珍惜
She treasures the family ring passed from her mother.
她很珍惜母親送給她的家傳戒指。

❽ mood **n.** 心情
Last night I was in bad mood.
昨晚我的心情不太好。

❾ sorrow **n.** (U) 悲傷
He tried to drink sorrow down, but he just couldn't forget sorrows.  Instead, he lost the health.
他整天借酒澆愁，不但沒有忘記煩惱，反而賠上了健康。

❿ comfort **v.** 安慰、安慰
It's comforting to be with my friends.
跟我的朋友們在一起就能得到安慰。

## 30 秒會話教室

當你不同意對方的想法時，你可以直接回應他 I don't think so.（我不這麼覺得。）如果你覺得這樣回答太過於直接的話你也可以說 I am not so sure.（我不確定耶。）

## Pub & Bar

Pub 其實是 public house 的簡稱，言下之意就是開放給大眾、全民皆可進入的酒館，歷史可回朔到羅馬時代的酒館（tarven），在英國、愛爾蘭等地 pub 可是相當重要的文化之一，在當地許多地方甚至是社區的重要聚會場所，英國不但有文人認為世間的任何樂趣都比不上人類重大發明 pub 所帶來的樂趣，更有政府官員認為這種酒館就是 the heart of England，由此足見 pub 在英國人心中的地位。那 bar 呢? Bar 在中文一樣多翻譯為酒吧，原意其實是『吧檯』，不知眼尖的讀者是否有發現吧檯其實是音譯加上一點中文輔助解釋？而酒保或調酒師英文則是 bartender（即照料吧檯的人）。Bar 後來則擴大指整間酒館。Bar 通常是指販賣酒精飲料和一些餐點的裝潢酒館，不同於 pub 的隨意、給人家的感覺，bar 的場合稍微正式，有人認為如果是要約會，就應該去 bar；要找酒伴，就得去 pub。

# 情境 10 幫女生看手相

## ⭐ Let's Talk in Love

Wesley and several **colleagues** are discussing the last night's fortune-telling show on TV.  When they are talking about **palm** reading, Olivia, a colleague from another department, seems interested and comes near...

Wesley 在公司的午休時間和幾位同事聊起了昨晚所看的命理節目話題，正當他們聊到手相時，另一個部門的女同事 Olivia 似乎感到很有興趣，便走了過來…

| | |
|---|---|
| Olivia | I heard that you are talking about palm reading. |
| | 我聽到你們在聊手相啊？ |
| Wesley | Yeah, we saw that on a fortune-telling show last night. |
| | 是啊，昨晚在命理節目中看到的。 |
| Olivia | I'm always interested in **divination**, signs, and **numerology**.  Can you tell how my romantic relationship goes **recently**? |
| | 我對占卜、星座、命理這些事情一向很有興趣，可以幫我看一下我最近的感情運勢嗎？ |
| Wesley | Well, sure.  Let me see your right hand. |
| | 嗯，好啊。請伸出妳的右手借我看一下。 |
| Olivia | Why the right hand? |
| | 為什麼是右手呢？ |

| | | |
|---|---|---|
| Wesley | Because the **palmist** on the show said the left hand **showed** your **innate** destiny and the right hand showed the **acquired** destiny. | 因為節目中的手相老師說左手代表先天；右手代表後天。 |
| Olivia | Can you tell when I will meet the right guy? | 看得出我甚麼時候會遇到對的人嗎？ |
| Wesley | You have strong potential for developing the relationship. Mr. Right is right before you. | 妳的感情運勢很旺，真命天子遠在天邊近在眼前。 |
| Olivia | What are you **hinting** at?  This is not palm reading! | 你這是在暗示甚麼？根本不是在看手相嘛！ |
| Wesley | That's how your relationship line shows.  You would never know if you never try. | 妳的感情線真的是這麼顯示的啊，不試試看怎麼知道呢。 |

## ⭐ Some Words to Know

❶ colleague **n.** 同事
My colleague and I are just close as family.
我跟同事就像家人一樣親密。

❷ palm **n.** 手掌
Father's palms are thick and warm.
爸爸的手掌厚實又溫暖。

❸ recently **adv.** 最近
I haven't visited my parents recently.
我最近都沒有去探望我的祖父母。

❹ palmist **n.** 看手相的人
That palmist knows a person's personality just from reading the palm.
那位手相老師光看手相就可以判斷一個人的個性。

❺ show **v.** 顯露 　字彙連結站　 reveal
It didn't take him too long to reveal great ambition after he comes to the company.
他才進公司沒多久就顯露出很大的野心。

❻ divination **n.** (U) 占卜
Do you believe divination?
你相信嗎占卜？

❼ numerology **n.** (U) 命理學
I'm very interested in numerology.
我對命理學很有興趣。

❽ innate **a.** 與生俱來的
The innate humor makes him a famous comedian.
他與生俱來的幽默感使他成了一位知名的喜劇演員。

❾ acquired **a.** 習得的
Teamwork is an acquired ability.
合作精神是一項後天習得的能力。

❿ hint **v.** 暗示
What is he trying to hint at?
他試著想暗示什麼？

## 30 秒會話教室

很多人對星座、命理等話題有興趣，也會將此拿來當作快速判斷一個人與自己是否契合的指標，因此下面這一句一定要學起來 Q：What is your sign?（你的星座是甚麼？）A：I'm a Scorpio.（我是天蠍座。）

附註：白羊 Aries 金牛 Taurus 雙子 Gemini 巨蟹 Cancer 獅子 Leo 處女 Virgo 天秤 Libra 天蠍 Scorpio 射手 Sagittarius 摩羯 Capricorn 水瓶 Aquarius 雙魚 Pieces

# 情境 11　和心儀同事留下來加班

 **Let's Talk in Love**

It is now past the regular working hour.  After buying light meal for dinner, Wesley is heading back to his desk to **continue** his work.  Most colleagues have left.  However, Wesley notices Olivia of another department stays in the office.

公司下班時間過後，Wesley 到附近買了簡便的晚餐準備回辦公桌前繼續加班。在同事們都走得差不多的公司裡，Wesley 看到另一個部門的 Olivia 也還在公司裡⋯

Wesley　Olivia, why are you still here?

Olivia　Oh, it's you.  The **supervisor** of our department said at the last minute that he wants to see the **shipment** of the last five years, so I have to stay and prepare for him.

Wesley　We are **in the same boat**.  When do you **assume** you will finish it?

Olivia　By myself...I'll be in luck if I can do it by eleven.  That's why I don't have dinner tonight.

Wesley　**Overwork** and no dinner would make **ill** your health.  You can have my hamburger.

Olivia，妳怎麼還在這？

喔，是你啊。我們部門的主管臨時說明天就要公司近五年來的出貨資料，所以我今晚要留下來整理給他。

我們真是同病相憐。妳預計要多久才做的完？

我一個人整理，11 點前能做完就要偷笑了，所以我今天不吃晚餐了。

工作過勞又不吃晚餐會弄壞身體的，我這份漢堡給妳吃吧。

| Olivia | You, too, have to stay and work **overtime**, right?  How about your dinner? | 你不是也要留下來加班嗎？那你的晚餐怎麼辦？ |
| Wesley | I have bought some extra fries and fried chicken, plus my job will be done in an hour. | 我有多買一些薯條和炸雞塊，而且我的工作大約再一個小時就能完成了。 |
| Olivia | I **envy** you for that.  It will be just me alone in the office after you leave. | 真羨慕你，等你走後公司裡就剩下我一個人了。 |
| Wesley | Don't be silly!  No way will I **leave** you alone.  Once my job is done, I will come to help you | 別傻了！我怎麼可能會放著妳一個人不管呢？等我的工作完成後就來幫妳。 |
| Olivia | Thank you!  It's so nice of you. | 謝謝你！你真好！ |

## ☆ Some Words to Know

❶ continue **v.** 繼續
Let's continue on the oil painting which was left unfinished last week.
讓我們繼續畫上周未完成的油畫。

❷ supervisor **n.** 上司；管理者
The new supervisor of our department looks so handsome.
我們部門新來的上司看起來好帥。

❸ shipment **n.** (U) （準備運送的）貨物；出貨
When will the first shipment arrive?
第一批出貨甚麼時候到？

❹ in the same boat **phr.** 同病相憐
You and I are in the same boat, having the allergy for pollen.
我和你同病相憐，都對花粉過敏。

❺ assume **v.** 認為
I assume your English is good since it's your major.
既然英文是你的主修，我想你的英文一定很好。

❻ overwork **n.** 過度工作、過勞
Many office workers in Japan are killed by overwork.
在日本有許多上班族過勞而死。

❼ ill **a.** 生病的、不健康的
She felt ill so she went home.
她覺得不舒服所以回家了。

❽ overtime **adv.** 加班
The employees in this company are asked to work overtime every day.
這間公司的員工被要求每天加班。

❾ envy **v.** 羨慕
Sophie envy that her brother is better at sports than her.
Sophie 很羨慕她的哥哥比她會運動。

❿ leave **v.** 遺棄、丟下
Some mean owners abandon their pets on the street.
一些狠心的飼主把不要的寵物直接遺棄在大街上。

## 30 秒會話教室

Don't be silly. 別傻了。可以表達叫人少做白日夢了、回到現實來的心情。也可以用在對方將事情往自己身上攬時，表達「別傻了，我怎麼捨得讓你那麼做呢？」的情緒。

## Overtime Working & System of Job Responsibility

加班在台灣似乎是很常見的現象，對資方而言應該很希望加班是項全民運動，但對勞工而言，加班等於犧牲自己和陪伴家人的時間。根據行政院勞工委員會資料整理，比較亞洲國家台灣、韓國、日本、新加坡，以及美國、加拿大、法國、德國、英國等歐美國家，發現整體而言，亞洲國家的工作時數大大超過歐美國家，台灣更是榮登榜上前三名。這幾個亞洲國家工時介於 2,100～2,402 小時，而歐美國家勞工一年僅工作 1,413～1,787 小時。雖然工作時數長，但台灣勞工加班卻有 70 萬人左右沒領加班費，其中一大原因是老闆說是責任制，這時或許有人會納悶責任制（system of job responsibility）不是從國外引進？怎麼國外工作時數仍是這麼還是遠低我們？這是因為一知半解知識的誤用，或是該說濫用，以規避付加班費給勞工。責任制相對於時間制，上下班是不打卡的，而非國內公司多現行的『上班打卡制、下班責任制』。

# 情境 12   新鄰居好帥！

## ⭐ Let's Talk in Love

Zoe hears from the **doorman** that the apartment building has a new comer **lately**, and he's a young handsome guy. **Being used to** greeting new neighbors, Zoe, **bashful** but exãted, goes to his apartment, A on the 16th floor, to give him a welcome.

Zoe 聽大樓管理員說這幾天搬來了一位新住戶，而且是個年輕英俊的帥哥，本來就習慣會跟新鄰居打聲招呼的 Zoe 聽了，也不免帶著既害羞又期待的心情到對方所住的 16 樓 A 座電鈴，準備歡迎對方搬進這棟大樓…

| | | |
|---|---|---|
| Zoe | Hi, I'm Zoe Kendrick. I live at B on the 14th floor. Just **drop by** and say hello. | 嗨，你好。我叫 Zoe Kendrick，是 14 樓 B 座的住戶，過來跟你打聲招呼。 |
| Trevor | Oh, hello. I'm Trevor Davis. | 喔，妳好，我是 Trevor Davis。 |
| Zoe | This is an apple pie I've just baked myself. I hope you will like it. | 這是我自己烤的蘋果派，我希望你會喜歡吃。 |
| Trevor | Wow! You are so **generous**. Let me get a **plate** for it so you can keep your own plate. Please come in. | 喔，妳真是大方，我找個盤子裝起來，好讓妳把妳的盤子帶回去，請進。 |
| Zoe | You don't have many things in your apartment. | 你房子裡的東西不多耶。 |

| | | |
|---|---|---|
| Trevor | Yup. 'Cause I live here alone. Sorry about the **mess** in here. I've just moved in and not got them **sorted** yet. | 對啊，因為我只有一個人住。不好意思，剛搬過來東西還沒整理好，裡面有點凌亂。 |
| Zoe | Alone? Will your girlfriend come and help you? | 一個人住？你的女朋友會過來幫忙整理嗎？ |
| Trevor | I'm **single** now. Here. I've washed your plate. Thank you. Do you want some coffee? | 我目前是單身，來，我把妳原本的盤子洗好了，謝謝妳。要不要順便泡杯咖啡給妳喝？ |
| Zoe | Don't worry about it. I should go. Just let me know **anytime** you want to have some more apple pies. | 不用麻煩了，我該走了。如果還想再吃蘋果派的話隨時跟我說。 |
| Trevor | No problem. Thanks a lot, new neighbor. | 沒問題，謝謝妳，新鄰居。 |

## Some Words to Know

❶ doorman **n.** 門房、警衛

As soon as I got off the car, the doorman came and helped me with the luggage.

一下車，門房就過來幫我拿行李。

❷ be used to  **v.** **phr.** 習慣於（接 n. 或動名詞）
The cat is not used to its new home.
這隻貓不適應牠的新家。

❸ bashful  **a.** 害羞的  字彙連結站  shy
The bashful boy dares not to greet the classmates.
那害羞的小男孩不敢跟同學打招呼。

❹ drop by  **v.** **phr.** 順便拜訪
We can drop by our grandma on our way to San Francisco.
去舊金山的路上我們可以順道拜訪奶奶。

❺ generous  **n.** 慷慨的、大方的  字彙連結站  kind
That mister is a very generous gentleman.
那位先生是個很大方的紳士。

❻ plate  **n.** 盤子
Please hand me an empty plate.  Thank you.
請遞給我一個空盤子，謝謝。

❼ mess  **n.** 混亂、凌亂
He's been in a mess since deserted by his fiancée.
被未婚妻拋棄後，他把自己搞的一團糟。

❽ sort  **v.** 分類
They sort the wine by grade.
他們依等級將葡萄酒分類。

❾ single  **a.** 單身的
It's really amazing that a beautiful woman like her is still single.
這麼漂亮的女生至今仍然單身，讓人覺得很不可思議。

❿ anytime  **adv.** 在任何時候
You can contact the police anytime you remember any clue about the case.
只要你想起了與案情有關的線索，任何時候都可以跟警方連絡。

## ⭐ **30 秒會話教室**

到別人家做客難免會遇到盛情難卻的狀況，這時可以說 I am fine, don't worry about it.（我很好，不用擔心）。也就是「不用麻煩了」的意思。較口語的說法可以說 Don't bother.（不用麻煩了）。不過這容易給人沒有禮貌的感覺，除了親近的朋友家人以外，建議不要隨口使用喔。

# 情境 13  女服務生打翻飲料

 **Let's Talk in Love**

Chris has an **appointment** with a client in a restaurant.  Chris is early and is looking at the menu.  A waitress who's walking near with a glass of water **stumbles** carelessly, **spilling** it over Chris and breaking the glass into pieces...

Chris 跟客戶約在一家餐廳吃飯。早到的 Chris 正在研究菜單，有一位端著水杯的女服務生走過來時不小心絆倒，將水打翻在 Chris 身上，玻璃杯也碎了一地…

| | | |
|---|---|---|
| Daisy | Oh, gosh! I'm so sorry! | 喔，天啊！真是對不起！ |
| Chris | It's all right.  Are you hurt? | 沒關係，妳沒受傷吧？ |
| Daisy | I'm OK.  I **tripped** over the carpet.  I didn't **mean** to spill the water. | 我沒事，剛剛不小心被地毯絆了一下，我不是故意要打翻的… |
| Chris | **Thank God** it's just water, not soup or wine. | 還好只是水，不是熱湯或紅酒。 |
| Daisy | But, sir, your shirt and pants are all wet.  Let me **dry** them up. | 可是先生您的襯衫和西裝褲都濕掉了，我來幫您擦乾。 |
| Chris | No.  Where's the restroom?  I can do something about them before my client comes. | 不用了，請問洗手間在哪裡？我趁客戶沒來之前先去整理一下就好。 |

Daisy　You have a client?  I can't let you meet him with these **wet** clothes on.

您還約了客戶啊？那我更不能讓您穿著這身濕衣服見客了。

Chris　You don't **happen to** have a man's suit for me, right?

妳該不會正好有一套男用西裝可以讓我替換吧？

Daisy　In fact, we have dryer and iron in our **staffroom**.  Let me show you the way.

事實上，我們店裡的員工休息室裡正好有吹風機和熨斗，我帶您過去吧。

Chris　OK.

好啊。

## ⭐ Some Words to Know

❶ appointment 　n.　約會
I have an appointment with my dentist on Sunday evening.
我禮拜日晚上和我的牙醫有預約。

❷ stumble 　vi.　絆倒、絆腳
Be careful and try not to stumble over the escalator.
小心不要被電手扶梯絆倒了。

❸ spill 　v.　使溢出
Who spilt the juice over the ground?  Now it's attracting the ants.
誰把果汁灑了一地？已經開始長螞蟻了。

❹ trip **v.** 絆倒
I tripped on the root of the tree which stuck out of the ground.
我被突出的樹根絆了一下。

❺ mean **v.** 意圖、打算
I didn't mean to eat your lunch. I was just too hungry.
我不是故意要偷吃妳的午餐的，我實在是太餓了。

❻ thank God **phr.** （慶幸或為某是開心時）感謝上天；還好...
Thank God it's Friday!
感謝上天今天是星期五！

❼ dry **v.** 弄乾
You must dry your hair after washing it, or you will have a migraine.
洗完澡一定要把頭髮吹乾，不然會有偏頭痛。

❽ wet **a.** 濕的、弄濕
Today's rain is too heavy. People get all wet even they use an umbrella.
今天的雨勢實在太猛，即使撐傘還是全身都濕透了。

❾ happen to **v.** **phr.** 碰巧
She happened to sit behind her idol when going to that movie premiere.
去看那場電影的首映時，她剛好坐在她的偶像後面。

❿ staffroom **n.** （學校或工作場合）職員休息室
You can take a break or read some newspaper in the staffroom.
你可以在員工休息室裡小作歇息或看看報紙。

## 30 秒會話教室

當你不小心做錯事情或是搞砸了的時候，可以馬上用以下句子表達自己的歉疚、獲得他人的諒解。如 I don't mean it!（我不是故意的。）或是在後方加上造成誤會的行為，如：I didn't mean to be rude.（我不是故意要無禮的。）其他還有：I didn't 'do it on purpose.（我不是故意要這麼做的。）It was not deliberate.（那不是蓄意的。）

## Tips

小費文化是歐美的特色，因此對很多台灣人來說有時是個很困擾的一件事，一方面我們本來就沒習慣給小費，另一方面就算給，也搞不太清楚到底是個怎樣的給法。首先我們要弄清楚為什麼要給小費。不同於台灣，甚至是亞洲國家，歐美許多從事服務業者的收入多來自小費，其服務單位像旅館或餐廳僅給予很少的小額薪水，如情境中的 Daisy 便是如此。那麼要付多少呢？這其實也沒有定論，以下倒是有個建議供你參考：在美國，為我們短暫的額外服務，如戲院帶位員、幫我們掛外套者、廁所服務生、泊車小弟、門房服務生等一般情況一次大多給一塊美金，而餐廳用餐、品酒師、理髮廳設計師專業服務等則給稅前消費額的 10%~15%（不同於台灣只看到一個總價錢，產品或消費金額會與稅額分開標示）。此外小費也是顧客對服務者的肯定，如果很滿意對方的服務，也可以給多一些。據調查，美國小費給的最大方的是紐約州，平均餐費給 20%小費，最小氣則是阿肯色州，只給 10%。而六成三的美國民眾就算不滿意服務，礙於面子仍會給小費，如果你是 Chris 不小心被服務生 Daisy 潑溼了體面的衣服，你是否還會給小費嗎？

# 情境 14　可以陪我挑禮物嗎?

## Let's Talk in Love

Tracy wants to buy a present for someone, but has no idea what he would like. **Thus**, she asks Phil to go to the department store with her and tries to help her out with the present...

Tracy 想送禮物給一個人,卻不知道男生會喜歡些甚麼。於是她約 Phil 一起到百貨公司去,幫她要買的禮物出主意⋯

| | |
|---|---|
| Tracy | Phil, how do you feel about this watch. Feels like something of good **taste**. |
| | Phil,你覺得這支手錶好不好?感覺很有品味。 |
| Phil | Yeah, it looks good, but are you sure that the person is used to wearing a watch? I don't wear one myself. |
| | 好看是好看,不過妳確定對方有戴錶的習慣嗎?像我就沒有。 |
| Tracy | Well, how about the tie? The thin **check pattern** seems to **go** well **with** every shirt. |
| | 那這條領帶呢?細格紋的圖案感覺很百搭。 |
| Phil | Women likes patterns or something, but men mostly like **plain** clothes. |
| | 女生都喜歡有圖案的,其實男生多半喜歡素色的。 |
| Tracy | And this blue **denim** shirt? I always feel men in these shirts look so **gorgeous**. |
| | 那這件藍色的牛仔襯衫呢?我覺得會穿牛仔襯衫的男生好帥。 |

| Phil | This is great! I want to get one for myself . It says it's the latest **design** for this fall. | 這件就不錯！連我也想買一件。上面寫著這是今年秋天的新款式。 |
| Tracy | You can **try it on** to see if it fits you. His body is pretty much like yours. | 你可以試穿一下看合不合身嗎？他的身材跟你差不多。 |
| Phil | Who has the body like me and is so lucky to get your gift? | 是誰的身材跟我一樣，又這麼幸運可以得到妳送的禮物啊？ |
| Tracy | As the matter of fact, it's for you! I want to thank you for lending me your umbrella so I didn't get home wet. | 其實…我正是要送給你的啦!感謝你上次借我傘讓我免於淋雨回家。 |
| Phil | Can't believe you still remember that! I'm so moved! | 妳竟然一直把那件事放在心上…我真是太感動了。 |

## ⭐ Some Words to Know

❶ thus **adv.** 因此　字彙連結站　therefore, hence
He didn't study hard. Thus he didn't pass the test.
他沒有認真讀書，因此他沒有通過測驗。

❷ taste **n.** 風雅、品味
A man of taste does not follow a fashion blindly.
有品味的人是不會盲目跟隨流行的。

❸ check **n.** 方格圖案、格子布
The check that goes with stripes is in fashion this year.
格子圖案搭配條紋是今年的新流行。

❹ pattern **n.** 花樣、圖案
He is already thirty years old and still carrying a backpack of cartoon.
他已經 30 歲了，還在背有卡通圖案的包包。

❺ go with **v.** **phr.** 搭配
What dressing would you want to go with your salad?
您想要用什麼醬料來搭配您的沙拉？

❻ plain **a.** 無花紋的
Mother wants me to buy a plain silk scarf to go with that evening gown.
媽媽要我幫她買一條無花紋的絲巾，她要來搭配那件晚禮服。

❼ denim **n.** (U) 單寧布；牛仔布
He likes to wear a denim jacket.
他喜歡穿著牛仔外套。

❽ gorgeous **a.** 極好的、好看的
What a gorgeous dress it is!
真是件漂亮的洋裝。

❾ design **n.** 設計、樣式
Some say every living creature is God's design.
有人說每一種生物都是上帝的設計。

❿ try on **v.** **phr.** 試穿
Do you need to try this on? The fitting room is at your right.
請問您需要試穿嗎？更衣間在您的右手邊。

## 30 秒會話教室

到服飾店購買衣服，可以詢問店員：May I try this on? 我可以試穿看看嗎？

## Clothes, Patterns, & Materials

英文中 top 可用來指上衣，褲子當然就是 bottoms（複數）。但就衣服的款式、圖案、以及材料其實是族繁不及備載，礙於篇幅，在此僅提供有關衣服比較常見的字彙：

| Clothes | Materials | Patterns |
|---|---|---|
| shirt 襯衫 | cotton 棉 | plain 素色 |
| T-shirt T 桖 | wool 羊毛 | plaid/tartan 蘇格蘭紋 |
| V-neck V 領 | linen 麻 | check 方格紋 |
| turtle-neck 長領 | ramie 苧麻 | polka dot 點點 |
| sweater 毛衣 | silk 蠶絲 | striped 條紋 |
| blouse 女上衣（胸口常有襯瓣） | leather 皮革 | flowered 花紋 |
| underwear 內衣 | fur 皮毛 | leopard print 豹紋 |
| jacket 外套 | suede 麂皮 | zebra print 斑馬紋 |
| coat 大外套 | nylon 尼龍 | |
| spaghetti strap 細肩帶 | polyster fiber 聚酯纖維 | |
| tank top 背心 | spandex 彈性纖維 | |
| shorts 短褲 | Lycra 萊卡彈性纖維 | |
| pajama 睡衣 | polypropylene 聚丙烯纖維 | |

# 情境 15 電梯停電好可怕

## Let's Talk in Love

Trevor, who's just got into the apartment building, is about to take the **elevator** up. Zoe, a **resident** who's welcomed him before long, also enters the elevator...

Trevor 剛搬進一棟公寓大樓不久。一天他從 1 樓準備搭電梯上樓回家，剛好有一位先前打過招呼的女住戶也進了電梯…

| | | |
|---|---|---|
| Trevor | Good evening, Zoe. You're going to the 14th floor, right? | Zoe 晚安，妳要到 14 樓對嗎？ |
| Zoe | Hi, Trevor. That's right. Thank you. Do you get used to the life here after moving in? | 嗨，Trevor，沒錯，謝謝。剛搬進來還習慣嗎？ |
| Trevor | Everything in this building is pretty good. Why does the elevator stop moving up? | 這棟大樓的環境很不錯……咦，電梯怎麼突然不動了？ |
| Zoe | How come? Will it fall and **crash**? I don't want to die! | 怎麼會這樣？電梯會不會往下墜呢！？我還不想死啊！ |
| Trevor | Take it easy! Let me talk to the doorman through the **interphone**. Hello, Sir? Can you hear me? We are **trapped** in the elevator. | 妳先別緊張，我來用對講機跟管理員聯絡。管理員先生，聽得到嗎？我們被困在電梯裡了。 |

| | | |
|---|---|---|
| Doorman | Don't worry. The **panel** shows it stops at the third floor. I'll get the **maintenance** guys right away and call the fire department to get you out. | 你們不要擔心，目前顯示電梯還停在 3 樓，我馬上找電梯維修人員和消防局過去救你們。 |
| Trevor | Hear that? It will be alright. We will be saved soon. My pocket happens to have some cookies. Do you want some? | 聽到了嗎？不會有事的，我們馬上就會得救了，我口袋剛好有些餅乾，要不要吃？ |
| Zoe | How can you be so calm and **optimistic** when you run into this? | 發生這種事你怎麼還能這麼冷靜樂觀啊？ |
| Trevor | At least I am not trapped in the elevator alone. I have your company. | 至少我不是一個人被困在電梯裡，我還有妳陪伴啊！ |
| Zoe | That's true. It's a **relief** to think this way. Oh, I think I hear something on the other side of the door. | 說的也是…這麼想的確安慰多了。啊！我聽到電梯門外有動靜了！ |

 ## Some Words to Know

**❶ elevator** 🔳 電梯
Some people take stairs, instead of the elevator, as exercise.
有些人不搭電梯改走樓梯以達到運動的功效。

❷ resident **n.** 居民

The residents on this island are quite hostile against outsiders.

這座島上的居民對外來的人充滿敵意。

❸ crash **v.** 墜毀

The airplane crashed and killed 250 passengers.

該飛機墜毀並使 250 乘客喪生。

❹ interphone **n.** 對講機

Average elevators have an interphone in case of emergency.

一般的電梯裡都會配備對講機以便緊急所需。

❺ trap **v.** 困住

The car broke down and we were trapped in the middle of nowhere.

車子拋錨了，我們被困在人煙罕至的地方。

❻ panel **n.** （如汽車儀表等）面板、顯示面板

The control panel is out of function.

控制面板已經壞了。

❼ maintenance **n.** (U) 維修

The old car needs a lot of maintenance.

這老房子需要很多維修。

❽ optimistic **a.** 樂觀的 字彙連結站 carefree

Optimistic people are always passionate about life.

樂觀的人總是對生活充滿熱情。

❾ relief **n.** (U) 慰藉；緩和

Knowing her son was safe from the war, she breathed a sigh of relief.

得知她兒子為從戰爭中倖存下來，她鬆了一口氣。

## 30 秒會話教室

Take it easy.（放輕鬆）、Don't be nervous.（別緊張）、Don't worry.（別擔心）、Chill out.（冷靜）、Don't Panic.（不要驚慌）以上都是在發生意外狀況時可以安撫對方情緒的短句。

## Elevator & Lift

Zoe 一度因受困於電梯而驚慌失措，英文中的電梯有兩種說法：elevator 和 lift，差別在於美國人用 elevator，而英國人使用 lift，因此馬來西亞、新加坡等曾被英國殖民過的地方也都稱電梯為 lift。名稱不同，但指的是一樣的。而你知道電梯是怎麼來的嗎？其實早在羅馬競技場建造時，當時的建築設計師就想設計出這樣的升降裝置，利用來運送猛獸或角鬥士，以增加競技場的效率，而當時是使用奴隸來拉動上下的運輸。似近代電梯的升降裝置的問世則是在 1845 年時發明的蒸氣升降機，到了 1853 年美國人奧的斯（Elisha Graves Otis）設計出安全、能防繩索斷裂而墜落的電梯，電梯至此進入真正現代化的階段。在老奧的斯將家業傳承兒子後，兒子成立的 Otis Brothers & Co.。這家公司仍世界上有關電梯、電手扶梯、自動走道等的最大供應商之一，就連台北捷運路線中很多電梯都是由 OTIS 承攬製作。此外，電手扶梯的英文是 escalator；而自動走道則是 moving walkway 或 moving sidewalk，英國人則稱作 travelator。因為現代電梯多有不錯的防墜落裝置，所以其實 Zoe 大可不用太擔心。

# 情境 16 陪我出席婚禮好不好？

 **Let's Talk in Love**

A buddy who often hangs out with Ivan in pubs is going to get **married** and gladly to see his good friends bring their dates to the **wedding**. So, Ivan **invites** Jessica to the wedding...

常跟 Ivan 一起去酒吧的好哥兒們要結婚了，非常歡迎親朋好友攜伴參加他們的婚禮。於是 Ivan 也邀請 Jessica 陪他一起出席…

| | | |
|---|---|---|
| Jessica | This wedding **ceremony** is so beautiful. It's **decorated** with flowers and pink balloons around the walls. It's like in a **fairyland**. | 婚禮好漂亮，四周都用鮮花和粉紅色氣球來佈置，宛如夢幻的國度。 |
| Ivan | Yeah. The wedding singer and **caterer** they hire are all good. | 對呀！他們請的婚禮歌手以及外燴餐點都很不錯。 |
| Jessica | The moment when the **bridegroom** and bride exchanged the vows before the **priest** was so **romantic**. | 剛才新人在神父面前宣讀誓言的那一刻真的好浪漫。 |
| Ivan | Thank you for attending the ceremony with me. | 謝謝妳今天願意陪我出席婚禮。 |
| Jessica | No, THANK YOU! I really like the air of wedding ceremonies. | 不客氣，我才要謝謝你。我很喜歡參加婚禮的氣氛。 |

| | | |
|---|---|---|
| Ivan | I can't express how I feel, seeing my best friend become a groom. | 看到自己最好的朋友成了新郎，真的有說不出的感動。 |
| Jessica | What's wrong with you?  You want to get married, too? | 怎麼了，你也想結婚了嗎？ |
| Ivan | I do, but that takes two people to work it out. | 想是想，那也得要先有對象才行啊。 |
| Jessica | People say the wedding ceremonies are great **occasions** for finding a date.  You can look carefully if there's any girl that you like. | 人家不是說婚禮是個認識對象的好場合嗎？你可以注意看看賓客裡面有沒有喜歡的人選。 |
| Ivan | I think I've found one.  She's standing right before me. | 我想我已經找到了，她就在我的眼前。 |

## ⭐ Some Words to Know

**❶ marry** `v.` 結婚
My sister is going to marry her boyfriend whom she's been dating with for ten years.
我姊姊要跟交往十年的男朋友結婚了。

**❷ wedding** `n.` 結婚典禮
Every girl dreams about a romantic wedding.
每個女孩都夢想擁有一個浪漫的結婚典禮。

❸ invite **v.** 邀請
My classmate invited me to his place to enjoy his new video game console.
同學邀請我去他家玩新買的電視遊樂器。

❹ ceremony **n.** 典禮、儀式
The ceremony will be held on December 10th.
這典禮將在 12 月 10 日舉行

❺ decorate **v.** 佈置
I decorate my room nicely and beautifully.
我把房間佈置的美輪美奐。

❻ caterer **n.** 承辦酒席、宴會的人
Do you know where to get a highly-recommended caterer?
你知道上哪裡可以找到風評好的承辦酒席業者嗎？

❼ bridegroom **n.** 新郎
The bride, drawing the groom's hand to her, received blessings from the crowd.
新娘挽著新郎的手接受眾人的祝福。

❽ priest **n.** 神父、牧師
The foreign priest has done many altruistic deeds.
來自國外的神父在台灣做了許多善事。

❾ romantic **a.** 羅曼蒂克的
He has prepared a romantic candlelight dinner for his girlfriend.
他為女朋友準備了一頓羅曼蒂克的燭光晚餐。

❿ occasions **n.** 場合、時刻
She seized the occasion to scare him for fun.
她抓住這個機會嚇他取樂。

## 30 秒會話教室

當我們要謝謝對方的某些行為或舉動時，可以用以下的說法，如：
Thank you for <u>your help</u>. 謝謝你的幫忙。Thank you for <u>your concern</u>. 謝謝你的關心。Thank you for <u>loving me</u>. 謝謝你愛我。

## Marriage Vows

相信披上美麗白色婚紗、接受眾人祝福下的浪漫婚禮是很多女孩憧憬，尤其是兩位新人交換結婚誓詞的那刻，更不知殺了多少包台上台下的衛生紙，美國愛情電影也常常出現神父帶領新人交換誓詞的場景，經典誓詞內容通常是：

"I, (speaker's name), take you, (partner's name), for my lawful (wife/husband), to have and to hold, from this day forward, for better, for worse, for richer, for poorer, in sickness and health, to love and to cherish, until death do us apart."

我，（說話者名），娶妳/嫁你，（對方名），為我合法的妻子/丈夫，今日以後，無論順境或逆境、富貴或貧窮、健康或疾病，我都會永遠愛著你、珍惜你，至死不渝。

其實誓詞會因為不同教派而有所不同，多大同小異，但也有將誓詞改為問題，讓神父一一分別問新郎與新娘，不過這樣似乎沒有從對方口中直接說出來的浪漫。

# 情境 17　無名指上的星光

 ## Let's Talk in Love

Raymond has been dating Helen since graduating from the college.　Now Helen is about to graduate, too.　However Raymond always feels Helen has been acting weird these days as she is **depressed** for something.　So, he asks her...

Raymond 從大學畢業就開始和 Helen 交往，如今 Helen 也要畢業了，但 Raymond 總覺得 Helen 最近的樣子都怪怪的，好像有甚麼事情悶悶不樂，於是他開口問道…

| | | |
|---|---|---|
| Raymond | What's wrong with you?　Still thinking about the ring we saw last time outside the **jewelry** store? | 妳怎麼了？還在想上次從珠寶店外面看到的那個戒指嗎？ |
| Helen | What?　Oh, you are talking about the jewelry store on Beck Street?　Yeah, the ring was really beautiful. | 甚麼？喔，你說上次在貝克街上的那家珠寶店嗎？對啊，那個戒指的確很美。 |
| Raymond | You stood and watched at that **display** window for a long while.　You almost had your face on the glass.　You must really want it, right? | 妳那個時候站在櫥窗外面看了好久，臉都快貼到玻璃上了，妳一定很想要對吧？ |
| Helen | **Absolutely**!　But I can only look at it.　After all, it's too expensive.　I am just about to graduate.　Where can I get the money? | 那是當然的囉！但是也只能看看而已，畢竟太昂貴了，我才剛要畢業而已，哪來的錢呢？ |

| Raymond | Da la! I saw you were so **eager** for it, so I went to buy it the next day. | Da la～妳看！上次看妳那麼渴望的樣子，我隔天就跑去買了。 |
| Helen | Raymond, didn't this cost you a 2- or 3-month salary? | Raymond，你…這樣不就花掉了你兩三個月的薪水！？ |
| Raymond | I will find the right time to **propose** to you. But now I just want you to be happy. Please take it. | 我會再找機會向妳做正式的求婚的，目前我只是希望妳能夠開心，妳就收下吧。 |
| Helen | I've been always happy for being with you. Besides, I would still **accept** it even if you didn't buy such an expensive ring. | 跟你在一起我一直都很開心啊，況且你不用買這麼昂貴的戒指，我也會答應的。 |
| Raymond | But, are you not always **moody** for not having the ring? | 可是妳最近不是為了這個戒指一直悶悶不樂嗎？ |
| Helen | I am moody because I am worried about the **job hunting** after graduation! | 我是因為畢業後找工作的事情在煩惱啦。 |

## ⭐ Some Words to Know

❶ **depressed** a. 沮喪的、消沉的
He became very depressed, knowing that he didn't pass the bar exam.
他知道自己沒通過律師考試後非常消沉。

**❷ jewelry** **n.** 珠寶、首飾
That notorious jewelry thief is still at large.
那個惡名昭彰的珠寶大盜至今還沒有落網。

**❸ display** **n.** 陳列、展示
That boss' house has collections from around the world on display.
那位大老闆的家中展示著從世界各地收集而來的收藏品。

**❹ absolutely** **adv.** （口）一點也不錯、完全正確
You are absolutely right! I just went to see a movie yesterday.
你說的一點也沒錯，我昨天正是去看電影。

**❺ eager** **a.** 渴望的
She's very eager to be a world-famous ballet dancer.
她非常渴望能當上世界知名的芭蕾舞者。

**❻ propose** **vi.** 求婚
The way he proposed to her was so romantic that she cried over it for two hours.
他跟她求婚的方式浪漫到讓她為此哭了兩個鐘頭。

**❼ accept** **v.** 接受、答應、（對求婚者）表示允諾
The teacher accepted to let us keep a turtle in the class.
老師答應要讓我們在班上養一隻烏龜。

**❽ moody** **a.** 悶悶不樂、鬱鬱寡歡
How can she get a boyfriend with that mood face?
她苦著那張悶悶不樂的臉怎會交的到男朋友？

**❾ job hunting** **n.** 找工作
How's your job hunting?
你工作找的如何？

## ⭐ 30 秒會話教室

表達「當然」、「沒錯」等意思，只要用以下幾個簡短的英文單字回答就可以了，如：absolutely（完全正確）、indeed（確實）、sure（當然）、definitely（肯定地）、certainly（無疑地），盡量少用帶有諷刺意味的 of course（當然），你也能成為英文口語達人喔。

## ⭐ Diamonds Are a Girl's Best Friend?

璀璨的鑽石其實真的很迷人，對女孩子們更是魅力無法擋，指定結婚戒指非得鑽戒不可，這份熱愛後來甚至發展成一股拜金心理。Diamonds Are a Girl's Best Friend 其實是一首 1953 年經典老歌的歌名，由一代豔星 Marilyn Monroe（瑪麗蓮夢露）在一部電影 Gentlemen Prefer Blondes（直譯意思是紳士愛金髮女郎）所歌唱，裡面一部分歌詞說到：

| | |
|---|---|
| Men grow cold | 男人會變冷漠 |
| As girls grow old | 在女孩們年華盡逝時 |
| And we all lose our charms in the end | 而我們終將失去我們的魅力 |
| But square-cut or pear-shaped | 但不論切割方正或梨狀 |
| These rocks don't lose their shape | 這些寶石都不會變形 |
| Diamonds are a girl's best friend | 鑽石才是女孩最好的朋友 |

在那個對比基尼穿著還有爭議的保守年代，這樣露骨的歌詞很受到大眾注意，不過女孩的魅力不是僅有外表，還有內涵，但只有內涵能經歷時間考驗，在生命河流裡慢慢地散發更多生命光彩。如果覺得男孩子們只看外表很膚淺，而女孩子們在意只愛追逐美麗的膚淺男性，不是也很傻嗎？

# 情境 18 妳看！有流星

 **Let's Talk in Love**

Wesley and Olivia, **privately** having an office romance, decide to go to the mountain and watch the Orionid meteor shower brought by the Halley's Comet. The couple is waiting quietly for the **magnificently brilliant meteors** under the silent night sky...

正在低調地談辦公室戀情的 Wesley 和 Olivia 兩人相約到山上去欣賞由哈雷彗星帶來的獵戶座流星雨。當兩人正在寂靜的夜空下等待壯觀絢麗的流星雨出現時…

| | | |
|---|---|---|
| Wesley | Look! A meteor! | 妳看！有流星！ |
| Olivia | Where? Why don't I see anything? | 在哪裡？我甚麼都沒看到啊！ |
| Wesley | Haha. Here it is! | 哈哈，流星在這裡。 |
| Olivia | What?! A diamond ring?! When... when did you buy this beautiful ring? | 甚麼，是鑽戒！？你…你甚麼時候買了這麼美的鑽戒？ |
| Wesley | Olivia Harper. I **swear** I will love you all the days of my life, **no matter** in bad, in sickness, and in health. Will you marry me? | Olivia Harper，我發誓會愛妳一生一世，不論貧窮或生老病死，妳願意嫁給我嗎？ |
| Olivia | Wow! How do you know I always want a romantic proposal? Of course I do. | 喔，你怎麼知道我從小就嚮往一段浪漫的求婚，我當然願意。 |

Wesley　Maybe I am not the Prince Charming that you've been imagining, but I will do everything to make you happy.

Olivia　This is the most **touching** words I've ever heard.  When our kids ask their Daddy's **proposal**, they will be touched too.

Wesley　Look!  The real meteors come out!  This is a real meteor shower!  It's the most beautiful scene I've ever seen in my life.

Olivia　Let's think about how to tell the office colleagues after we finish watching it.  After all we haven't made **public** our relationship.

或許我不是妳想像中的那種白馬王子，但是我會盡全力讓妳幸福的。

Wesley，這真是我聽過最動聽的一段話，以後如果我們的孩子問起當初爸爸是怎麼求婚的，他們聽了一定也會很感動。

妳快看！流星真的出現了，原來這就是流星雨！這真是我這輩子所看過最美麗的景色了。

等我們欣賞完，再來思考要怎麼告訴辦公室的同事吧。畢竟我們連在一起這件事都沒有公開呢。

## ⭐ Some Words to Know

❶ privately　**adv.**　低調地、不公開地
That superstar keeps what he does privately.
那位大明星的行事作風非常低調。

❷ romance ｎ. 戀愛、風流韻事
Everyone has some romances in his/her youth.
每個人年輕的時候都有些風流韻事。

❸ magnificently ａｄｖ. 壯麗地、宏偉地
The polar lights shine magnificently through the night sky.
北極的極光將夜空閃耀得非常壯麗。

❹ brilliant ａ. 光輝的、明亮的
This five-carat diamond is quite brilliant.
這顆五克拉的鑽石非常光輝明亮。

❺ meteor ｎ. 流星、隕石
Usually it's hard to see a meteor in the sky of cities.
平常在城市的夜空中很難看得到流星。

❻ swear ｖ. 發誓
I swear that I never eat the cookies you left in the fridge.
我發誓，我真的沒有偷吃妳放在冰箱的餅乾。

❼ no matter 不論、不管怎樣
No matter how wealthy or powerful one is, he would never buy time.
不管一個人有多有錢有勢，都沒有辦法買到時間。

❽ touching ａ. 動人的、感人的
I've never heard of such a touching story.
我從沒聽過這麼感人的故事。

❾ proposal ｎ. 求婚
She has accepted her foreign boyfriend's proposal and is moving to the U.S. to start a new life.
她已經接受了外國男朋友的求婚，準備搬到美國展開新生活。

❿ public ａ. 公然的、眾所皆知的
After the clerk was sacked, he made the company's illegal secret public.
那位小職員被開除之後，公開了那間公司違法的秘密。

## 30 秒會話教室

想表達「這是我所～最～的事物」可以套用以下文法，如：This is the most wonderful thing I have ever seen.（這是我所看過最美好的事物），或是 This is the best song I have ever heard.（這是我聽過最棒的歌曲。）

## Shooting Star

流星在口語英文也就做shooting star。流星劃過深邃的暗夜，實在是讓人奪目窒息的美麗瞬間，有個名叫Owl City個人樂團做了一首名為Shooting Star的歌曲，其中一段歌詞如下

| | |
|---|---|
| When the sun goes down, and the lights burn out, | 當太陽西下，光線散去 |
| Then it's time for you to shine. | 便是你展現光芒的時刻 |
| Brighter than the shooting star, | 比流星更亮 |
| so shine no matter where you are. | 無論你在何處，閃耀吧 |
| Fill the darkest night, with a brilliant light, | 讓耀眼的光芒充斥最暗的夜 |
| 'cause it's time for you to shine. | 因為這是你展現光芒的時刻 |
| Brighter than a shooting star, | 比流星更亮 |
| so shine no matter where you are, tonight. | 無論你在何處，閃耀吧，就在今晚 |

其實地球每天都會吸引一堆隕石，但很多是在白天，肉眼無法觀察，因此沒有黑暗的夜空，便無法襯托流星的光芒；當人身處困境時，其實就是淬鍊自我、展現內心自信光芒的最佳時機！

# 超芭樂的誤會

## ···冰釋

# 情境 1　不小心走進女廁

 **Let's Talk in Love**

Wesley and his colleagues go to a dinner party, celebrating their **annual performance goal achieved**. He comes home after the party is over. What awaits him at home is his wife, Olivia, who's just got hot and bothered...

Wesley 下班後跟同事去參加部門慶祝年度業績達成的聚餐。聚餐結束後一回到家，等待著他的卻是氣沖沖的妻子 Olivia…

| | | |
|---|---|---|
| Olivia | You really **disappointed** me. We've just got married! | 你真是讓我太失望了！我們才剛結婚耶！ |
| Wesley | What's going on here? I just went to the department party. You know that! | 發生甚麼事了？我剛剛是去參加部門的聚餐，這件事妳也是知道的啊！？ |
| Olivia | You thought you had told me and could just do whatever you wanted. | 你以為跟我報備過就可以放心亂來了嗎？ |
| Wesley | Do whatever I want? I've been hanging out with the guys. | 我哪有亂來？我一直都跟男同事們混在一起啊。 |
| Olivia | Debby of your department has just called and told me everything. She said you followed her into the **restroom** and tried to harass her! | 你們部門的 Debby 剛剛都打電話跟我說了，她說她一進廁所，你隨後就進來想要騷擾她！ |

| Wesley | Oh, that!  I mistook women's restroom for men's.  I was also shocked to see her in there and ran out right away. | 喔，那是我把女廁跟男廁搞錯了啦！我看到她的時候也嚇了一跳，就趕快跑出去了。 |

Olivia　How come you mistook the restrooms?  Don't they have signs to show men's and women's outside the restrooms?

怎麼可能會走錯廁所！？廁所外面不是都會有標明男、女的記號嗎？

Wesley　That's because the restaurant is of **concise** design.  They even only use **triangle** and **rectangle** to **indicate** the restrooms.  People who go there for the first time certainly can't get a clue.

因為那間餐廳的設計是走簡約風，連廁所外面都只用三角形和長方形標示，第一次去當然會摸不著頭緒。

Olivia　Is that real?

你說的都是真的嗎？

Wesley　Definitely.  If you don't believe me, I can take you to that restaurant tomorrow and buy you a dinner and make you feel smooth, all right?

當然是真的，不信我明天就帶妳去那家餐廳看看，順便請妳吃晚餐讓妳消消氣，好不好？

## ⭐ Some Words to Know

**❶ annual** **a.** 每年的、全年的
Every year the Mid-autumn Festival is like a barbeque party for each family.
一年一度的中秋節宛如全台灣家家戶戶的烤肉會。

**❷ performance** **n.** 業績、成果　字彙連結站　sales
I might get fired quite possibly if my performance doesn't reach the standard by the end of the month.
若這個月底的業績再沒有達到標準，我很可能就會被開除了。

**❸ achieve** **v.** 完成、達到
A party of old grandpas achieved the goal of rounding the island on bike.
一群年邁的老爺爺達成了機車環島的夢想。

**❹ disappointed** **a.** 失望的
Many people are disappointed about many social systems.
許多人都對現今社會的諸多制度感到失望。

**❺ restroom** 廁所、洗手間　字彙連結站　lavatory、toilet
I hadn't noticed that a grain of rice was on my face until I walked into the restroom.
我進到洗手間才發現我的臉上黏著一顆飯粒。

**❻ concise** **a.** 簡潔的
The concise style of the designer begins to draw attention.  Many magazines want to interview him.
那位設計師的簡潔風格開始受到注目，許多雜誌爭相採訪他。

**❼ triangle** **n.** 三角形
She decided to buy the triangle earrings.
她決定買那三角形的耳環。

**❽ rectangle** **n.** 長方形、矩形
Can you help me to arrange these stones around the flower bed and make it into a rectangle?
你能幫我把這些石頭繞著花圍排成矩形嗎？

**❾ mistake** **v.** 弄錯、誤認為…

I always mistake my friend's phone number and call someone who I don't know.

我一直記錯了朋友的電話號碼，打到完全不認識的人家裡去了。

**❿ indicate** **v.** 指示、表明

The index on the panel indicates the car is running out oil.

儀錶板上的指標顯示，車子快要沒油了。

### ⭐ 30 秒會話教室

當我們對某個人的表現感到失望時，可以用下列兩句來表達，如：You really disappointed me. 或是 You really let me down. 你真是讓我太失望了。但這樣的話很重，建議失望完之後還是要好好與對方溝通比較好喔。

# 情境 2    我不是色狼！

 **Let's Talk in Love**

Owen asks Gill, a girl who he just met not long ago, to go to an **exhibition** together.  They take a very **crowded** train to the **destination**.  Gill feels that Owen, standing behind her, is seemingly touching her **hips**, and later she feels again something hard is pushing against her.  Thus, she speaks silently but with rage to Owen...

Owen 約剛認識不久的 Gill 一起去看展覽。兩人搭上了一班擁擠的列車前往目的地，兩人剛站定沒多久，Gill 就覺得身後的 Owen 好像在摸她的屁股，隨後便感覺到有硬硬的東西抵著自己，於是她很憤怒地回頭小聲地對 Owen 說…

| | | |
|---|---|---|
| Gill | Would you please give me some **respect**? Can't believe this is what you really are! | 真沒想到你是這種人，請你放尊重一點好嗎？ |
| Owen | What?  What I really am? | 甚麼事情？我是哪種人？ |
| Gill | You still don't **admit** it?  I have not screamed yet for you helped me. | 你還不承認！我是看在你幫過我的份上才沒有大叫的。 |
| Owen | What have I done?  You totally **confused** me! | 我到底做了甚麼？妳把我搞糊塗了。 |
| Gill | You have not only touched my hips but also pushed me with something strange! | 你剛剛不但摸我的屁股，還用奇怪的東西頂我。 |

| Owen | Something strange?　Oh, you are saying these keys in my pocket, right?　The key to the gate is larger.　It kind of sticks out when put in the pocket. | 奇怪的東西…喔，妳說的應該是我口袋裡的這串鑰匙吧？我家大門的鑰匙尺寸比較大一點，整串放進口袋總是會突出來。 |
| Gill | Well, ...the thing that touched my hips? | 那…那剛剛摸我屁股的是…？ |
| Owen | It should be my hand which acãdently touched them when I was putting the keys in the pocket.　I should apologize for that. | 應該是我伸手要把鑰匙放進口袋的時候不小心揮到的，這我就要向妳道歉了。 |
| Gill | That's OK.　I **misunderstood** you. | 沒關係的，是我誤會你了。 |
| Owen | Thank God you didn't yield "**Pervert!**" or we could only get fun in the police station. | 好險妳剛才沒有大聲叫：「有色狼」，不然我們今天可能就要到警察局去玩了。 |

## ⭐ Some Words to Know

**❶ exhibition**　**n.** 展覽

The exhibition of Salvador Dali is very popular in Taiwan.

超現實主義大師—瘋狂達利的展覽在台灣很受歡迎。

❷ crowded  **a.** 擁擠的
The little boy and his parents were separated in a crowed street.
小男孩跟父母在擁擠的大街上被人群擠散了。

❸ destination  **n.** 目的地
The plane will arrive at our destination, Tokyo, Japan, after ten minutes.
飛機再過 10 分鐘就要抵達我們的目的地——日本東京。

❹ hip  **n.** 臀部
The baby is so cute when his hips dance to the rhymes of music.
看小嬰兒隨著音樂扭腰擺臀真是有趣又可愛。

❺ rage  **n.** 狂怒、盛怒
On knowing her loved car was smashed, she flew into a fit of rage.
得知她的愛車被人砸毀時,她憤怒的不得了。

❻ respect  **n.** 尊重、尊敬
Everyone should learn to show respect to different opinions from others.
每個人都要懂得尊重他人的不同意見。

❼ admit  **v.** 承認
The young brother just doesn't admit he broke the window.
弟弟始終不承認玻璃是他打破的。

❽ confused  **a.** 困惑的、惶恐的
She is so confused about the difficulty she has that she comes to discuss with me.
她對於眼前的難題感到非常困惑,於是來找我商量。

❾ misunderstand  **v.** 誤會
That juvenile was misunderstood to be the thief.
那個少年被誤會成小偷。

❿ pervert  **n.** 色狼  字彙連結站  satyr
If you are harassed by a pervert, you must cry out for help immediately.
如果遇到色狼一定要馬上呼救。

**30 秒會話教室**

如果真的遇到某些很過份的舉動，可以先嚴厲地警告對方 Give me some respect.（給我放尊重一點。）如果對方還是不知節制，那就可以說 Leave me alone, or I will call the police.（快走開，否則我要叫警察了。）

# 情境 3 父母安排相親

 **Let's Talk in Love**

Stella, a pet-lover, **remains** single.  Her mother is more eager to **arrange** a **blind** date for her.  For her mother's sake, Stella shows up with a 'making friends' **notion** in mind.  She doesn't find out her date is the man who has saved the kitten on the tree until she gets there.

喜歡動物的 Stella 目前是單身，比她還著急婚事的媽媽擅自為她安排了一場相親。Stella 看在媽媽的面子上，也抱著交朋友的心態出席。到了現場才發現相親的對象竟然是之前幫忙拯救樹上小貓的男子…

| | | |
|---|---|---|
| Stella | It's you!  Aren't you the man who climbed up the tree and saved the kitten?  What a coinãdence! | 是你！你不是上次幫忙爬到樹上將貓咪救下來的那位男士嗎？怎麼這麼巧！ |
| Gordon | I remember you, too.  The name's Gordon Smith.  How's the kitten going? | 我也記得妳！我叫 Gordon Smith。上次那隻小貓後來還好嗎？ |
| Stella | I'm Stella Johnson.  I took it to the vet and had it examined.  It was just a little **frightened**.  I took it home and keep it. | 我是 Stella Johnson。我當天帶牠去獸醫那裡診斷，只是有點受到驚嚇，我把牠帶回家收留了牠。 |
| Gordon | It really met the angel of its life. | 牠真是遇到了生命中的天使。 |

| Stella | You **overpraise** me! I am just **fond** of cats. Plus, without your help, I wouldn't be able to save it. | 過獎了！我只是喜歡貓咪而已。而且要不是有你的幫忙，也無法成功救牠下來呀。 |
| Gordon | My colleague arranged this date for me. I wasn't interested. Never thought I can meet you who also like cats. | 我同事幫我安排了這場相親，本來我還興趣缺缺呢！沒想到可以遇到同樣喜歡貓咪的妳。 |
| Stella | I feel lucky likewise. I named it Lucky. Now it feels like it's **destined**. | 我也一樣覺得很幸運，當初我把貓咪取名為「Lucky」，現在感覺就像命中注定一樣呢！ |
| Gordon | **Toast** Lucky! And our **matchmakers**, too! | 我們敬 lucky 吧！也敬幫我們牽線的媒人！ |
| Stella | Cheers! By the way, how did your colleague and my mom get connected? | 乾杯！對了，你的同事和我媽媽是怎麼搭上線的呢？ |
| Gordon | We can talk about that after ordering. | 等點完餐後，我們再來好好地聊聊這個問題吧。 |

## ⭐ Some Words to Know

**❶ remain** `vi.` 仍然
Although ten years has gone, she remains young.
雖已過了十年,她依舊年輕。

**❷ arrange** `v.` 安排,約
I've arranged with her to meet at the movie theater.
我已經和她約好在電影院見面。

**❸ blind** `a.` 盲目的
People in love are all blind.
戀愛中的人都是盲目的。

**❹ notion** `n.` 想法、見解、概念
I have a vague notion of what a director does to make a film.
我對導演怎麼製作一部電影有個模糊的概念。

**❺ frightened** `a.` 受到驚嚇的
That little girl was so frightened at the sight.
驚見那幕,那小女孩飽受驚嚇。

**❻ overpraise** `v.` 過度誇獎
You overpraised me. I was just in luck.
您過獎了,我只不過是運氣好而已。

**❼ fond** `a.` 喜歡的、愛好的
She is very fond of horses.
她非常喜歡馬。

**❽ destined** `a.` 命中注定的
His repeatedly irresponsible personality is destined to fail.
他總愛逃避責任的個性是註定要失敗的。

**❾ toast** `v.` 敬酒
Let's toast the host for this perfect party.
讓我們向主辦人敬酒,謝謝他舉辦了這場完美的派對。

⑩ matchmaker **n.** 媒人

Dad said if it were not for the matchmaker, he and mom would not have been together.

爸爸說當初要不是有那位媒人，他跟媽媽也不會在一起了。

## ✨30 秒會話教室

當你遇到跟偶像劇一樣不可思議的重逢場景時，可以說：What a coincidence! Never thought I'd see / meet you here. 怎麼這麼巧？從沒想過會在這裡遇見你。

# 情境 **4** 交往才發現男方是 GAY

 **Let's Talk in Love**

Gill and Owen just starts dating each other. However, she finds that Owen is often **sneaky**, leaving her and talking on the phone during the date. One time during their meals, Owen goes to a corner for **answering** the phone. She couldn't **resist** to **overhear** from behind. Surprised at hearing Owen saying "Love you, too, baby" to the other person on the phone, she questions him angrily right after he hangs up.

Gill 與 Owen 才剛開始交往沒多久，她就發現 Owen 在約會中經常丟下她跑到一旁偷偷講手機。一次用餐時 Owen 又到角落接電話，她忍不住跟在後頭偷聽，竟然聽到 Owen 對著電話另一頭的人說：「寶貝我也愛你啊⋯」等 Owen 掛了電話她馬上生氣地質問⋯

| | | |
|---|---|---|
| Gill | Who were you talking to? | 你剛剛跟誰通電話？ |
| Owen | You...why do you follow me here? Have I just told you I need to leave for a while to answer the phone? | 妳⋯妳怎麼跟來了！？我不是告訴妳我暫時離開接個電話嗎？ |
| Gill | Is that your mom? The child of you and ex-wife? Or you pet just called? | 是你媽媽、你跟前妻生的小孩，還是寵物打給你的嗎？ |
| Owen | Uh, no. | 嗯⋯都不是耶。 |
| Gill | Then the only **possibility** is that you have another girlfriend! | 那麼唯一的可能就是你還有其他的女人！ |

| Owen | I don't have any other girlfriend. | 我沒有其他女人啊。 |
|------|-----------------------------------|------------------|
| Gill | I just heard you call her baby! I've been feeling you weird since we started dating. You are always sneaky whenever the phone rings. Speak up! What do you see in her better than I am? | 我明明就聽到你叫她寶貝。從我們一開始交往我就覺得你怪怪的了，只要手機一響你就鬼鬼祟祟的。說，她到底哪一點比我好？ |
| Owen | (Sigh)... there's no way to **conceal** from you anymore. Actually, it is him. I feel really sorry but I like men. | 哀，事到如今我也無法再隱瞞妳了，其實，她是個「他」，對不起，我真正喜歡的是男人。 |
| Gill | What?! Then...why do you go out with me? | 甚麼！？那…你為什麼還要跟我交往？ |
| Owen | I thought I might use you as **cover** to hide my **underneath sexual orientation** from my family. I am sorry. I made a terrible mistake, and I will do anything to make it up to you. | 我想或許可以用妳當作幌子，隱藏我私底下真實的性向來給周遭的親友一個交代。對不起，我犯下了很嚴重的錯誤，我願意用任何方法補償妳，以表達我的歉意！ |

## ⭐ Some Words to Know

**❶ sneaky** **a.** 鬼鬼祟祟的
Girls must be careful when renting houses if the landlord is sneaky.
女生在外租屋，如果遇到鬼鬼祟祟的房東千萬要小心。

**❷ answer** **v.** 接（電話）
Could you help me answer the phone?
妳可以幫忙接一下電話嗎？

**❸ resist** **v.** 抗拒
It's very difficult to resist ice cream on such a hot day.
這麼熱的一個日子要抗拒不吃冰淇淋是很困難的。

**❹ overhear** **v.** 偷聽、竊聽；無意中聽到
Bella's mom just couldn't help overhearing her conversation with Jason.
Bella 的媽媽忍不住偷聽她和 Jason 的交談。

**❺ possibility** **n.** 可能性
The police wouldn't want to let go of any possibility for cracking the case.
警察不願意放過任何破案的可能性。

**❻ conceal** **v.** 隱瞞　字彙連結站　hide
That parent seems to conceal something.  Maybe she's abusing her own child.
那位家長似乎在隱瞞些甚麼，或許正是她虐待自己的小孩。

**❼ cover** **n.** (U) 掩護（物）、掩蔽處
If any earthquake occurs, remember to hide right away under the closest and stongest cover.
如果遇到地震，記得馬上躲到最近且最堅固的掩護物底下。

**❽ underneath** **prep.** **adv.** 在⋯之下，底下的、底層的
Underneath that cold exterior, he is actually a warm person.
在那個冷漠的外表下，他其實是一個溫暖的人。

❾ sexual  **a.** 性別的、性的
AIDS is passed on by sexual contact.
AIDS 藉由性接觸而傳播。

❿ orientation  **n.** 定位、傾向
Some people think sexual orientation isn't a problem for fatherhood.
有些人認為性傾向對成為父親而言不是個問題。

## ⭐ 30 秒會話教室

知錯能改，善莫大焉，如果知道自己鑄下了大錯，千萬要向及時對方承認：I can't hide it anymore.  I made a terrible mistake.（我無法再隱瞞下去了，我犯了很嚴重的錯誤。）

# 情境 5　被素顏的枕邊人驚醒

 **Let's Talk in Love**

Raymond and his **fiancée**, Helen, move into a new house for marriage life and have been **preparing** the coming wedding ceremony.　At the very first night, Raymond and Helen sleep in each other's arm.　However, when Raymond gets up for a glass of water, he finds it's a female stranger lying beside him...

Raymond 跟未婚妻 Helen 搬進了兩人婚後共同的新家，準備迎接不久後的婚禮。當晚 Raymond 和 Helen 甜蜜地相擁入眠。不過當 Raymond 夜半起床喝水時，卻發現枕邊躺的是個陌生的女人…

| | | |
|---|---|---|
| Raymond | What the earth are you?　Why are you sleeping in my bed?　Where's my fiancée, Helen? | 妳…妳是誰？為什麼睡在我的床上？我的未婚妻 Helen 呢？ |
| Helen | What are you talking about?　I'm Helen!　Did you have a **nightmare**? | 你在說甚麼啊？我就是 Helen 啊！你做惡夢了嗎？ |
| Raymond | Your voice does sound like Helen.　Let me look **closely** at your face.　Hmmm.　Why is there something different? | 妳的聲音的確是 Helen 沒錯呀…讓我仔細看看妳的臉…咦，怎麼有點不太一樣？ |
| Helen | Ah!　I just removed the **makeup**.　Don't you **exaggerate**, alright?　That would hurt my feelings. | 唉唷，人家只是卸了妝而已，你別那麼誇張好不好，這樣會傷了我的自尊耶！ |

| Raymond | That reminds me of something. I haven't seen you without makeup when dating you. | 這麼一說，我們之前交往的時候的確沒有看過妳的素顏。 |

| Helen | That's because we lived apart from each other. We never spent the night together, so I didn't have any chances to remove makeup before you. | 因為我們當時分隔兩地，沒有一起過夜、需要卸妝的機會啊。 |

| Raymond | No wander people say women wearing makeup is like wearing **enchanted** cloak. | 難怪聽人說女生化妝後就像施了魔法一樣。 |

| Helen | Is it really that horrible when I don't wear any makeup? | 我的素顏真的有那麼可怕嗎？ |

| Raymond | Actually, you look **innocent** and pretty without the makeup. I am just used to you wearing it, so my **reaction** may be a little **intense**. Never mind. | 其實妳不化妝看起來比較清純，一樣很漂亮，只是我看習慣了妳平常的樣子，所以當下的反應比較激烈一點，妳別在意。 |

| Helen | I thought you were so scared that you regreted to propose. | 我還以為你被嚇到想悔婚了呢！ |

## ⭐ Some Words to Know

**❶ fiancée** 🔲 未婚妻
This dessert is made by my fiancée.  Please enjoy it, everyone.
這是我的未婚妻親手做的甜點，請大家嚐嚐看。

**❷ prepare** 🔲 準備
It's very unwise to attend job interviews without preparing.
毫無任何準備就去參加工作面試是非常不明智的事情。

**❸ nightmare** 🔲 惡夢
That big shiny supermarket is small shopkeeper's nightmare.
那家大又明亮的超市是小店家的惡夢。

**❹ closely** 🔲 仔細地、接近地
Please look closely.  Is this really your handwriting?
請再看仔細一點，這真的是你的筆跡嗎？

**❺ makeup** 🔲 化妝
Wearing makeup can bring confidence to females.
化妝可以帶給女性自信。

**❻ exaggerate** 🔲 誇大其辭
The media exaggerates the effects of the policy.
媒體誇示了該政策的效果。

**❼ enchanted** 🔲 被施法的、被迷惑的；迷人的
Is that song enchanted?  I just can't stop listening to it over and over again.
這首歌被施加魔法了嗎？我就是忍不住一次又一次地聆聽。

**❽ innocent** 天真的、單純的
The innocent eyes of that kitty make me want to take it home so badly.
小貓咪天真無辜的眼神讓人好想把牠帶回家。

**❾ intense** 🔲 劇烈的、強烈的
She has intense passion for ballet.
她對芭蕾舞有著強烈的熱愛。

**⓾ reaction** **n.** 反應

Good drivers have quick reactions.
好駕駛都有快速的反應。

 **30 秒會話教室**

當你遇到別人的玩笑開得過火的時候，或是對某些事實的反應太過激烈，可以用以下這句提醒一下對方：Don't be so exaggerating.　It will hurt my feelings.（別這麼誇張好不好？這會傷到我的心！）

# 情境 6  原來兩人是兄妹

 **Let's Talk in Love**

Matt and Grace seem to have a thing about each other after they helped a kid to find his parents in an **amusement park**.  They share the **situation** that others might not be able to understand - their parents died and they were both **adopted** when little.  Therefore, they are getting closer and closer.  One day when Matt shows the only family portrait for Grace, it comes to her that they could be brother and sister.

Matt 與上次在遊樂園一起幫助迷路小孩找父母的 Grace 正處於曖昧期。都是父母雙亡，從小被人領養的兩人有著外人所無法理解的相同處境，也因此感情越來越深厚。一天 Matt 拿著自己唯一的一張全家福給 Grace 看，Grace 赫然發現，兩人有可能是親生兄妹…

Grace  You are saying this is your family **portrait**?

你說這張照片是你們的全家福？

Matt  Yup.  My parents died in a car **accident**.  This is all that they left, only this family portrait.

是啊！我的父母在一場車禍意外中過世，當時留下的遺物裡，全家福合照就只有這張。

Grace  This picture has your parents, you, and a little girl.  She is...?

這張照片裡除了你的父母、你、還有一個小女孩，她是…？

Matt　She's my sister.  After my parents died, we didn't have any **relatives**. Through the soāal **welfare** organization, we were adopted by two separate families.  I was just 7 and could only recall **vaguely**.  These were told by my **adoptive** parents.

她是我的妹妹，父母過世之後，我們也沒有其他親戚，就經由社會福利單位的幫助，分別被兩個好心人家收養了。不過我當時才 7 歲，記憶很模糊，這些都是我的養父母事後才告訴我的。

Grace　Have you ever tried to find your sister?

你曾經試圖找過你的妹妹嗎？

Matt　I did!  But her name seemed changed after adopted.  I couldn't find any information by her real name and I don't even know the last name of her adoptive family.

有啊！可是她被收養之後好像連名字都改了，因為我用她的本名完全查不到任何資料，而且我也不知道收養她的人家姓甚麼。

Grace　Do you still remember your sister's name?

你還記得你妹妹本來的名字嗎？

Matt　Her name's Milly.  Our family name was Evans.

她叫做 Milly，我們家原本姓 Evans。

Grace　Ever since I could remember, this necklace has been with me and the **lettering** on its back is "Milly Evans."

從我有記憶以來，我的脖子上就掛著這條項鍊，項鍊背後正是刻著 Milly Evans！

Matt　That means...you are my sister?!

這也是說…妳就是我的親妹妹！？

## ⭐ Some Words to Know

**1** amusement park　**n.** 主題樂園
I am going to the popular amusement park with kids on Sunday.
禮拜天我要和小孩去那個很受歡迎的主題樂園。

**2** situation　**n.** 處境、境遇
The financial situation of this company is now in crisis.
公司的財政狀況陷入了危機。

**3** adopt　**v.** 領養
The animal refuges have lots of stray dogs and cats waiting to be adopted.
收容所裡有很多等待領養的流浪貓狗。

**4** portrait　**n.** 照片、肖像
Many portraits are hanged on the walls of Grandpa's home.
外公家裡的牆上掛了許多照片。

**5** accident　**n.** 意外
A car accident took his left leg.
一場車禍意外讓他失去了一條左腿。

**6** relative　**n.** 親戚
The aunt who moved to Australia is our only relative.
搬到澳洲的阿姨是我們唯一的親戚。

**7** welfare　**n.** (U) 福利事業
She worked for the social welfare section after graduation.
她一畢業後就進入社會福利部門工作。

**8** vaguely　**adv.** 模糊不清地
I vaguely remember having seen her somewhere.
我模糊地記得在哪裡看過她。

**9** adoptive　**a.** 收養的
One factor whiched affects potential adoptive parents is age.
一個影響潛在養父母的因素是年齡。

**❿ lettering**  寫字、刻字
This picture has lettering "1995" on the back.
這張照片背後寫著「拍攝於 1985 年」。

## ⭐30 秒會話教室

當想問別人是否曾做過某些努力時，可以用以下句型：Have you ever tried to <u>find your sister</u>?（你有試圖尋找過你的妹妹嗎？）

# 情境 7 交往後食量大增？

 **Let's Talk in Love**

Joseph and Rebecca have connected to each other for a while. After Joseph finally tells her that he has a thing for her, they become sweetheart friends. However, Joseph finds that Rebecca seems more and more **gluttonous**...

Joseph 跟 Rebecca 經歷過一段互有好感的曖昧期，Joseph 終於向 Rebecca 告白，兩人成了男女朋友。不過 Joseph 卻發現，Rebecca 的食量好像越來越大…

| | | |
|---|---|---|
| Joseph | Darling, you eat like you haven't had food for days. Too busy working? | 親愛的，妳看起來好像幾天沒吃東西了，是工作太忙了嗎？ |
| Rebecca | No. I am just hungry. Can I order one more spaghetti? | 沒有啊，我只是還覺得餓，我可以再點一份義大利麵嗎？ |
| Joseph | This is not a problem for me. I am just afraid you might **ruin** your stomach. | 這倒是沒問題，我只是怕妳把胃撐壞了。 |
| Rebecca | Relax! It won't happen. I usually have to eat at least two main courses. | 放心，不會的，我平常至少要吃兩份主餐才會飽。 |

| | |
|---|---|
| Joseph | Do you remember that we got to know each other because you forgot to bring your purse? In fact, I'd noticed you before you paid the tab. You just ordered a Caesar salad and a **potage**. I thought this woman **ate like a bird**. | 妳還記得我們認識是因為妳忘了帶錢包嗎？其實那天在妳去結帳之前，我就注意到妳了，妳只點了一份凱薩沙拉和濃湯，我還覺得這個女生的胃口真小。 |
| Rebecca | Oh, that was because I went out for lunch too late. That restaurant is the closest one to my company but **serves** the food really slow. So I just made the two fast convenient **orders**. | 喔，那是因為我那天太晚出來吃午餐了，那間餐廳離公司最近，但是上菜速度卻很慢，所以我只點了那兩樣方便快速的餐點。 |
| Joseph | So you weren't really full! I thought you begin to eat like a horse after we get together. | 原來妳在那個時候是沒有吃飽的，我還以為妳是交往以後才突然食量大增。 |
| Rebecca | Yes, so right after I returned to my office, I ate chocolate and crackers which I **stocked** in my drawer to **refresh** myself anytime. And we called the delivery during afternoon tea time. | 對啊，所以我那天回到辦公室，又吃了我擺在抽屜裡隨時可以補充體力的巧克力和餅乾，當天還跟同事們在下午茶時間一起叫外送來吃。 |
| Joseph | It's really hard to tell that you are a **fresser** since you are so **petite**. | 妳的個子這麼嬌小，一點都看不出來是個大胃王。 |

Rebecca　Come on!  You have never heard people say that using the brains causes hunger?

嘿，你沒聽人家說過，動腦也是會餓的嗎？

## ⭐ Some Words to Know

**❶ gluttonous** **a.** 貪吃的
Mark's gluttonous.  That's why he can't lose weight.
Mark 太貪吃了。這就是為什麼他瘦不下來的原因。

**❷ ruin** **v.** 毀壞、破壞
The shops have ruined the old elegant town.
商家已經破壞這老而優雅的城鎮。

**❸ potage** **n.** (U) 濃湯
I love potage more than any kind of soup.
我喜愛濃湯勝過任何湯類。

**❹ eat like a bird** **v.** **phr.** 食量很小、吃的很少
If you want to become as fat as Mark, you can't eat like a bird.
如果你想變得跟 Mark 一樣胖，你就不能吃這麼少。

**❺ serve** **v.** 提供
This dinner serves the best hotdog in town.
這家小餐館提供市區中最棒的熱狗。

**❻ order** **n.** 訂購、點（餐）
May I tak your order, sir?
先生，我能為您點餐嗎？

**❼ stock** v. 儲存、庫存

Some animals stock meat in the ground during the winter.

有些動物在冬季時會將肉儲存在地底下。

**❽ refresh** v. 消除疲勞、使⋯提起精神

I need a shower to refresh myself.

我需要沖個澡消除疲勞一下。

**❾ fresser** n. 愛吃的人、食量大的人

I have never seen a fresser like him.

我從沒看過像他一樣這麼愛吃的人。

**❿ petite** a. 嬌小的

That petite girl is the board chairman's daughter.

那位嬌小的女孩是董事長的千金。

## 🌟 30 秒會話教室

以下三種都是叫人「放輕鬆、別緊張」的說法，如 Take it easy.（別緊張）、Relax.（放輕鬆）、Chill out!（冷靜、放輕鬆）。

# 情境 8   男方電腦中發現秘密檔案

 **Let's Talk in Love**

One day when Stella is using Gordon's computer at his place, she gets an email **notification** from Angel with "The **naked hairy** file you desire is done!" as the title.  A file is **attached** to it.  As Stella is about to open it **suspiciously**, Gordon walks near...

某天 Stella 在男友 Gordon 家中隨意地使用著他的電腦時，正好收到一封署名 Angel、標題是「你要的全裸露毛檔案好了喔」的信件通知，並夾帶了一個附檔。Stella 正懷疑地要打開信件來看時，Gordon 正好走近她的身旁…

| | | |
|---|---|---|
| Stella | **Shame** on you!  I want to break up with you! | 你這個不要臉的傢伙，我要跟你分手！ |
| Gordon | Baby, what happened?  Why are you so angry all of a sudden? | 寶貝，怎麼了？突然這麼生氣！ |
| Stella | Tell me how I can not get angry when you want a woman named Angel to send her naked **image** to you! | 你要一個叫做 Angel 的女人傳她的全裸影像給你，叫我怎麼能不生氣！ |
| Gordon | Oh, Angel has sent the file?  Let me check it out. | 喔，Angel 把檔案寄來了啊？我來看看。 |

| Stella | You totally ignore me! This is way out of line! I'll leave right now. | 你…你竟然完全不把我放在眼裡，實在是太過份了，好，我現在馬上就走。 |
| --- | --- | --- |
| Gordon | Hold on a second. Just let me **explain**. We often **record** adorable Lucky with the cellphones, right? Angel is a friend of mine who is good at **editing** films. I gave her all video and asked her to make a speãal edition of Lucky. | 等一下，聽我解釋啦，我們不是常常用手機把 lucky 可愛的模樣錄下來嗎？這個 Angel 是一位很會處理影像的朋友，我把錄下來的影像都交給她，請她幫我們剪輯成一段 lucky 特輯。 |
| Stella | So...it's actually the film of our kitty? Why such a strange file name? | 所以…這其實是我們家貓咪的影片？那為什麼要取這種奇怪的檔名呢？ |
| Gordon | You know I like to be different and Lucky is really naked and hairy. | 妳也知道我喜歡跟別人不一樣，而且 lucky 的確是全裸又露毛呀。 |
| Stella | You idiot! | 你這個笨蛋！ |
| Gordon | OK. Don't get mad. Now let's watch the film. | 好啦，別生氣了，我們現在就來看看完成後的影片吧。 |

## ⭐ Some Words to Know

**❶ notification** **n.** 通知
Everyone in the community receives the notification of an electronic power cut.
社區裡的每個人都收到了停電的通知。

**❷ naked** **a.** 裸體的
The boy is naked to the waist.
那男孩裸露上半身。

**❸ hairy** **a.** 多毛的
The little girl got a hairy stuffed toy for a Christmas gift.
小女孩收到了一隻毛茸茸的娃娃做為聖誕節禮物。

**❹ attach** **v.** 附加、裝上、貼上
I will attch the map with the invitation, so you'll know the way to the restaurant.
我會在邀請卡上附上地圖，這樣你就知道到餐廳的路。

**❺ suspiciously** **adv.** 猜疑地
She suspiciously followed her husband.
她疑心尾隨跟蹤她老公。

**❻ shame** **n.** 羞恥
His disease makes him look different from others, but he doesn't take it as a shame; he's very optimistic.
他的疾病讓他長得跟別人不太一樣，但是他一點也不覺得羞恥，反而非常開朗。

**❼ image** **n.** 影像
After watching the images, please tell me how many key words you remember.
看完這段影像，請告訴我你記得多少個關鍵字。

**❽ explain** **v.** 解釋
He told to the new colleague about the job description.
他向新來的同事解釋工作內容。

❾ record　**v.**　紀錄

I like recording everything in my life with pictures.

我喜歡用照片紀錄我生活中的點點滴滴。

❿ edit　**v.**　剪輯

He spent the whole night editing that film.

他花了一整晚剪輯那支影片。

## ★30 秒會話教室

英文中說人不要臉的類似說法有：Shame on you.（你真可恥）、You are shameless.（你真不要臉）、How cheeky you are!（你真是厚顏無恥）。

# 情境 9　手機中出現可疑號碼

## Let's Talk in Love

One day, when Tracy, during a date, is playing Phil's cellphone, it rings **without** Caller ID **Display**.  Tracy does not take it **seriously** and hand the phone to Phil.  Surprisingly, as Phil sees the call, he walks away in an **unnatural** way and takes the call quietly...

一天 Tracy 在約會中把玩著男友 Phil 的手機，這時一通沒有顯示名稱的電話打了過來，Tracy 不以為意地將手機遞給 Phil 接聽，沒想到 Phil 看到來電之後反而不自然地躲到一旁小聲接聽…

| | |
|---|---|
| Tracy　Dear, who was that? | 親愛的，剛剛是誰打來的啊？ |
| Phil　Uh... nothing.  Just some insurance **salesperson**. | 沒…沒有啊，只是拉保險的業務。 |
| Tracy　Why are you so **nervous** if that's the insurance salesperson. | 既然是拉保險的業務何必那麼緊張？ |
| Phil　I... I am not nervous.  Next time don't play with my phone. | 我…我哪有緊張，妳下次不要再隨便拿我的手機去玩了啦！ |
| Tracy　You are so weird today.  You always let me see what's in your cellphone and now you are **mad** at me because of the call.  Something's going on here. | 你今天好奇怪喔，本來都很大方地讓我看你的手機，這次卻因為那通來電而對我動怒，一定有問題！ |

| | | |
|---|---|---|
| Phil | It's really nothing! Stop bothering me with it. | 我說沒有就是沒有，妳別再追問這件事情了。 |
| Tracy | You think I would never be able to find out what you are doing? I've **memorized** the number at the glance. Now I am calling to see who that is!<br>(Dials the number) | 你以為這樣我就不知道你在搞甚麼鬼了嗎？我剛剛看過一次就記下了那個號碼，我現在就打過去看對方是誰！<br>（播電話） |
| Female | Hi, this is Royal Travel **Agency**. How may I help you?<br><br>(Hangs up the phone) | 您好，這裡是皇家旅行社，請問有甚麼可以為您服務的嗎？<br>（掛電話） |
| Tracy | How come it's the travel agency's number? | 怎麼會是旅行社的電話？ |
| Phil | Because I'm planning a secret trip to Hawaii for us. They just called to tell me the flight tickets and hotel room have been **successfully** booked. | 我為了我們兩個，秘密計畫了一次夏威夷之旅，剛剛對方就是打來跟我報告機票和飯店已經順利訂到位了。 |
| Tracy | What?! I'm so surprised! You are so sweet, but you make me feel guilty now. | 甚麼？！我好驚訝! 你真貼心，但現在你讓我感到內疚了。 |
| Phil | Don't feel guilty. Feel happy! The happy smiles on your face are all I want. | 不要覺得內疚。覺得快樂就好! 見到妳臉上快樂的笑容才是我所想要的。 |

## ⭐ Some Words to Know

**❶ without** `prep.` 沒有
The younger brother went to bed without brushing his teeth.
弟弟沒有刷牙就上床睡覺了。

**❷ display** `n.` (U) 顯示、顯露
There isn't much display of his feelings on the face.
他臉上沒有顯露太多感情。

**❸ seriously** `adv.` 嚴肅地、認真地
The teacher takes seriously the reports handed by every student.
老師很嚴肅地看待每一位同學交的報告。

**❹ unnatural** `a.` 不自然的、造做的
The man's unnatural action caused the police's suspicion.
那個人不自然的舉動引起了警察的懷疑。

**❺ salesperson** `n.` 業務
She's now working as a salesperson in a car company.
她現在在一家汽車公司裏頭做業務。

**❻ nervous** `a.` 緊張
Don't be nervous, students. This exam isn't as difficult as you think.
同學們別緊張，這次的考試沒有你們想像中的困難。

**❼ mad** `a.` 惱火的
Dad was mad at Mom because the dinner did not have his favorite beef.
爸爸因為晚餐沒有他最喜歡的牛肉而對媽媽大發脾氣。

**❽ memorize** `v.` 記住、背熟
I have to memorize the lines of the next week's play.
我必須把下周的話劇表演的台詞背熟。

**❾ agency** `n.` 代辦處、經銷處
I was a salesperson in a travel agency for one year.
我曾在旅行社擔任過一年的業務。

**❿ successfully** adv. 順利地、成功地

That baseball team defeats the enemy and wins the champion of the year successfully.

那支棒球隊順利地擊敗對手,得到今年的總冠軍。

 **30 秒會話教室**

Don't be mad at me. 別對我發火。Don't be angry with me. 別對我生氣。
Don't get cross with me. 不要對我發怒。

# 情境 10 口袋中出現可疑名片

 ## Let's Talk in Love

Chris **drives** his girlfriend, Daisy, home.  He takes off the suit coat and is going to make some simple dinner in the kitchen.  As Daisy tries to **hang** his coat, a business card falls from the pocket...

Chris 載著下班的女友 Daisy 回家，一踏進家門，他就隨手脫下西裝準備到廚房弄個簡單的晚餐，Daisy 便想順手幫他將西裝掛好，此時卻有一張名片從 Chris 的西裝口袋掉了出來…

| | |
|---|---|
| Daisy | I thought you said you would never go to any pub for drinking again, Chris. |
| Chris | Yeah.  I have never gone to those places for drinking since the doctor **warned** me. |
| Daisy | Then why is this card in your pocket? |
| Chris | **Which** card?  Let me see. |
| Daisy | This card with "333 Restaurant & Bar" on it. |

Chris，你不是說以後都不會再到 pub 喝酒了嗎？

對啊，自從醫生告誡我之後，我就沒有再去那些地方喝酒了。

那你的口袋裡為什麼會有這張名片？

哪一張？我看看。

就是這個，上面寫著「333 restaurant &Bar」。

Chris　Oh. I was waiting for an **appropriate** time to give you a surprise. But since you have found out, I might just tell you now as well.

喔，這本來是我要等一個適當的時機再告訴妳的驚喜啦！不過既然妳發現了，就先告訴妳也無妨。

Daisy　A surprise?

驚喜？

Chris　You told me that you are a waitress in the restaurant because you want to be a chef one day? So I show some of your **recipes** and menus to several restaurants and this one gets interested and wants to talk to you.

妳不是曾說過，會到餐廳當服務生就是希望有一天能進入廚房當上廚師嗎？我把妳寫的一些食譜和菜單拿給幾間餐廳看，這間餐廳的人看了之後非常有興趣找妳談談。

Daisy　So that's how it is. That's **wonderful**! I don't know you've **quietly** done so much for me.

原來如此，那真是太好了，我都不知道你默默為我做了這麼多。

Chris　This is a pub **run** by a hotel. I'll tell you about the **detail** after I get the dinner ready.

這是一間由飯店經營的酒吧，等我準備好晚餐再跟妳說詳情吧。

## ⭐ Some Words to Know

**❶ drive** **v.** 開車載…
Who drove you home last night?
昨晚誰在你回家？

**❷ hang** **v.** 把…掛起
Can you hang up the coat for me?
可以請你幫我把大衣掛起來嗎？

**❸ warn** **v.** 警告、告誡
Riots occur in the capital recently, so the police have warned us not to go out at night.
最近首都發生暴動，警察告誡我們晚上不要出門。

**❹ which** **deter.** **pron.** 哪一個
Which do you prefer, coffee or black tea?
咖啡和紅茶，妳喜歡哪一個？

**❺ appropriate** **a.** 適當的
The teacher picked an appropriate film for pupils to watch in the classroom.
那位老師挑了一部適當的影片在教室內播放給學童看。

**❻ recipe** **n.** 食譜
Even we follow the recipe, we may not be able to make gourmet dishes.
就算是照著食譜做，還是不一定能做出大師級般的口味。

**❼ wonderful** **a.** 極好的、精彩的
Those two actors' performance is just wonderful.
那兩位演員的演出實在是太精采了。

**❽ quietly** **adv.** 暗中、秘密地
The revolutionary army is planning quietly to overthrow the government.
革命軍正在暗中地計畫要推翻政府。

**❾ run　v.　經營**
I often help in the restaurant run by my mom.
我經常到媽媽經營的餐館幫忙。

**❿ detail　n.　細節、詳情**
Before he gives the detail, the police will not let him go.
在他沒有說明詳情以前，警察是不會放他回去的。

## ⭐ 30 秒會話教室

So that's how it is.（原來如此。）I got it.（我懂了。）I see.（我知道了。）以上三種都有恍然大悟的感覺喔。

# 情境 11  誰種的草莓？

 **Let's Talk in Love**

Today John goes out of the dorm for the class as usual. However, there seems many people who **point** and talk about him on the way. Some even **snicker** evilly, which makes him feel quite **uneasy**. In the classroom, Linda, his girlfriend who is also in the same class, first looks at him surprisingly and then **ignores** him for the rest of the class. He tries to stand with that until the break...

John 今天像往常一樣步出宿舍準備去上課，但一路上一直有人對他指指點點，甚至報以不懷好意的微笑，讓他感到很不自在。進到教室之後，同班的女友 Linda 一看到他也先是驚訝，而後整堂課都不理他，他忍到下課後…

| | | |
|---|---|---|
| John | Lind, people on campus are so **odd** today, and why do you try to ignore me? | Linda，今天全校的人都好奇怪，而且怎麼連你也不理我？ |
| Linda | You know what you have done. | 你做了甚麼自己心裡有數。 |
| John | What I've done today is as usual, nothing particular. Do I get something on my face? | 我今天的作息跟往常一樣，沒甚麼特別的啊，難不成是我臉上沾到了甚麼東西？ |
| Linda | Not on your face. It's your neck that has two super **showy zits**! | 不是你的臉，是你脖子上那兩個超顯眼的吻痕！ |

| | | |
|---|---|---|
| John | Zits? How could it be possible? Do you have a **mirror** with you? Can I borrow it for a minute? | 吻痕？怎麼會？妳身上有帶鏡子嗎？借我一下！ |
| Linda | Don't you know she left them on you? Humph! Do not bother to **remind** her next time. You can make her your girl! | 你不知道她會在你身上留下吻痕嗎？哼，下次也不用提醒她了，你直接去跟她交往吧！ |
| John | Wait! I really never fool around with any girls. These should be the bites caused by **mosquitoes** when I slept last night. I scratched them and they got red and swollen. | 等等，我真的完全沒有跟任何女生亂來，這應該是我昨晚睡覺時被蚊子咬，自己抓到紅腫的。 |
| Linda | Do you really think I will fall for that? | 你覺得我會這麼容易就相信你嗎？ |
| John | For real! Look closer. The red swollen skin has not only small scratch, but also a hole bit by the mosquitoes. | 真的！妳靠近一點看，紅腫的皮膚底下不但有細小的抓傷，還有一個蚊子叮的小孔。 |
| Linda | It's true! Well, your room must be too dirty then. | 真的耶！那一定是你的宿舍房間太髒了！ |

## ✦ Some Words to Know

**❶ point** v. 把…指向
Do not point your finger at people. It's very rude.
不要隨便用手指指人，這樣很不禮貌。

**❷ snicker** v. 竊笑
When the annoying colleague was scolded by the supervisor, others in the office were snickering.
那個討人厭的同事被主管叫去罵之後，辦公室裡的人都在竊笑。

**❸ uneasy** 拘束的、不自在
I feel uneasy to have a speech in front of all students of the school.
在全校同學面前演講讓我感到很不自在。

**❹ ignore** v. 不理會、忽視
Everyone ignores the vagabond lying at the corner.
沒有人理會躺在街角的那位流浪漢。

**❺ odd** a. 奇特的、古怪的
It is said there are many odd foods for foreigners in Southeast Asia.
聽說東南亞有很多在外國人眼中古怪的食物。

**❻ showy** a. （過份）顯眼的、引人注目的
That girl means to wear a showy, revealing clothes to the night club.
那個女孩故意穿上引人注目的暴露服裝到夜店去。

**❼ zit** n. 吻痕
Some zits were left on her neck after she and her boyfriend had a date.
她和男友約會後，脖子上留下了吻痕。

**❽ mirror** n. 鏡子
Many girls always carry a small mirror with them so take care of their appearance anytime.
許多女生都會隨身攜帶一面小鏡子，以便隨時整理服裝儀容。

**❾ remind** **v.** 提醒
The timer's sound reminded me of taking the cake out of the oven.
定時器的聲音提醒了我該把蛋糕從烤箱裡拿出來了。

**❿ mosquito** **n.** 蚊子
There's a mosquito in the room, making me sleepless with the noise.
房裡有一隻蚊子，吵的我睡不著覺。

## 30 秒會話教室

有時候意料外的情形就是會降臨在自己身上，這時可以用 How could it be possible? (那怎麼可能？)來表達自己不明所以的情緒喔。

# 情境 12　不明開銷花哪去？

 **Let's Talk in Love**

Olivia starts to keep records of the family livelihood after married.  She finds that, however, during these past few months some **expense** has been **deducted** from Wesley's, her husband, bank **account**.  It's about one-third of his payment.  Therefore, she asks him about it...

結婚後開始掌管家計的 Olivia 發現，從最近幾個月開始，老公 Wesley 的銀行戶頭裡每個月都會多扣一筆費用出去，約是他的薪水的三分之一，於是她詢問 Wesley 那筆錢的流向⋯

| | | |
|---|---|---|
| Olivia | Darling, how are your parents going? Do we not give them enough money every month? | 親愛的，你父母他們那邊最近還好嗎？是不是我們每個月寄的生活費不夠用？ |
| Wesley | No.  They are quite fine.  They even say we don't have to give them money. | 沒有啊，他們過的都很好，還說可以不用給了呢。 |
| Olivia | Well, are you lately **into** something expensive, like a diamond watch or some accessories? | 這樣啊，那你最近是不是看上了甚麼昂貴的東西，比如鑽錶、皮件等等？ |
| Wesley | I don't need those things.  Why?  Why are you talking about money all of a sudden? | 那些東西我都不需要，怎麼了嗎？怎麼突然提起錢的事情？ |

| Olivia | We work for the same company, so I know you don't have to spend money soãalizing with customers. Then, the only possibility is that you have the other person! | 我們在同一間公司工作，我也知道你不需要跟客戶應酬花錢，那唯一的可能就是你在外面有女人了！ |
|---|---|---|
| Wesley | What are you talking about?　We almost leave the office and go home together.　You see me around on holidays.　How can it be possible for me to have someone else? | 妳在說甚麼啊？我們每天幾乎都一起下班回家，假日妳也都看的到我，我怎麼可能會有其他的女人？ |
| Olivia | Why is there an **amount** of money deducted from your bank account these three months?　And this is not a small amount of money! | 那你這三個月來的銀行戶頭為甚麼個別扣了一筆錢，而且還不是個小數目耶！ |
| Wesley | Oh, that's my new **investment** insurance **policy**.　It's my **fault** that I did not **discuss** with you before making the deãsion.　And then, I really forgot to tell you. | 喔，那是我買了新的投資型保單啦！沒有先跟妳商量就做決定是我不對，不過我後來是真的忘了跟妳說了。 |
| Olivia | Investment?　I thought you had done something to me. | 投資…？害我以為你做了甚麼對不起我的事情！ |
| Wesley | Alright.　I'm sorry.　But since you know it already, can you help me figure out what the chance for us to make a **profit** is? | 好啦，對不起嘛！既然妳都知道了，那可以請妳幫我看看我們賺到錢的機率有多少，好不好？ |

## ✦ Some Words to Know

**❶ expenses** **n.** 費用、支出

Jenny has extra expense monthly for keeping a stray dog.

Jenny 因為收養了一隻流浪狗，所以每個月多出了一筆費用。

**❷ deduct** **v.** 扣除

Wage will deduct the amount of same value if any dish is broken.

若有任何打破碗盤的情形，將從工資內扣除相當價值的費用。

**❸ account** **n.** 帳戶

Do you know what it needs to open an account in a bank?

妳知道到銀行開一個帳戶需要準備甚麼資料嗎？

**❹ into** **prep.** 喜愛、入迷、熱中

She is really into pop music.

她真的很愛流行樂。

**❺ amount** **n.** 數額

Five hundred thousand U.S. dollars isn't a small amount of money.

50 萬美金不是一筆小數目。

**❻ investment** **n.** 投資、投資額

Stocks are seen as good long-term investments.

股票被視為良好長期的投資。

**❼ policy** **n.** 保險單、保險

My brother bought a new accident policy for his new car.

哥哥為新買的車辦理了一份意外保單。

**❽ fault** **n.** 錯誤、責任

The family think it's the drunk driver's fault that Heath died.

家屬認為 Heath 的死是酒醉駕駛的錯。

**❾ discuss** **v.** 討論

Shutting the door, Mom is apparently unwilling to discuss this with Dad.

媽媽關上了房門，顯然不想再跟爸爸討論這件事。

**⑩ profit** **n.** 利潤、益處

Students gained a lot of profit from the teacher's speech.

老師的一席話讓學生們獲益匪淺。

## ⭐ 30 秒會話教室

What are you talking about?（你在說甚麼東西啊？）這句話有時並非聽不懂對方所說的話，而是帶不認同、有反駁的意思，有時也會使用 What did you (just) say? 來表達。

# 情境 13 原來妳是特務！？

## Let's Talk in Love

Tracy never lets Phil touch any of her mails or cellphone. One day, a blank mail without writing a receiver or sender's address shows up in the mailbox...

Tracy 平常都不讓 Phil 碰她的郵件和手機，一天，信箱裡又出現一封全白的、沒有註明任何收、送件資料的郵件…

| | | |
|---|---|---|
| Phil | You got a mail, Tracy. It's all blank except for the **signature** of "J" on the back. | Tracy，這裡有一封妳的郵件喔，除了背面署名「J」以外，甚麼都沒有。 |
| Tracy | Thank you, dear. Just leave it on the desk. | 謝謝你親愛的，放在桌上就可以了。 |
| Phil | You never tell me who sends these mails or what's in it every time? I must open it up this time. Uh, what's this? It says "Press your **fingerprint**"... | 妳每次都不告訴我這些郵件究竟是誰寄來的、甚麼內容？我這次一定要拆開來看…咦？這是甚麼東西？上面寫著「請按上您的指紋」… |
| Tracy | Wait, Phil! Don't **press**! It will **explode** if it finds it's not my fingerprint by contrast! | 等等，Phil，不要按，如果比對之後發現不是我的指紋的話那可是會爆炸的！ |

| Phil | Explode?! Who on earth sent this stuff? And can you try to explain what's going on here? | 爆炸！？這到底是誰寄的啊？還有妳能不能解釋一下這究竟是怎麼一回事？ |
| --- | --- | --- |
| Tracy | Please keep your voice down first. (Sigh...) I actually work for the Secret **Intelligence Service** of the **government**. | 請你先把音量放小一點！唉…其實我是隸屬於政府秘密情報組織當中的一員。 |
| Phil | The Secret Intelligence Service? So you are a spy sent to kill me? | 秘密情報組織？所以妳是被派來暗殺我的臥底嗎？ |
| Tracy | I just keep **illegal commercial** activities under **surveillance**. Plus, the intelligence agents are allowed to have romantic relationships. | 我只是負責監控有無非法商業活動的啦！而且情報員也是容許戀愛的。 |
| Phil | Does that mean you are not going to kill me? | 也就是說妳不需要殺我滅口囉？ |
| Tracy | I don't have any gun assigned to me. But seriously, you must keep it a secret. | 我沒有配槍。不過說真的，請你一定要保密。 |

## ⭐ Some Words to Know

**❶ signature** **n.** 簽署、簽名
It requires both signatures of parents to participate in the science contest.
需要有父母兩人的簽名才能報名參加科學競賽。

**❷ fingerprint** **n.** 指紋
His fingerprints were all over the gun.
他的指紋佈滿整支槍。

**❸ press** **v.** 按、壓
Press the button and the devices of the whole product line will be activated.
按下這個鈕，整條生產線上的機器設備就會啟動。

**❹ explode** **v.** 爆炸
The firework factory suddenly exploded.
那家爆竹工廠突然爆炸了。

**❺ intelligence** **n.** 情報工作、情報機關
Vigilance and intelligence are the best weapons against terrorism.
警覺性和情報工作是對抗恐怖主義的最佳利器。

**❻ service** **n.** 部門、單位
The ambulance service, health service, and postal service are all necessary for urban development.
緊急救護單位、社會保健單位、郵政單位對都市發展都是必要的。

**❼ government** **n.** 政府
Every year a lot of people compete to work officially in government departments.
每年都有許多人搶著進入政府機關工作。

**❽ illegal** **a.** 非法的
LSD, cocaine, and heroin are illegal drugs.
迷幻藥、古柯鹼和海洛因是非法藥物。

**❾ commercial** a. 商業的
That art school working at cutting edge design has attracted strong commercial interest.
那所從事尖端設計的藝術學院一直吸引強大的商業興趣。

**❿ surveillance** n. 監視
The police keep that casino under surveillance for suspected illegal activity.
因為懷疑非法活動，警方監視著那家賭場。

## 30 秒會話教室

我們經常把秘密告訴某個人，卻又希望他能保密，此時就可以說 Seriously, please keep it a secret.（我是認真／嚴肅的，請幫我保密）。

# 情境 **14** 原來你是有錢人

 **Let's Talk in Love**

Zoe goes to Trevor's place, the neighbor who lives in the same building, with cookie she has just baked.  Stepping out of the elevator, she sees a man in a suit and with a **suitcase** just walking out from Trevor's apartment...

Zoe 拿著剛烤好的餅乾到住在同一棟公寓的 Trevor 家，卻在電梯外看到一個穿西裝、拿著手提箱的男子從 Trevor 家離開…

| | | |
|---|---|---|
| Zoe | I'm coming in, Trevor.  I have cookies just hot from the oven for you. | Trevor，我進來囉，我拿剛烤好的餅乾過來給你吃。 |
| Trevor | Oh, it's you.  Thank you.  Just leave them on the **countertop**.  By the way, do you want to join me to watch the DVD tonight? | 喔，是 Zoe 啊，謝謝妳，放在流理台上就可以了。對了，妳晚上要不要過來一起看 DVD 呢？ |
| Zoe | OK.  I'll bring some food later.  Who was the man who just left? | 好啊，那我待會再準備一些食物過來。對了，剛剛從這裡離開的那個人是誰啊？ |
| Trevor | Oh, that's a lawyer. | 喔，那是一位律師。 |
| Zoe | A lawyer?  What happened? | 律師？發生甚麼事情了嗎？ |

| Trevor | My father is actually an owner of a big company.  He always hopes I will **take over** the company after I graduate but I hope I can live on my own. | 其實我父親是一間大公司的老闆，他一直希望我大學畢業後可以接手掌管公司，但我希望能靠自己的能力過生活。 |

| Zoe | I didn't know you are from the rich second **generation**!  So your father sends the lawyer to **force** you to **give in**? | 原來你是有錢人家的第二代啊！所以你父親是派律師來逼你就範的嗎？ |

| Trevor | I've tried to talk to my father for so long that he finally agrees to let me do it with my own way.  He hires the lawyer to **transfer** a house to me, but I turned it down. | 我跟父親溝通了很久，他終於同意讓我自己闖闖看，剛剛他是請律師來要把一棟房子過戶給我，但是我拒絕了。 |

| Zoe | It is worth respect for someone who is born with a **silver** spoon in the mouth can do this.  I'm so impressed by you. | 含著金湯匙出生的人能夠這麼做真的很值得尊敬耶，我對你刮目相看了。 |

| Trevor | But, giving it a second thought, now I feel kind of **regretful**.  Should I have taken the house? | 但我想一想又有點後悔，我是不是該收下那棟房子啊？ |

# Some Words to Know

**❶ suitcase** **n.** 手提箱
This is the lastest suitcase with a password lock to prevent theft.
這款最新型的手提箱附有密碼鎖，可以防止竊賊。

**❷ countertop** **n.** 流理臺
She selected the milky countertop with slight silver sparkle in it.
她選了那款乳白色，泛著微微銀色亮光的流理台。

**❸ take over** **v.** **phr.** 接管
It's just a matter of time before they take over the area.
他們接管這地區是遲早的事。

**❹ generation** **n.** 世代、一代
The young generation smokes heavierthan their parents did.
年輕世代比他們父母那一代抽更多菸。

**❺ force** **v.** 逼迫、強迫
The police forced the robbers to give up their arms.
警方迫使搶匪放棄槍械。

**❻ give in** **v.** **phr.** 讓步
He finally gave in to his kid's demand for a new bike.
他最後讓步買了一台新的腳踏車給小孩。

**❼ transfer** **v.** 轉讓、過戶
I have transferred the outlay of the ordered product to the seller.
我已經將訂購商品的款項轉帳給賣家。

**❽ silver** **a.** 銀製的
It is said that silver bullets can kill vampires, but this is unable to prove.
聽說用銀子彈可以消滅吸血鬼，但根本無法證明。

**❾ agree** v. 同意

Mom has agreed that I can fly by mesylf to Astralia for my aunt and spend the summer vacation.

媽媽同意讓我一個人搭飛機到澳洲找阿姨過暑假。

**❿ regretful** a. 後悔的

I am so regretful to say such bad words to Mom.

我很後悔對媽媽說出這麼不好聽的話。

## ⭐ 30 秒會話教室

You made me impressed. 或 I'm impressed by you. 你讓我印象深刻。這兩句話也就是「你讓我刮目相看」的意思。

# Part 3

# 情轉淡？
# 小三出場？

# 情境 **1**    和異性單獨出門

 **Let's Talk in Love**

Since Ivan starts seeing Jessica, who he's admired, he's been worried about his beautiful girl would be stolen by others.  And, Jessica always goes out alone with other boy friends....

Ivan 自從跟心儀的 Jessica 交往之後，就一直擔心外型出眾的女友會被其他人搶走，偏偏 Jessica 也毫不避諱地經常跟異性單獨出門…

| | | |
|---|---|---|
| Ivan | Are you going out again today, Jessica? | Jessica，妳今天又要出門啊？ |
| Jessica | Yes.  I am going out with Nathan for **indoor** rock climbing.  I told you. | 對呀，我要跟 Nathan 去室內攀岩，我之前跟你說過了。 |
| Ivan | I know, but... just you and Nathan? | 我知道，可是…只有妳跟 Nathan 兩個人嗎？ |
| Jessica | Nathan is my **fitness trainer**.  He is the only person I know who is interested in this sport, so I can only go with him. | Nathan 是我的健身教練，我認識的人當中只有他對這項運動有興趣，所以當然是找他囉。 |
| Ivan | I know, but I feel worried when I know you go out with another man alone. | 我知道…可是妳跟另一個男人單獨出去，我很不放心。 |

| | |
|---|---|
| Jessica | If you are worried about what he is, I know him long before I met you. I can **guarantee** you that he's not some kind of **serial** killer. You can come if you want to. |
| | 如果你是擔心他的人品的話，我認識 Nathan 比認識你還要久了，我可以保證他不是什麼變態殺人魔。如果你想去的話也可以一起來呀。 |
| Ivan | I am not worried about that, but you and your other male friends might **have a thing**. |
| | 我擔心的不是那個，而是怕妳跟其他男性擦出火花。 |
| Jessica | He's just a **like-minded** friend and happens to be the **opposite** sex. I hope you can understand I am not **fooling around**. |
| | 他只不過是一位志同道合的朋友，剛好又是異性而已，希望你能了解我並不是想亂來。 |
| Ivan | I am not having a doubt about you. I think I am just not that confident so I am jealous of him. |
| | 我並沒有要懷疑妳的意思，我想我只是對自己沒有自信，才會對他吃醋。 |
| Jessica | Do you think I am that kind of woman? If I am interested in other males, I wouldn't have dated you then. |
| | 你認為我是那種隨便的女生嗎？如果我對其他男性有意思，當初就不會跟你交往了，不是嗎？ |

## ⭐ Some Words to Know

**❶ indoor** **a.** 室內的
It's raining heavily, so the PE teacher has s doing indoor sports.
外面下著傾盆大雨，因此體育老師帶我們進行室內的運動。

**❷ fitness** **n.** 健康、體適能
I try to improve my fitness by swimming.
我試著藉由游泳改善健康。

**❸ trainer** **n.** 教練員
My fitness trainer is a muscular female.
我的健身教練是一位肌肉結實的女性。

**❹ guarantee** **v.** 保證、擔保
We guarantee our customers top-quality service.
我們承諾提供我們的客戶最高品質的服務。

**❺ serial** **n.** 一連串的、一系列的
He is charged with serial rapes.
他因連續強暴被控訴。

**❻ have a thing** **v.** **phr.** 有情愫
I think your sister has a thing for Stanley.
我覺得你妹妹對 Stanley 有意思。

**❼ like-minded** **a.** 看法相同的、志趣相投的
This club is established for like-minded students.
這社團是為了志趣相同的學生而成立的。

**❽ opposite** **a.** 相反的、相對的
The twins have opposite personalities.
這對雙胞胎有著相反的個性。

**❾ fool around** **v.** **phr.** （男女感情上）亂搞
She's been fooling around with many men.
她一直和很多男人亂來。

### ⭐30 秒會話教室

對某人或某事有興趣共有以下數種說法，feel/have/show/express/ interest in sb or sth。例：He showed interest in reading when he was a child.（他從小就顯露出對閱讀的興趣。）

# 情境 2　吃任何東西都要加調味料

 **Let's Talk in Love**

It doesn't hurt Joseph and Rebecca's relationship when he finds out she's a fresser.  However, Joseph cannot **live with** it when he learns of the habit that Rebecca has to put lots of **condiments** into everything she eats.

自從 Joseph 知道女友 Rebecca 的食量頗大之後，倒也無損於兩人之間的感情，不過 Rebecca 不管吃任何東西都要加許多調味料的習慣卻讓 Joseph 很難接受…

| | |
|---|---|
| Rebecca | Dear, can you pass the ketchup for me?  Thank you. |

親愛的，可以幫我把番茄醬遞過來嗎？謝謝。

| | |
|---|---|
| Joseph | Rebecca, the fries have salt on it. They are quite salty.  I suggest you stop adding that much ketchup, or you might **absorb** too much **salinity**. |

Rebecca，薯條上面撒了鹽，已經很鹹了，妳就不要再加那麼多番茄醬了，這樣鹽分會攝取過量的。

| | |
|---|---|
| Rebecca | I can't help.  They are tasteless without any condiments. |

我沒辦法呀，不加調味料總覺得吃起來沒有味道嘛！

| | |
|---|---|
| Joseph | And you eat pizza with a lot of **mayonnaise**, let alone the powdered cheese you keep spraying on your spaghetti.  These are hazardous to your health. |

妳吃披薩的時候還要加一大堆美乃滋，更別提吃義大利麵時還要不停地撒上大量的起司粉，這樣對健康是有害的。

| Rebecca | I don't get any disease and still keep fit.  What are you complaining about? | 我又沒有甚麼疾病，身材也維持在標準之內，你有甚麼好抱怨的？ |
| --- | --- | --- |
| Joseph | I am worried about you.  And you eat a lot.  You may have taken more condiments than others.  In the long run, it will burden your **kidney**. | 我是為妳擔心，更何況妳的食量比較大，這樣算下來，吃進去的調味料也比別人多了許多，長期下來會對腎臟造成負擔的。 |
| Rebecca | So what do you want me to do? Always eat boiled eggs or vegetables? | 那你要我怎麼樣嘛？以後都吃水煮蛋或燙青菜嗎？ |
| Joseph | Every kind of food has its unique **original flavor**.  Many **seasonings** have been added when food are cooked.  You can try to add less and less extra condiments. | 其實每種食物都有它獨特的原味，在烹調的過程中也加過不少調味料了，妳可以慢慢減少添加額外的調味料試試看。 |
| Rebecca | Hmm.  Condiments just **grow on** you and finally you just can't quit. | 嗯，調味料這種東西真的是只會越加越多，到最後就無法戒掉了呢。 |
| Joseph | Yeah, so we should be careful when using them. | 對啊，所以真的要小心呢。 |

## ⭐ Some Words to Know

**❶ live with** **v.** **phr.** 忍受
I can't live with his singing!
我無法忍受他的歌聲！

**❷ condiment** **n.** 調味品、佐料
There are unique representative condiments in each food culture.
各種飲食文化當中都有各具風格的代表性調味料。

**❸ absorb** **v.** 吸收
Use the sponge to absorb the spilled water.
用海綿吸濺灑出來的水。

**❹ salinity** **n.** (U) 鹽分
The sea water is salty because of salinity.
海水因為含有鹽分所以是鹹的。

**❺ mayonnaise** **n.** (U) 美乃滋
Mayonnaise is one of Japanese favorite condiments.
美乃滋是日本人最愛的一種調味料之一。

**❻ kidney** **n.** 腎臟
Everyone of us has two kidneys.
我們每人都有兩個腎臟。

**❼ original** **a.** 最初的、原始的
The original idea of that café's logo comes from the mermaids in the ocean.
這間咖啡廳 logo 最原始的設計靈感來自於海上的美人魚。

**❽ flavor** **n.** 味道、風味
The restaurant releases its new noodle of strawberry flavor, which is very creative.
這間餐廳推出了帶有草莓風味的麵條，非常創新。

**9** seasoning　**n.** 調味料

Can you help me taste the dish and adjust the seasoning?

你能幫我是這菜的味道並調整調味料嗎？

**10** grow on　**v.** **phr.** 使…越來越喜歡

The funny cartoon on TV starts to grow on him.

他開始喜歡電視上那好笑的卡通。

## ★ 30 秒會話教室

I can't help it. 我沒辦法。這句話並非只有單純的做不到的意思，而是引申為「我控制不了」、「禁不住」的意思。

# 情境 3　比女生還愛美的花美男

## ⭐ Let's Talk in Love

Gill gets to know Vincent through a friend.  This boyfriend, though straight, is a **metrosexual** who cares more about beauty than women.  This often makes Gill feel between tears and laughter.

Gill 經由朋友介紹認識了一位新對象 Vincent，這次的男友性向正常，但卻是一位比女生還要愛美的花美男，常常讓 Gill 啼笑皆非⋯

| | | |
|---|---|---|
| Vincent | Gill, lend me your makeup mirror.  I left mine in the car.  I want to set up my **fringe**. | Gill，妳的化妝鏡借我，我的放在車上忘了拿，我想整理一下我的瀏海。 |
| Gill | There you go. | 嗯，拿去。 |
| Vincent | Do you think my **skin** lacks glow?  I have been staying up lately.  It appears that I should have a nice **facial treatment**. | 妳覺得我的皮膚看起來會很沒有光澤嗎？我最近經常熬夜，看來晚上應該好好敷個臉了。 |
| Gill | A faãal treatment?  Aren't you exaggerating?  I am a woman and can't **compete** with you in skin care. | 敷臉？你會不會太誇張了？我身為一個女人，保養都沒有你來的勤快。 |

| Vincent | Skin care is no longer the **preserve** of women. Men also need to take care of their faces. This is also one part of appearance. | 保養不再只是女性的專利了，男生也是需要好好照顧自己的門面的，這也是服裝儀容的一環。 |
| Gill | You are right. Skin care is OK, but I will doubt your sex orientation if you start wearing makeup. | 你說的沒錯，保養是沒關係，但你要是開始在臉上化妝，我一定會懷疑你的性向。 |
| Vincent | You are too **subjective**. What's wrong with men who wearing makeup? Many male artists put on makeup to look better on **screen**. | 妳這樣就太主觀了，誰說會化妝的男生性向就有問題呢？有許多男藝人為了上鏡頭好看，也是會在臉上化妝的呀。 |
| Gill | OK. I'm wrong. I am just not used to seeing men who concern beauty more than women. This is not about **sexism**. | 好，是我不對。我只是不太習慣看到男生比女生還愛漂亮而已，並沒有性別歧視的意思。 |
| Vincent | From deep inside my heart I definitely like women. You can bet on it. | 我的內心絕對是喜歡女生的，妳可以放心。 |
| Gill | I will have a faãal treatment tonight. I don't want my face to have less glow than my boyfriend's. | 晚上我也要跟你一起敷臉，我才不想輸給自己的男朋友。 |

## ⭐ Some Words to Know

**❶ metrosexual** n. 都會美型男
Metrosexuals have taken the fashion by storm.
時尚圈吹起了一股都會美形男的熱潮。

**❷ fringe** n. 瀏海
She has a frindge aligned to the eyebrows.
她有著齊眉的瀏海。

**❸ skin** n. 皮膚
The skin is the biggest organ of a human body.
皮膚是人體身上最大的器官。

**❹ facial** a. 臉部的
That rich woman goes to the beauty shop for facial treatment every week.
那位貴婦每周都會定期到美容院進行臉部的保養。

**❺ treatment** n. 對待、處理
The whole series of the treatment cost 100 thousand dollars.
這樣一套護膚療程要價 10 萬元。

**❻ compete** v. 競爭
Both girls compete for their parents' attention.
兩個女孩都爭搶父母親的注意。

**❼ preserve** n. 保護區、禁獵區（此延伸為專利）
Being a politician is not any longer the preserve of men.
當政治人物早已不再是男性的專利。

**❽ subjective** 主觀的
It is severely prohibited to take a subjective view on the results in scientific experiments.
在科學實驗當中嚴禁以主觀的角度看待實驗結果。

**❾ screen　n.　螢幕**

He has always dreamed about being a superstar on the screen.

他一直夢想成為螢幕上的大明星。

**❿ sexism　n.　(U)　性別歧視**

We have less and less sexism in Taiwan.

在台灣，我們性別歧視越來越少。

## 30 秒會話教室

當你不相信對方如同吹牛般的言詞時可以說 You are exaggerating.（你太誇張了）、You must be exaggerating.（你一定是在誇大）。

# 情境 4　請男性友人幫忙修電腦

 **Let's Talk in Love**

Trevor plans to go to Zoe's place to have some fun.　But as he is about to ring the bell, the sound of talk between Zoe and a strange guy comes from the other side of the door.　After he leaves in anger to his own apartment, Zoe comes to his place...

Trevor 本想到同棟樓的 Zoe 家去玩，卻在按電鈴前就聽到門內傳來 Zoe 和陌生男性的交談聲音，Trevor 只好悻悻然地回到家裡後，不久 Zoe 去找他…

Zoe　Trevor, I thought you are coming over to play the new video game?　I've been waiting for you but you didn't **show up**.　So, here I am.

Trevor，你不是說今天中午要來我家玩新買的電玩遊戲嗎？我等了好久都沒等到你出現，所以我就跑來了。

Trevor　Humph!　Tell me about it.　How can I **interrupt** you when you bring some guy home?

哼，妳還說呢，妳自己帶了其他男生回家，我怎麼好意思去打擾你們。

Zoe　Some guy?　Oh, my computer had a **breakdown** last night.　I asked the friend to **fix** it.

男生？喔，我的電腦昨晚突然故障了，我是請朋友來幫我修電腦啦。

Trevor　So you let some guy enter you apartment when you are alone?

因為這樣就讓男生單獨進妳家？

Zoe　What else can I do?  It's Sunday today.  The repair shops are not open and he lives nearby.  I could only ask him to do me this favor.

不然我能怎麼辦？今天是禮拜天，維修店家沒有營業，剛好那位朋友就住附近，當然只能請他來修理囉。

Trevor　Is it necessary for you to **fetch** him right at the time we meet?  If you want to reject me **indirectly**, you can just say it.

那妳有必要在跟我約好的時間點同時找他來嗎？如果妳是要給我軟釘子碰，那妳就直說吧！

Zoe　What are you talking about?  I asked him to fix the computer just because we had made a deal to play the new video game.  Wait.  Reject you indirectly?  Does that mean you are **pursuing** me?

你在說甚麼啊？我就是因為跟你約好要玩新的電玩遊戲，才趕快請他來修理電腦的呀。等等…軟釘子？這也就是說你一直在追我囉？

Trevor　It's just my misunderstanding anyway.  Forget what I've just said.

反正一切都是我的誤會，妳就當我沒說吧。

Zoe　I will not **turn down** if it's you.

如果是你的話，我可是不會拒絕的喔。

Trevor　Can I ask you one thing then - from now on, any man except me is **disallowed** to enter your place?

那我可以要求妳一件事，從今以後除了我以外的男人，都不准進妳家嗎？

## ☆ Some Words to Know

**❶ show up** v. phr. 出席、露面
Almost every star I know shows up in this big event.
幾乎每個我認識的明星都出席了這場盛會。

**❷ interrupt** v. 打擾
Sorry to interrupt you, but who makes this extra order?
很抱歉打擾您們，請問這是哪一位加點的餐點？

**❸ breakdown** n. 故障、損壞
Father always diligently puts the car in service, so it never has any breakdown halfway.
爸爸總是很勤勞地保養車子，從來沒有在半路上故障過。

**❹ fix** v. 修理　字彙連結站 repair
Can you fix the broken clockwork toy?
你能幫我修理這個壞掉的發條玩具嗎？

**❺ fetch** v. 拿取
Can you fetch my book for me from my room?
你可以到我房間幫我拿書嗎？

**❻ indirectly** adv. 間接地
He knows about her getting married indirectly.
他間接得知她結婚一事。

**❼ pursue** v. 追求
Pretty girls always attract a lot of boys to pursue.
漂亮的女孩總是吸引眾多男孩的追求。

**❽ turn down** v. phr. 拒絕
It is not the first time that my colleague's proposal get turned down.
同事的提案被上司拒絕已經不是第一次了。

**❾ disallow** **v.** 不許

The girl's father disallows her to stay with friends overnight.
那女孩的父親不許她陪朋友過夜。

 **30 秒會話教室**

Tell me about it!（就是說嘛！）有時可以表達贊同對方的意思；有時也可表達不耐煩的意思，如「這還用得著你說嗎？」。

# 情境 5　畢業即分手？

 **Let's Talk in Love**

John and Linda, his girlfriend in the same school, is about to graduate from the university.  They live in different **states** in America; there can only be break-up ahead of them.  Therefore, John **screws up his courage** and says to Linda...

John 跟同校的女友 Linda 即將從大學畢業，原本就住在美國不同州的兩人勢必要走上分手一途…於是 John 鼓起勇氣開口…

| | | |
|---|---|---|
| John | Linda, I will have to go back to California after I graduate and you will go back to Montana, right? | Linda，畢業以後我就要回到加州去了，而妳還則是會回到蒙大拿州對嗎？ |
| Linda | Yeah.  We have **discussed** this when we started dating each other.  It just hardly **occurs** to me that time flies like an arrow and now we have no choice but to face it. | 是啊，想當初我們剛交往的時候有討論過這個問題，沒想到時間過得這麼快，已經不得不面對了呢！ |
| John | If possible, I hope we can be together.  But the distance between us is too **faraway**. | 如果可以的話，我也希望能繼續跟妳在一起，但是畢業以後我們相隔的距離實在是太遙遠了。 |

| | | |
|---|---|---|
| Linda | That's true.  And I am not confident about having a **long-distance relationship**.  It certainly feels terrible when you want to see someone so bad but just can't. | 對啊，連我也沒有把握可以談好遠距離戀愛，想見面卻不能隨時見面的感覺一定很難熬。 |
| John | Unless we both stay in Washington, get a job, and live together. | 除非我們兩人都留在華盛頓州，各自找分工作一起過生活。 |
| Linda | But I promised my father to take over the family's little **rangeland** before going to college. | 可是我上大學前就答應過我父親，回家接手經營家裡的小牧場。 |
| John | So did I.  My cousin always hopes I can establish a website for his surf shop and run the online business. | 我也是，我的表哥一直希望我能幫他的衝浪用品店架設一個網站，經營網路的生意。 |
| Linda | So, we can just break up **peacefully**? | 所以，我們就真的只能和平地分手囉？ |
| John | I **regret** to say that.  But it seems the only way.  I'm so happy to have your company during these four years in college.  I hope you can find a better guy in your hometown.  Don't forget that we are still friends. | 我很遺憾地說，也只能這樣了。很高興大學四年來有妳的陪伴，祝福妳在家鄉找到更好的人，也別忘了我們可以繼續當朋友。 |

Linda　Me, too.　Keep in touch.

你也是，那我們就保持聯絡吧。

## ☆ Some Words to Know

❶ state　**n.**　美國的州
Which state in the U.S. is the biggest?
美國面積最大的州是哪一州？

❷ screw up one's courage　**v.**　**phr.**　提起勇氣
He finally screw up his courage to talk to her.
他終於鼓起勇氣跟她說話。

❸ discuss　**v.**　討論
Classmates used the break to discuss secretly the gift of Teacher's Day for the teacher.
班上同學利用下課偷偷討論要送給老師的教師節禮物。

❹ occur　**vi.**　浮現、被想起；發生
It occured to him that he had left the pizza in the drawer for 3 weeks.
他想到他已經把比薩放在抽屜裡三個禮拜了。

❺ faraway　**a.**　遙遠的、遠方的
This kind of migrant bird comes from a faraway forest in the north.
這種候鳥是來自於一座遙遠的北方森林。

❻ long-distance　**a.**　長距離的
It's tiring for old men to have a long-distance flight.
長距離的飛行對上了年紀的老年人來說非常吃力。

**❼ relationship** **n.** 人際關係、戀愛關係

I can see that my brother values a lot the relationship he and his girlfriend have.

我看的出來哥哥非常重視他與現任女友間的感情。

**❽ rangeland** **n.** 牧場

Their family rangeland is very large.

他們家的牧場很大。

**❾ peacefully** **adv.** 和平地

Can the mouse and cat live peacefully?

老鼠與貓可以和平的相處嗎？

**❿ regret** **v.** 遺憾

I regret so much that I was never able to say 'I love you' to my dad before he passed away.

我很遺憾在我爸去世前我一直無法對他說我愛你。

## ⭐30 秒會話教室

Time flies like an arrow. 光陰似箭。不過平常若想表達時間過得很快，只要簡略為 Time flies 就可以囉。

# 情境 6　購物狂的異想世界

 **Let's Talk in Love**

After returning home, Raymond finds a box of **TV home shopping** product on the floor and several bags of a department store on the bed, and his wife, Helen, is trying on her new clothes one by one...

Raymond 回到家中發現客廳地上放著一箱電視購物台寄來的商品，房間床上又放著好幾袋百貨公司的提袋，而妻子 Helen 正在鏡子前一件件衣服地試穿…

| | | |
|---|---|---|
| Raymond | You went shopping again, Helen? | Helen，妳今天又去逛街購物啦？ |
| Helen | Yeah, today is the first day of the annual sale in the department store. I ran and bought so many beautiful clothes. Do they look good on me? | 對啊，今天是百貨公司週年慶的第一天，我跑去搶了好多漂亮的衣服，你看，穿在我身上好不好看？ |
| Raymond | Yeah, they do but don't you think you bought too many things? Did you not tell me that you have to save money since the wedding and honeymoon cost lots of money in the **deposit**? | 好看是好看，不過妳也買太多了吧！？妳不是跟我說結婚和蜜月旅行花掉了妳不少銀行存款，之後要省一點嗎？ |

| Helen | But there are so many things I want to buy! They become cheaper with the sale discount. | 可是人家還有好多想買的東西啊，周年慶打折的時候買比較便宜嘛！ |
|---|---|---|
| Raymond | You have too many clothes in your closet. You don't wear them very often, so you don't have to buy new ones. | 妳衣櫃裡的衣服已經夠多了，每一件都沒看妳穿過幾次，妳不必一直買新的其實沒關係的。 |
| Helen | Just some extra clothes. Since they don't cost you a penny, you don't have to talk on and on. | 只是多一些衣服而已，花的又不是你的錢，你不必一直嘮叨吧。 |
| Raymond | Just some extra clothes? Then what is the TV home shopping stuff in the living room? | 何止一些衣服？客廳那箱電視購物台寄來的東西又是甚麼？ |
| Helen | That's the exerāse **equipment** which allows you to watch TV and exerāse at the same time. Don't you think I seem to **gain** weight after getting married? I'm afraid you might **cold-shoulder** me so I have to be as slender as I was before our marriage. | 喔，那是標榜可以邊看電視邊瘦身的運動器材啦，你不覺得我結婚之後好像有點變胖嗎？我怕你嫌棄我，所以我要趕快瘦回結婚前的樣子。 |

Raymond　You look just perfect like the days before we are married, but you are not the **sensible** and wise Helen that I used to love.

妳的外表仍舊跟結婚前一樣完美，不過妳已經不是我原本愛的那個理性又懂事的 Helen 了。

Helen　I don't know this would make you so mad.  Can you stop saying the **harsh** words?  Can we talk?

我不知道這件事會讓你這麼生氣，你可以先不要說這麼重的話，我們好好談談嗎？

## ⭐ Some Words to Know

**❶ TV home shopping** `n.` `phr.` 電視購物
The TV home shopping saves lots of trouble, so it's getting popular.
電視購物因省去很多麻煩，所以越來越受歡迎。

**❷ annual** `a.` 一年一次的
The annual sales of department stores are just like warzones for women.
一年一度的百貨公司週年慶簡直就像女人的戰場一樣。

**❸ deposit** `n.` 存款
That kind old man donated all his deposit which he has saved during most of his life to the orphanage.
那位善心的老先生將存了大半輩子的存款全數捐給孤兒院。

**❹ equipment** `n.` (U) 裝備、器具
We should exam the equipment carefully before we set out for mountain climbing.
在出發登山之前一定要仔細檢查裝備。

❺ gain **v.** 增加

I gain much weight every time the winter comes.

每到冬天我就會增加不少體重。

❻ cold-shoulder **v.** 冷落

He found himself being cold-shouldered by some of his friends.

他發現他被部分的朋友冷落。

❼ sensible **a.** 明智的、合情理的

I think you can talk to him directly. He is a sensible man.

你可以直接跟他談談看，他是個明理的人。

❽ harsh **a.** 嚴厲的；惡劣的

He said some harsh words about his classmate.

他說了關於同學的惡言。

## ⭐ 30 秒會話教室

She talked on and on, I couldn' t throw in a word or two. 她一直說個沒完，我連一句話也插不上。

# 情境 7 可以和紅粉知己保持距離嗎？

 **Let's Talk in Love**

Chris and his **confidante**, Gill, get alone quite well.  They usually spend some time talking on the phone or having a cup of coffee together.  This brings up Chris' girlfriend, Daisy, **grienvances**...

Chris 和紅粉知己 Gill 感情很好，兩人經常會通電話或是相約一起喝咖啡，這讓 Chris 的正牌女友 Daisy 感到相當不悅…

| | | |
|---|---|---|
| Chris | Darling, I will hang out with Gill tonight so I'm not coming home for dinner. | 親愛的，我今晚出門陪 Gill 聊聊天，晚上不回來吃晚餐囉。 |
| Daisy | But I have prepared a new dish.  I want you to be the first to taste it. | 可是我準備了新的菜色想讓你第一個品嘗耶！ |
| Chris | I can't.  Gill appears to worry about something.  I will go listening to her and let her air her grievances to see if I can help solve the problem.  I'll be back soon. | 沒辦法，Gill 好像很煩惱的樣子，我去聽她訴苦，看能不能幫她解決問題就回來。 |
| Daisy | Why on earth does she have so many worries to tell you? | 為什麼她老是有那麼多煩惱要找你訴苦？ |

| | |
|---|---|
| Chris | I don't know why she has such bad luck in love. Last time she was **fooled** by a gay, and now she is dating with a man of **femininity**. She wants to know my **point of view** as a male about how I look at her boyfriend. |

我也不知道她的感情運怎麼那麼差？上次被一個男同性戀耍，現在又跟一個行為陰柔的男人交往，她想知道以我這個男性的觀點，對她男朋友的看法是如何。

| | |
|---|---|
| Daisy | Can she not just find any other boy friends? |

難道她沒有其他男性朋友可以找了嗎？

| | |
|---|---|
| Chris | Yes, she can. But most of them are into her, or just some **undependable** guys. The only one she can talk to is me. |

有是有，不過大多是對她有意思的，或是根本靠不住的人，真的能夠聊得來的就只有我了。

| | |
|---|---|
| Daisy | You don't think she's actually interested in you? |

你不怕她其實是對你有意思嗎？

| | |
|---|---|
| Chris | Don't you worry. She **is not my type** and **vice versa**. That's why we can simply be friends. If you care, maybe I should introduce you to each other sometime and then you will understand. OK? |

這妳放心，我們都不是對方喜歡的類型，所以才能單純當好朋友啊！如果妳很介意的話，有機會我介紹妳們認識，妳就會明白了，好不好？

| | |
|---|---|
| Daisy | OK. But **promise** me one **condition**——never go to her place alone! |

好吧！不過你要答應我一個條件，千萬不可以單獨去她家喔！

## ⭐ Some Words to Know

**❶ confidante** **n.** 知己女友
Every man has one or two confidantes.
每個男性或多或少都有一、兩位紅粉知己。

**❷ grievance** **n.** 不滿、牢騷
Don't keep the grievance to yourself.  You can talk to your friends.
有甚麼不滿不要放在心裡，你可以找親朋好友傾訴。

**❸ fool** **v.** 愚弄、欺騙
People usually get fooled by their own eyes and can't not see the truth before them.
人們經常被自己的雙眼愚弄，看不見近在眼前的真相。

**❹ femininity** **n.** (U) 陰柔、女性化
Long hair is traditionally a sign of femininity.
傳統上長髮是女性化象徵。

**❺ point of view** **n.** **phr.** 觀點、見地
Everybody's point of view is different from each other.
每個人的觀點都不同。

**❻ undependable** **a.** 不可靠的
It's better to believe in oneself's ability than others' undependable words.
與其相信他人不可靠的閒言閒語，不如相信自己的能力。

**❼ be one's type** **v.** **phr.** …喜歡的類型、…的菜
Benson's quite handsome and strong, but he's not my type.
Benson 是很帥也很強壯，但就不是我的菜。

**❽ vice versa** **adv.** 反之亦然
She doesn't want to talk to him again, and vice versa.
她不想再跟他說話，反之亦然。

**❾ promise** **v.** 答應

Granny has promised me to make a nice and warm scarf for me.

奶奶答應我要織一條好看又保暖的圍巾給我。

**❿ condition** **n.** 條件

That ma'am wanted the child to accept her condition, so she would buy him ice cream.

那位女士要孩子答應她的條件，才準買冰淇淋給他吃。

## ⭐ 30 秒會話教室

on earth 是一種加強語氣的方式，代表「究竟、到底」的意思，要放在疑問句中。如：Why on earth did you do that?（你到底為什麼要那麼做？）

# 情境 8　開車習慣大不同

 **Let's Talk in Love**

Both Phil and Tracy like going on a trip on holidays.　However, it always needs driving a car no matter they want go to to a scenic spot or a famous local food dinner on streets.　Thus, they usually fight over the driving habits...

Phil 與 Tracy 都很喜歡利用假日出門旅遊，不論是到風景區遊玩、或是在巷弄間尋找美食小店都需要開車，也因此兩人經常因為開車習慣問題而吵架…

Tracy　Dear, you should take the right turn at that road.

親愛的，剛剛那條路應該要右轉才對。

Phil　Why don't you say it earlier?　We've already passed!　Now we can only find a place for a **U-turn**.

妳怎麼不早說？都已經過頭了！現在只好找地方迴轉了。

Tracy　There was a **signpost**!　I thought you would notice it.　Hey!　Wait!　Why do you make a U-turn without flicking the turn signal?　We could be easily **bumped** by the cars coming behind us!

前面明明就有指標啊，我以為你會注意到。喂，等等，你迴轉怎麼不打方向燈啊？這樣很容易被後方來車追撞耶！

**Phil** I **am very aware of** them through the side mirrors. Can you stop talking when I am driving? If you are that good, you drive!

我已經有透過後照鏡看清楚後方來車了，我在開車妳不要多嘴好不好？講得那麼厲害不如換妳來開呀！

**Tracy** If I had a driving **license**, I would just say yes. I would absolutely notice the signposts.

要不是我沒有駕駛執照，不然我還真想答應呢！我一定比你會注意路標。

**Phil** Aren't you an intelligence agent? How come you don't have a driving license? How **ironic**!

妳不是情報單位的嗎？怎麼可能會沒有駕駛執照呢？還真是諷刺。

**Tracy** Sorry. I am not the agent who needs to **deal with** danger. I just **investigate** commerãal activities.

不好意思喔，我不是電影裡面那種出生入死的情報員，我只是調查商業活動的而已。

**Phil** So stop being a **backseat driver** before you get your own license. That just gets me **distracted**. Where should we go after turning right from the road?

所以在妳考到駕駛執照以前請不要在我開車的時候囉嗦了，會害我分心的。剛剛那條路右轉以後接下來怎麼走呢？

**Tracy** Humph, didn't you just tell me to stop being a backseat driver?

哼，你不是叫我不要囉嗦了嗎？

**Phil** **Pathfinding** doesn't count. Don't be mad. Don't you have the map? Give me a hand.

報路不算啦，妳不要嘔氣了，地圖不是在妳手上嗎？幫我看一下嘛！

## ⭐ Some Words to Know

**❶ U-turn** **n.** 迴轉
Some car racers bumped into crash barriers when taking a U-turn on the track.
某位賽車選手在賽道上迴轉時不慎失速撞上護欄。

**❷ signpost** **n.** 路標、指示牌
Just follow along the signpost, and you will find the scenic view restaurant.
只要依照指示牌前進，就可以找到那家景觀餐廳。

**❸ bump** **v.** 碰撞
I bumped my head to the desk when I stood up.
我要站起來時，我的頭撞到桌子。

**❹ be aware of** **v.** **phr.** 知道、意識到
Jess was not ware of any reason that his young brother acted so strangely.
Jess 並不知道他弟弟行為奇怪的原因。

**❺ license** **n.** 執照、許可
Every man dreams about being James Bond who always looks cool and has a killing license.
每個人都夢想成為既帥又擁有殺人執照的詹姆士龐德。

**❻ ironic** **a.** 具有諷刺意味的
How ironic it is that the chicken farmer says he never eats chickens.
養雞的人說自己不吃雞肉，真是諷刺。

**❼ deal with** **v.** **phr.** 應付、處理
Relax! See how I deal with the frequent picky customers.
別緊張，看我怎麼應付這位經常上門都百般挑剔的顧客。

**❽ investigate** **v.** 調查
The stubborn policeman just won't quit investigating this case.
那頑固的警察就是不放棄調查這案子。

**9** backseat driver **n.** **phr.** 後座駕駛人（指給予多餘的駕駛意見的乘客）
I don't want be a backseat driver but shouldn't you stop to let pedestrians pass first?
我不想當個後座駕駛人，但你是不是應該停下來禮讓行人先行。

**10** distracted **a.** 思想不集中的
His dog is missing, getting him distracted all day and unable to focus on the lesson.
他養的小狗不見了，害他整天無法集中精神上課。

**11** pathfinding **n.** (U) 找路
He is good at pathfinding.
他很會找路。

## 30 秒會話教室

以下這句話可以用在當對方放了某些馬後炮的時候，例：Why didn't you say so? 你為什麼不早說？

# 情境 9　不做家事的魚乾女

 **Let's Talk in Love**

Wesley and Olivia who work in the same **workplace** usually go home together after work.  However, when at home, Olivia does not do any **housework** but just turns into a couch potato...

在同一個職場上班的夫妻檔 Wesley 和 Olivia 通常是一起下班回家，不過回到家的 Olivia 卻甚麼家事也不做，就只知道賴在沙發上看電視…

| | | |
|---|---|---|
| Wesley | Can you do some housework, Olivia? | Olivia，妳也好歹做一下家事吧！ |
| Olivia | We ate dinner in the restaurant, didn't we?  What else housework to be done? | 晚餐不是已經在外面吃過了嗎？還要做甚麼家事？ |
| Wesley | Don't you know that there are so much work to do to keep the house clear and clean?  Can't imagine how you lived before we got married. | 要維持一個家的環境整潔，有很多工作要做，妳不知道嗎？真不曉得妳結婚前是怎麼活過來的。 |
| Olivia | Oh, you mean like doing the **laundry**, mopping the floor, cleaning the bathroom? | 喔，你說洗衣服、擦地、清洗浴室這些家事嗎？ |

Wesley　Yes.  You sit before TV when getting home but the laundry hasn't been done for one week.  Don't tell me you will wear them again without washing?

對呀，妳一回家就坐在電視機前面，髒衣服已經累積到一個禮拜的分量了，難道妳要重複穿嗎？

Olivia　But I am so tired after a long day of work.  Just let me take a rest.

可是我上了一整天班，已經很累了，你就讓我先休息一下嘛！

Wesley　I am tired from the work, too.  But we have to work together to **maintain** the family.  Sharing out the housework **equally** can **prevent exhausting** one of us.  I am open-minded enough.  Some men leave all housework to their wives!

我上班也會累啊！可是一個家是需要夫妻兩共同維持的，平均地分攤家事才不會讓我們的其中一個人累上加累。我已經很開明了，有些男人是把家事全都丟給老婆的耶！

Olivia　Alright, alright.  But it's the best part of the show on TV right now.  I will do the laundry during the commerãals, OK?

好啦好啦！現在電視正演到最精彩的地方，我等進廣告的時候就去洗衣服，好嗎？

Wesley　Let's make a deal: you use the breaks to do some simple, petite work or I will go telling the colleagues in office how lazy you are at home.

那我們約定，以後妳要利用看電視的廣告時間做一些簡單、零碎的家事，不然我就去告訴辦公室的同事說妳在家裡有多麼懶散！

Olivia  OK, I've got it.  Don't **destroy** my hard-earned **reputation**.

好啦，我知道了，你不要破壞我辛苦建立的形象。

## ⭐ Some Words to Know

**❶ workplace** n. 工作場所
Don't take personal feelings to the workplace.
請不要把私人情感帶到工作場所中。

**❷ housework** n. 家事
I know I shouldn't but I hate doing housework.
我知道不應該但我就是討厭做家事。

**❸ laundry** n. （洗好或未洗好的）衣服
It's raining now so there's no place to hang the laundry.
下雨了，洗好的衣服沒地方曬。

**❹ maintain** v. 維持
It's not easy for a woman who has three children to maintain such a good body.
生過三個小孩的媽媽還能維持那樣的好身材，真是不容易。

**❺ equally** adv. 平均地
The farm owner gave his two sons eaqually the income which earned by selling the farm.
農場主人把賣地的所得平均分給兩個兒子。

**❻ prevent** v. 避免
It seemed that there was no other way to prevent war at that time.
當時似乎沒有其他可以避免戰爭的方式。

**❼ exhaust** **v.** 使精疲力盡

The long-distance marching exhawsted the soldiers.
長距離的進軍讓士兵疲憊不堪。

**❽ destroy** **v.** 毀滅、破壞

A serious forest fire destroyed the whole town at the foot of the mountain.
一場森林大火毀滅了山腳下的整個小鎮。

**❾ reputation** **n.** (U) 名譽、聲望

She is a politician of good reputation.
她是個富有聲望的政治人物。

## ⭐30 秒會話教室

想跟人約法三章的話，以下這兩句很好用喔。Let's make a deal. 我們來做個約定。Let's make a promise. 我們來做個承諾。

# 情境 10 小事也要生氣？

 **Let's Talk in Love**

Joseph and Rebecca have started losing **patience** after being together for a long while. Impatient words occur when they talk to each other and the little issues in their daily life are getting bigger and bigger...

Joseph 跟 Rebecca 這對情侶交往久了之後，開始對彼此失去耐心，兩人對話時經常出現不耐煩的言詞，生活上的小問題也逐漸放大…

Joseph　Can you please stop putting things on your face? I'll be late for work.

> Rebecca，妳能不能別再往臉上塗塗抹抹了？我上班已經要遲到了！

Rebecca　Can you just wait for another ten minutes? Were if not for you who used the bathroom first, I would have my makeup done already.

> 你就不能再等十分鐘嗎？剛才要不是你先佔用浴室，我早就化好妝了。

Joseph　I got up first. I used it first as **a matter of course**. Since it takes you so long to put on the makeup, you should get up earlier than me. If you do this again, you will have to go to work by yourself.

> 是我先起床的，先用浴室是天經地義的事情，既然妳化妝需要那麼久的時間，更應該比我早起床才是啊！以後妳再這樣的話，就自己想辦法去上班吧。

Rebecca　I can't sleep well and get up early because you **snore** all night.

> 還不都是你晚上睡覺會打鼾，害我晚上睡不好，早上爬不起來。

| Joseph | How **dare** you **incriminate** me when you like to **sleep in**? Did you just sleep well in the first year we dated each other? | 妳自己愛賴床，竟敢賴在我頭上？交往頭一年妳不是一樣照睡不誤？ |
| Rebecca | Anyway, let's stop blaming each other, OK? Think about it. Don't you feel we've been impatient to each other? | 反正我們別再互相指責對方了好嗎？認真想想，你不覺得我們倆最近對彼此很沒有耐心嗎？ |
| Joseph | Kind of. The little **issues** that were OK now appear to become big **eyesores**. | 是有一點，感覺以前沒問題的小事情，現在看起來都很不順眼。 |
| Rebecca | Are we now in the so-called tired relationship? | 我們是不是進入所謂的倦怠期了啊？ |
| Joseph | Perhaps. Let's discuss this when we come back later, OK? I am almost late. | 或許吧，等我們晚上回家再好好討論，好嗎？我真的已經要遲到了。 |
| Rebecca | OK. I'm coming. | 好，這就來。 |

## ⭐ Some Words to Know

**❶ patience** **n.** (U) 耐心
You need more patience.  We almost get the tickets.
有耐心一點，快輪到我們買票了。

**❷ a matter of course** **n.** **phr.** 理所當然的事
It's a matter of course to yield seats to the elder, pregnant women, the weak, and the children.
讓位給老弱婦孺是理所當然的事。

**❸ snore** **vi.** 打鼾
I am so glad that my other half doesn't snore.
真高興我的另一半不會打呼。

**❹ dare** **vi.** 敢、竟敢
How dare you insult my family!
你竟敢辱罵我的家人！

**❺ incriminate** **v.** 歸咎於
The setback of the government's policies should not incriminat the people.
政府的施政失敗不應該歸咎於人民。

**❻ sleep in** **v.** **phr.** 比平時起得晚、賴床
Most office workers allow themselves to sleep in on holidays.
每到假日，多數的上班族就會容許自己比平時晚起床。

**❼ issue** **n.** 問題、議題
The same-sex marriage issue remains quite sensitive in some states of the U.S.
同性婚姻議題在美國的某些州仍然相當敏感。

**❽ eyesore** **n.** 看起來不順眼的東西
As long as Mom is in anger, everything is an eyesore to her.
只要媽媽生起氣來，任何東西看起來都不順眼。

## 30 秒會話教室

put on 強調的穿戴、塗抹的動作，而非要穿戴或塗抹的物品。如：My sister <u>puts on</u> some lipstick.（我姐姐擦了些口紅。）<u>Put</u> your coat <u>on</u>.（把你的外套穿上。）

## ⭐ Makeup & Cosmetics

Makeup 和 cosmetics 中文都翻譯成化妝，但意思其實不相同，簡單的說，makeup 多為加抹於臉上的物品，好讓面子更加出色；而 cosmetics 除了這意思之外，更包含臉部、身體的保養，因此意思更為廣泛。所以 Rebecca 一早起來塗抹的便是 makeup。

愛美的確是人的天性，據考古研究，西元前 4000 年的古埃及就有化妝品的證據，古希臘與羅馬人也會使用化妝品，而且化妝品成分含有水銀，cosmetics 一字即是源於希臘，原意是『穿著與裝飾的技巧』。中國化妝的歷史也是淵遠流長，據說商周時代宮廷婦女為了獲得君王的賞識，便開始化妝打扮、彼此爭豔，至春秋時代，民間也開始化起妝來。無獨有偶，此時中國的化妝品製作時同樣使用到水銀。綜觀人類活動，只要有文明幾乎都有化妝的文化，箇中巧妙不同就是。一路算下來，人類化妝的歷史也有 6000 年了！人類對化妝的觀念也隨著時代不停地改變，18 世紀英國維多利亞女王認為使用化妝品是不禮貌、粗鄙的行為，因此只有戲子與妓女才會化妝，現代卻有人提倡化妝是種禮貌，不知始作俑者是否為化妝品公司，但人為樂己者容卻是千年來不變的道理啊！甚至連男性也開始畫起裝來了不是？

# 情境 11 牙膏怎麼擠也要吵？

 **Let's Talk in Love**

Gill and her boyfriend, Vincent, stay **overnight** at a hotel in a scenic **resort** for the first time after they got together. This is when Gill realizes how her boyfriend pays much attention to little habits...

Gill 跟男友 Vincent 交往後，兩人第一次一起到風景區的飯店過夜，卻也是在這個時候，才讓 Gill 發現男友對於一些生活小習慣非常注重…

| | | |
|---|---|---|
| Vincent | Gill, you've just brushed your teeth, right? | Gill，剛剛妳先刷了牙對吧？ |
| Gill | Yes. I've washed my face and brushed the teeth when you were sleeping and I'm awaiting you for breakfast. Why? | 對啊，你還在睡的時候我就梳洗好了，等著跟你去吃早餐呢。怎麼了嗎？ |
| Vincent | The way you **squeeze** the toothpaste is incorrect. How can you just **grasp** and squeeze? You should squeeze it from the **bottom**. | 妳擠牙膏的方式不對，怎麼可以牙膏握著就隨手一擠呢？應該要從最底下推上來才對。 |
| Gill | What's the difference? Can we just use sāssors to cut it in the middle and **scrape** the rest of it with toothbrushes? | 有甚麼差別嗎？反正用到最後，再拿剪刀從中間剪開，用牙刷伸進去把剩下的牙膏刮乾淨不就可以了嗎？ |

| | | |
|---|---|---|
| Vincent | But before that, the middle part of the paste will become flat and unable to stand on the holder. | 可是在那之前，牙膏的中段就會被妳越捏越扁，這樣就無法直立放在牙刷牙膏架上了。 |
| Gill | Why not just lay it on the sink? | 那麼平放在洗手台上不就好了嗎？ |
| Vincent | Then it will get wet. I don't like it wet. | 這樣牙膏會整條弄得濕濕的，我不喜歡這種感覺。 |
| Gill | You are quite a **handful**. We are not living together anyway. You can do whatever you want at home and you don't **interfere**, OK? | 你很難搞耶，反正我們又沒有住在一起，等回到你家，你喜歡甚麼樣的方式就隨你，你也別干涉我的方式好嗎？ |
| Vincent | You shouldn't put the used towel **randomly**. That would grow **mold**. You should find a place to hang it. | 妳用過的毛巾也不應該隨便亂放，這樣會發霉的，應該找個地方掛好。 |
| Gill | This is a hotel! Housekeepers will come and take care of it after we check out. | 這裡是飯店耶，待會我們退房就會有服務人員進來處理了啦。 |

## ⭐ Some Words to Know

**❶ overnight** `adv.` 整夜、整夜的
It's very late.  We need to find a place to stay overnight.
很晚了，我們需要找個可以過夜的地方。

**❷ resort** `n.` 休閒度假地、名勝地區
Jiu Fen is a very popular vacation resort in north Taiwan.
九份是北台灣相當受歡迎的假日景點。

**❸ squeeze** `v.` 擠、壓、榨
It's not easy to squeeze out every drop of the lemon juice by hand.
用手不容易把每滴檸檬汁都擠出來。

**❹ grasp** `v.` 抓
Mark grasped a coat in a hurry and rushed out.
Mark 急急忙忙地抓了一件外套就衝出家門。

**❺ bottom** `n.` 底部、下端
My classmate found a bug after she almost drank up the beverage.
我同學喝完飲料才發現瓶底有一隻蟲。

**❻ scrape** `v.` 刮
Scrape your shoes clean before you come in.
進來之前把你的鞋子刮乾淨。

**❼ handful** `n.` 難控制的人、事
The young boy is quite a handful.
那小男孩真是個麻煩的傢伙。

**❽ interfere** `vi.` 介入、干涉
We should not interfere in others' business.
我們不該介入他人的家務事。

**❾ randomly** `adv.` 隨便地、隨機地
The toys are randomly placed on the ground.
玩具被隨意的擺在地上。

**⑩ mold** **n.** (U)　霉、黴菌

There is mold on the toast.

土司上有霉。

**30 秒會話教室**

當你想知道事物兩者間的差異時可用下列問法：What's the difference between jail and prison?（監獄跟監牢有甚麼差別？）

# 情境 12　男方出國深造

 **Let's Talk in Love**

The relationship of Zoe and Trevor is getting clear. They could be a couple as long as one of them **expresses** the love for one another. Trevor, however, is bringing a bad news for her...

Zoe 跟住在同一棟公寓的 Trevor 的關係正逐漸明朗化，只差開口告白兩人就是情侶了，此時 Trevor 卻帶來了一個令人難過的消息…

| | |
|---|---|
| Zoe | Come on in, Trevor. You said on the phone that you have something to tell me. What is it? |
| | Trevor，快進來，你在電話裡說有重要的事情要告訴我，是甚麼呢？ |
| Trevor | Do you still remember I made a deal with my father? He said if I **achieve** success by myself, he will not force me to take over the company. |
| | Zoe，妳還記得我跟我父親之間的約定嗎？他說如果我自己闖出名堂，就不逼我接手經營公司？ |
| Zoe | Yes. I remember. Does your father **go back on** his words? |
| | 記得啊，難不成你父親反悔了？ |
| Trevor | No. A **master** has **taken a fancy to** my painting. He said I have **potential** and asked me if I want to pursue **advanced studies**. |
| | 不是，我畫的油畫被一位名家相中，他說我很有潛力，問我願不願意到巴黎深造？ |

| | |
|---|---|
| **Zoe** | Really?  That's just great!  What did you say to him? | 真的嗎？那太好了，你怎麼回答？ |

Zoe　Really?  That's just great!  What did you say to him?

真的嗎？那太好了，你怎麼回答？

Trevor　I think this is a wonderful opportunity, but I have to discuss this with you first so I can reply him.

我覺得這是一個大好機會，但我還是想先跟妳討論再回覆對方⋯。

Zoe　Oh, why do you have to discuss with me since we are not a couple?  Go following your dreams bravely.

哎呀，我們又不是男女朋友，怎麼會需要跟我討論呢？你還是勇敢地去追求你的夢想吧。

Trevor　Zoe, I am grateful to have you around these days.  I know we can be together if I express my feelings to you now.  But I can't be this **selfish**.  If you are willing to wait until I finish studies and return, I will formally ask you to be my girlfriend.

Zoe，這些日子以來很感謝有妳的陪伴，我知道只要現在開口向妳表白，我們就能在一起了，但我不能這麼自私，如果妳願意等我學成歸國的話，我一定會慎重請妳當我的女朋友的。

Zoe　I am willing to wait for you.  We can talk about it after you come back.  You just go developing your career.

我願意等你。交往的事情等你回來再說，利用這段時間好好地去闖出一片天吧。

Trevor　OK.  I'll go and reply him then.

好的，那我這就去給對方回覆。

## ⭐ Some Words to Know

**❶ express** [v.] 表達、陳述
His eyes express deep sadness.
他的雙眼透露深沉的哀傷。

**❷ achieve** [v.] 達成
You will achieve nothing if you spend all your time playing video games.
如果你盡把你的時間花在玩電動上，就永遠都不會有成就。

**❸ go back on** [v.] [phr.] 不履行
The government looks likely to go back on its political promises.
政府可能要對於它的政策承諾跳票了。

**❹ master** [n.] 名家、大師
He's is a tae kwon do master.
他是一位跆拳道的大師。

**❺ take a fancy to** [v.] [phr.] 愛上
I've taken a fancy to Japanese pop culture.
我喜歡上日本流行文化。

**❻ potential** [n.] (U) 潛力
I don't feel I'm achieving my full potential in my present work.
我覺得我在目前的工作中沒有發揮全部的潛力。

**❼ advanced** [a.] 高等的、進階的
After the employees in this factory passed the beginning level exam, they can go further to learn some advanced work skills.
工廠的員工通過初級考試後，就可以進階學習一些高等的工作技能。

**❽ studies** [n.] (plural) 學業、研究
Albert should spend more time on his studies.
Albert 應該多花點時間在他的研究上。

**❾ selfish** [a.] 自私的

A selfish person would never be welcomed in any place.

自私的人在任何地方都絕對不會受到歡迎。

**30 秒會話教室**

A real man never goes back on his words. 一言既出、駟馬難追。go back on one's word 就是「食言」的意思喔。

# 情境 13 　宗教信仰不同

##  Let's Talk in Love

Ivan and his girl, Jessica, **get along** well, but they have a little fight every time Jessica wants Ivan to go to church with her on holidays...

Ivan 跟女友 Jessica 的感情非常融洽，但每當假日 Jessica 要找 Ivan 一起上教堂的時候，兩人就會發生一點小爭執…

Jessica　I am going to the church tomorrow. Are you sure you are not coming with me?

我明天要去教堂做禮拜，你確定不跟我一起去嗎？

Ivan　I've told you. I am not a believer of **Catholicism**. Why not you go by yourself and I'll wait outsides.

我已經說過了，我不信天主教，妳自己去就可以了，我會在外面等妳。

Jessica　People without **faith** are just like boats **drifting** aimlessly in the wide ocean. Are you really sure you don't want to come and listen to the Father's **preach**?

內心沒有信仰的人就像沒有目標在汪洋上漂泊的船一樣，你真的不來聽聽神父講道嗎？

Ivan　In fact, I am not a real **atheist**. All my family follow **Buddhism**.

其實我也不算是無神論者，我的家族全都是信奉佛教的。

| | | |
|---|---|---|
| Jessica | Buddhism? So you believe in **transmigration** and the like? | 佛教，所以你相信輪迴轉世那些說法囉？ |
| Ivan | In fact, I am not a very **religious** Buddhist. I have followed people to burn **incense** since my childhood, so I know some of the **doctrines**. | 其實我也不是非常虔誠的佛教徒啦，只是從小都會跟著拿香拜拜，當然或多或少相信其中的一些道理。 |
| Jessica | Will your family allow us to have the wedding in a church when we get married? | 那以後如果我們結婚，你的家人願意讓我在教堂舉辦婚禮嗎？ |
| Ivan | In fact, Buddhism does not deny other religions. Buddhists don't force others to believe it, so I think it's not a problem. | 其實佛教並不排斥其他宗教，佛教徒也不會強迫別人硬要信一樣的宗教，所以我想是沒問題的。 |
| Jessica | In fact various religions try to make people altruistic. It's a good thing that religions can communicate with each other. | 其實不同宗教都是以勸人向善為出發點，彼此之間能夠互相交流、了解也不錯呢。 |
| Ivan | Yeah. It's OK to hear you share doctrines, but don't make me go to the church. I feel it will sacrifice lots of pastime. | 是啊，不過聽妳說說教義可以，別再逼我上教堂了，我覺得會占用好多休閒的時間。 |

## Some Words to Know

❶ get along **v.** **phr.** 相處得來、喜歡與對方相處
I don't really get along with my brother-in-law.
我和我姊夫相處不來。

❷ Catholicism **n.** (U) 天主教
Most people don't understand the difference between Catholicism and Christianity.
大部分的人對天主教以及基督教的差別都不是很了解。

❸ faith **n.** (U) 信念、信仰
Even in time of trouble, we should never lose faith.
即使在困境中也不能失去信念。

❹ drift **v.** 漂流
Losing power, the boat drifted in the ocean for a couple of days.
失去動力後，這船在海上漂流了好幾天。

❺ preach **n.** 講道、訓誡
That Father's preach was quite interesting.
那神父的講到很有趣。

❻ atheist **n.** 無神論者
Communists are wolrd-famous atheists.
共產主義者是世界著名的無神論者。

❼ Buddhism **n.** (U) 佛教
Buddhism is the religion that most Chinese believe.
佛教是華人信仰最多的宗教。

❽ transmigration **n.** (U) 輪迴
The idea of transmigration is kind of romantic to some level.
就某程度而言，輪迴的概念是蠻浪漫的。

**❾ religious** a. 宗教的、虔誠的
She is a very religious Catholic.
她是一位非常虔誠的天主教徒。

**❿ doctrine** n. （宗教的）教義
Since he learned of Catholic doctrine, he has been very interested in the related fields.
自從他接觸過天主教的教義之後，就開始對相關領域非常感興趣。

## 30 秒會話教室

宗教信仰的問答法如下，但觸及這種敏感議題的時候要特別小心喔。
Q：Are you religious? 你有宗教信仰嗎？A：I am a _____（我是一個 _____ 教徒。）或 A：I am not religious.（我沒有宗教信仰。）

# 情境 14　未來婆媳大戰

 **Let's Talk in Love**

Gordon takes Stella to see his parents and tells them about their plan of getting married.  **Out of the blue**, Gordon's mother turns **hostile** suddenly, leaving everyone quite embarrassed...

Gordon 帶女友 Stella 回家拜見父母，並向父母報告兩人有意結婚的消息，沒想到 Gordon 的媽媽當場翻臉，讓現場氣氛好不尷尬⋯

| | | |
|---|---|---|
| Gordon's mother | I would never allow you to marry a woman of ordinary origins.  We are a **prominent** family in our hometown. | 我絕對不答應你娶一個出身這麼平凡的女人，我們家好歹也是地方上的望族啊。 |
| Gordon | Mom, that's just a name.  We are not public **figures** or some rich family.  We don't need to put us on that prominent **position**. | 媽，望族也只是個虛名而已，我們又不是甚麼公眾人物或有錢人家，不需要把自己看的高高在上。 |
| Gordon's mother | How silly it is.  So many local girls from good families are waiting in line to marry you.  Why do you get such an ordinary woman in the city? | 你說甚麼傻話，地方上想要嫁進我們家的好人家女孩多到要排隊了呢，你怎麼反而到城市裡認識了這麼一個普通的女孩回來。 |

| Stella | Sorry, Mrs. Smith. Although where I come from isn't a match to yours, I have parents. Is it necessary that you have to **humiliate** me? | Mrs. Smith，不好意思，雖然我的出身配不上妳們家，但是我好歹也是有父母的，您有必要如此羞辱我嗎？ |

| Gordon | I have to marry her anyway. If you don't **consent**, I will have a **civil** marriage with her. | 對啊，媽，反正我這輩子非她不娶，如果妳硬是不答應的話，我就跟她去公證結婚。 |

| Gordon's father | Dear, you are being **unreasonable**. Ever since Stella entered our home, I can tell she's a bright, sensible girl. Besides, this is our son's life, you should let go and let him make his own deāsion. | 老婆啊，妳說這話也太過分了，從 Stella 一進我們家作客，就可以看出她是個聰明懂事的好女孩，而且這是兒子的人生，妳應該放手讓他自己作主。 |

| Gordon's mother | Well, I just dislike any powerful business woman. Can she still spare energy and thoughts to take care of her husband and children when at home? | 哼，反正我就是看不慣工作能力強的女人，這種人回到家還有心思照顧好丈夫跟孩子嗎？ |

| Gordon | Mom, Stella isn't only good at working but also sweet and thoughtful. She takes good care of me. She's a **respectable** modern woman. | 媽，Stella 不僅工作能力強，平常也很溫柔體貼，把我照顧的很好，是個值得敬佩的新時代女性。 |

| Stella | I can understand how you love your son, Mrs. Smith, but can you give me a chance and judge me after spending some time with me? | Mrs. Smith，您愛護兒子的心情我能體會，但能否請您給我機會，實際跟我相處、了解我之後再來判斷呢？ |
| Gordon's father | That's right. You two just come home whenever you have time, so your mom and Stella can get to know each other. | 是啊是啊，你們倆有空就回來家裡吃飯，讓你媽媽跟 Stella 多了解彼此吧。 |

## ✦ Some Words to Know

**❶ out of the blue** adv. phr. 意外地
Lady Gaga came to the party out of the blue.
Lady Gaga 意外地來到舞會現場。

**❷ hostile** a. 敵意的、不友善的
A hostile neighbor has just moved to the next door.
隔壁搬來了一位很不友善的鄰居。

**❸ prominent** a. 卓越的、著名的
This prominent alumnus came back again to the shool to give a speech this year.
這位卓越的校友今年又回到學校來演講。

**❹ figure** n. 人物、名人
She finally became a figure known to the world.
他終於變成世界知名的人物。

**❺ position** **n.** 身分、地位

Don't forget your position as a waiter even when facing a customer who is hard to deal with.

即使在面對難纏的客戶的時候，也不要忘記自己的身分是個服務生。

**❻ humiliate** **v.** 使丟臉

Parents should avoid humiliating children in front of people.

父母應避免在眾人面前汙辱小孩。

**❼ consent** **v.** 同意

The deal will be complete if you consent.

如果你同意，這交易就完成了。

**❽ civil marriage** **n.** **phr.** 公證結婚

Many newly-weds choose to have a civil marriage in the court.

有許多新人選擇了到法院公證結婚。

**❾ unreasonable** **a.** 過分的、不講理的

The English teacher is so unreasonable that he wants us to hand out 3 articles in a day.

英文老師真是太不講理了，要我們在一天內交出三篇作文。

**❿ respectable** **a.** 值得尊敬的

He is a very respectable gentleman.

他是一位值得尊敬的紳士。

## ⭐ 30 秒會話教室

tell 有「辨別」的意思，如：You are a good man, I can tell from your eyes.（你是個好人，我從你的眼睛裡看的出來。）I can't tell what's real.（我無法分辨甚麼是真的。）

# 情境 15　腳踏兩條船

 **Let's Talk in Love**

Kenneth and his girlfriend, Irene, live separately in two different āties. They hardly get together but live apart a lot. So Kenneth begins to get closer with the colleague, Grace, in the company...

Kenneth 與女友 Irene 分別住在兩個不同的城市，聚少離多，因此 Kenneth 開始與公司裡的女同事 Grace 越走越近…

| | | |
|---|---|---|
| Kenneth | Are you available after work today, Grace? Do you want to get a drink at my place? | Grace，妳今天下班後有事嗎？要不要到我家去喝一杯？ |
| Grace | Don't you have a girlfriend? Will she not care about this? | 你不是有女朋友嗎？她不會介意嗎？ |
| Kenneth | (Sigh) I meet her just one time one or two months. I am kind of unable to **stand** this long-distance relationship **anymore**. | 哀，我跟她一、兩個月才見面一次，我已經有點受不了這種遠距離的關係了。 |
| Grace | Why don't you just break up with her? | 那為什麼不乾脆跟她分手呢？ |

| Kenneth | I still like her a lot.  It's just that I feel empty and lonely when we can't see each other.  It feels **horrible** when I need **company** and she is not around. | 我還是很喜歡她呀，只是無法見面的時候總是會感到空虛寂寞，需要有人陪的時候女朋友卻不在身邊，這種感覺很難受。 |
|---|---|---|
| Grace | So you want me to fill your **emptiness**, taking me as your **backup** plan? | 所以你就想找我填補這份寂寞、把我當成你的替代女友？ |
| Kenneth | If you think so...didn't you have a crush on someone before?  No further **development**? I think you, too, have some **ineffable** difficulties, right? | 妳要這麼想也可以…妳很久之前不是說有了喜歡的人嗎？後來怎麼就沒下文了？我想妳應該也有一些苦衷吧？ |
| Grace | (Sigh) That's really a tragedy.  I can't get over him but it's our destiney that we can't be together. | 哀，那件事簡直是個悲劇。我的確忘不了他，但又注定無法跟他在一起。 |
| Kenneth | So let's go.  Let's fill the emptiness for each other. | 所以我們走吧，讓我們填補彼此的寂寞。 |
| Grace | Alright.  I accept your suggestion. | 好，我接受你的提議。 |

## ⭐ Some Words to Know

**❶ stand** `v.` 忍受

How can you stand the noise, living beside the train station?

你要怎麼忍受住在火車站旁的吵雜聲？

**❷ anymore** `adv.` 再也（不）、（不）再

I don't want to make friends who lies anymore.

我再也不要跟會說謊的人交朋友了。

**❸ horrible** `a.` 糟透的

That food at that restaurant was so horrible.

那家餐廳的食物糟糕透了。

**❹ company** `n.` 陪伴

We can tell from her smiles that she enjoys the dog's company.

從她的笑容我們可以知道她喜歡這隻狗的陪伴。

**❺ emptiness** `n.` 空洞、空虛

No one but her best friend can understand her emptiness inside her heart underneath the fame.

除了她最好的朋友外沒有人能理解掩藏在她名氣底下的內心空洞。

**❻ lonely** `a.` 寂寞的、孤單的

My daughter said she felt very lonely when I was working away from home. I felt so sorry to hear that.

女兒說我因工作不在家時她感到非常寂寞，對做爸爸的人來說真是不捨。

**❼ backup** `n.` 備案、後援、支援

Your colleagues are your backup system.

你的同事們都是你的後援系統。

**❽ development** `n.` 發展

Smart phones have great development over the three years.

智慧手機在近三年來有了長足的發展。

**❾ ineffable** `a.` 說不出的

There's ineffable joy when I am with her.

當我和她在一起時，有一種說不出的喜悅。

**❿ tragedy** `n.` 悲劇

The prisoner's childhood is such a tragedy.

那位受刑人的童年簡直是一場悲劇。

## ⭐ 30 秒會話教室

以下兩種說法都是詢問對方是否有空閒的時間，如：<u>Are you available tonight?</u> 或 <u>Are you free tonight?</u>（你今晚有空嗎？）

# 情境 16　抓到出軌證據

 **Let's Talk in Love**

Gill has returned from a trip to a scenic resort for a weekend with her boyfriend, Vincent.  She happily **updates** all the pictures they have took on Facebook and **tags** Vincent on them.  At this point, a strange woman leaves an **ambiguous** message on one of the pictures but deleted it right away.  Therefore, Gill **estimates** the time he gets home from work and makes a call to him...

與男友 Vincent 到風景區度過一個周末回來的 Gill，開開心心地將兩人出遊所拍的照片上傳到臉書，並將 Vincent 標註在照片上。此時有張照片出現了一位陌生女子曖昧的留言，但隨即又刪掉了，於是 Gill 算準男友應該下班到家的時間，打了電話過去…

| | | |
|---|---|---|
| Vincent | Do you call me this late for anything serious? | 妳這麼晚還打電話來，有急事嗎？ |
| Gill | Vincent, I've got to ask you.  Who is the woman who uses Cutie Lin as her Facebook account? | Vincent，我有事情要問你，在臉書上一個帳號為「Cutie Lin」的女生，是你的甚麼人？ |
| Vincent | Cutie Lin?  She's just a friend.  Why do you ask? | 她喔，只是一個普通朋友啦。妳問這個做甚麼？ |
| Gill | Are you sure you are just friends?  No particular **fellowship**? | 你確定只是普通朋友？交情沒有特別好？ |

| Vincent | No. I am **unacquainted** with her. We just talked for couple of times on Facebook. | 對啊，我跟她不熟啦，在臉書上沒講過幾次話。 |

Gill Then why did she leave "Dear, I miss you so much. You have not come to my place for going out with your girlfriend. I am so lonely. Can you go to your place?" beneath one of your photos I uploaded to Facebook?

這樣啊，那為什麼我今天上傳完你的照片後，她在某張照片底下留言「親愛的我好想你，你為了帶正牌女友去玩，這個周末都沒來我家找我，我好寂寞，今晚可以去你家嗎？」。

Vincent Uh...well...

這…這。

Gill She **either** wanted me to know your relation on purpose **or** had not realized I would see the message so she deleted it right away. Wait! I hear some woman's calling you on the phone...you are with that woman now!?

我想她要不是故意讓我知道你們的關係；就是一時沒發現留言會被我看見，所以那則留言馬上就被刪掉了…等等，我在電話中聽到有女人在叫你…原來你現在根本就跟那個女的在一起！？

Vincent (Sign) **Busted**. I guess I have to **confess** everything, then.

哀，既然被妳發現了，那我就只好坦承了。

Gill I just know it. A **narcissistic** man like you should love yourself much more than me. Let's break up right now so you two can be together. But I don't want to see you from now on!

我就知道！像你這種自戀的人，一定是愛自己比愛我還要多。我們馬上分手，成全你跟那個女人，從今以後你再也不要出現在我面前了！

## ⭐ Some Words to Know

❶ update **v.** 更新
That model updates her Facebook every day.
那位模特兒每天都會更新她臉書上的個人近況。

❷ tag **v.** 給…加標籤
Every patient's blood sample is tagged in the hospital.
在醫院裡每一位病患的血液樣本都會貼上標籤。

❸ ambiguous **a.** 含糊不清的
The government has been ambiguous on this issue.
在這議題上，政府一直很曖昧。

❹ estimate **v.** 預計、估計
They estimate that forty five people have been killed in this accident.
他們估計 45 人在這意外中喪生。

❺ fellowship **n.** 交情、友誼
The banker bears the minister of the Ministry of Finance strong fellowship.
那位銀行家跟財政部長有著深厚的交情。

❻ unacquainted **a.** 不熟悉的、不認識的
We are unacquainted with foreign cultures.
我們不太瞭解外國人的風土民情。

❼ either...or 要不…或者
He either forgets our appointment or oversleeps.
他要不是忘了我們的約定，就是睡過頭遲到了。

❽ busted **a.** 被逮補、被抓到
He was busted cheating on his girlfriend.
他背著女友偷吃被抓到了。

**❾ confess** **v.** 坦白、承認

I have to confess that I don't understand what that famous painting is good about?

我必須承認我完全無法理解名畫的魅力何在？

**❿ narcissistic** **a.** 自戀的

A narcissistic man never cares about how others feel.

自戀的人總是不在乎別人的感受。

## ⭐ 30 秒會話教室

Either or 為兩者間任一個的意思。用法如：Either you or I must wash the dishes.（總該有個人去洗碗，不是你就是我。）

# Part 4

# 誰都要來參一腳

## 情境 1　星座說我們不合

 **Let's Talk in Love**

Gill, who just broke up with a player, meets Matt through a friend's introduction.  This time she makes sure he is not just a pretty face who only care about the looks, and also a person has some normal past relationships.  She **shrinks** back at the **sight** when she finds out more about the signs though...

跟花心男友分手的 Gill 經由朋友介紹認識了 Matt，這次她先確定對方不是愛美的花美男、感情史似乎也很正常，但當問到星座這一關時就讓她望而卻步…

Gill　Did you say you are a Scorpio?

你說你的星座是天蠍座？

Matt　Yah, I was born in November 5th. What's wrong?

對啊，11 月 5 號生的，怎麼了嗎？

Gill　I am a Libra...Let me see...Look, the horoscope says the **matching** point of a Libra and a Scorpio is only 70.

我是天秤座…我看看…你看，星座書上說天秤跟天蠍的速配指數只有 70 分耶。

Matt　I think 70 is pretty good.  The signs can only be used for **reference** only.  It's so **narrow-minded** to **divide** the people in this whole world into only 12 categories.

我覺得 70 分不低了啊，而且星座只能當參考啦，把世界上所有的人只分成 12 種未免太狹隘了。

| | |
|---|---|
| **Gill** | But don't you agree some of the characteristics of the zodiac signs here?  For example, Scorpios are very mysterious with much charisma, **faithful** to love, and affectional... | 可是你不覺得星座說的都很準嗎？比方說天蠍座的人渾身充滿神秘魅力、對待感情專一又深情… |
| **Matt** | Alright, alright!  If you only acknowledge the good qualities, why should I deny any of them? | 好好好，妳故意挑優點說，我怎麼好意思否認呢？ |
| **Gill** | Huh, so do you also acknowledge some dark sides of yourself?  Like easy to get **jealous**, always get revenge on people, crafty minded, and defensive. | 呵呵，那缺點你也承認囉？愛吃醋、報復心強、城府又深，感覺不好惹。 |
| **Matt** | Most Scorpios I've know are simple and kind people, with much sense of humor.  Maybe it's also about my **blood** type B personality. | 我所認識的天蠍座大多是單純又善良的人，而且都很有搞笑天分，可能因為血型是 B 型的關係吧。 |
| **Gill** | You're right!  I forgot matching the blood types and the **symbols** of Chinese Zodiac besides the signs. | 也對，忘了除了看星座，還要搭配血型跟生肖。 |

Matt　See, I told you!  After all, there are many factors that have influences on a person's characters, including the family environment and the educational background.  The zodiac signs should only be used as references.  Don't categorize and label people before you get to know him or her well.

妳看吧！說到底，影響一個人性格的因素還是很多的，包括家庭環境和求學背景都有差，星座這種東西看看可以，千萬別在深入了解一個人之前就先將大家分類了。

## ⭐ Some Words to Know

**❶ shrink** [vi.] 退縮、畏懼
That little girl shrinks whenever hugged by a stranger.
那個小女嬰很畏懼給陌生人抱。

**❷ sight** [n.] (U) 視界、視線所及的範圍
The contestants all speed up when the finish line is in sight.
當終點線進入視線範圍內時，選手們紛紛加快腳步衝刺。

**❸ match** [vi.] 相配
Red pants don't match with green tops at all.
紅褲子跟綠上衣極不相配。

**❹ reference** [n.] 參考
The references of the book are listed at the last page.
撰寫本書的參考書目列於最末頁。

**⑤ narrow-minded** [a.] 胸襟狹窄的

Those narrow-minded people always feel bitter when seeing someone else's success.

那些心胸狹窄的人總是見不得別人好。

**⑥ divide** [v.] 劃分、分成

Out department is divided into three teams that are in charge of different marketing plans aimed for different target markets.

我們部門被劃分成 3 個小組，分別負責對不同的目標市場執行不同的行銷企劃。

**⑦ faithful** [a.] 忠誠的

A faithful partner will never spontaneously agree to see another opposite sex alone with giving a notice in advance.

一位忠誠的另一半不會隨意答應異性的單獨邀約並且還不敢告訴事先告知。

**⑧ jealously** [adv.] 愛吃醋地

He jealously and furiously went questioning their relation when he saw his girlfriend hugging another man.

看到女友摟著其他男人時，他又忌妒又生氣地跑上前質問兩人的關係。

**⑨ blood** [n.] (U) 血、血液

Please ask healthy adults to donate blood more often for those in need.

請身體健康的成年人多多捐血，幫助需要幫助的人。

**⑩ symbol** [n.] 象徵、符號

A white dove is a symbol of freedom and peace.

白鴿是自由與和平的象徵。

## ⭐ 30 秒會話教室

中文的「速配」該怎麼表達呢？其實只要用 match 這個單字就行囉，例：He / She is a perfect match for me. 他／她是跟我最速配的人。

# 情境 2 誇張的潔癖

## ☆ Let's Talk in Love

After Vincent got caught with cheating, he thought he might as well let Bella, the one he cheated together, move into his place. Nevertheless, the outrageous **mysophobia** Vincent has almost drives Bella crazy for the first few days they live together...

Vincent 偷吃被抓包後，索性就讓偷吃對象 Bella 搬進他家一起住，但 Vincent 誇張的潔癖在同居的頭幾天就快把 Bella 給逼瘋了⋯

Vincent  Bella, how come you brought and ate the food in the room? This would attract **ants**!

Bella  Oh, there's no TV in the kitchen, so I brought in the room some **microwave** food that I just heated and ate here.

Vincent  Please only have food in the kitchen. Also, bring the kitchen **waste** and **garbage** down to the assorted garbage cans in the **basement** of the building once you finish.

Bella，妳怎麼把食物拿到房間裡面吃？這樣會長螞蟻的！

喔，因為廚房裡沒有電視，所以我剛弄好微波食品就拿進來吃了。

拜託妳到廚房裡去吃，還有，吃完要馬上把廚餘和垃圾拿到大樓地下室的垃圾分類區去丟。

| | |
|---|---|
| Bella | It's late already. I'll bring it down tomorrow before I go to work. What's the rush? I don't feel like moving around after eating! |
| | 這麼晚了，明天要出門上班再拿下去就可以了啦，為什麼要這麼急呢？人家剛吃完東西不想動嘛！ |
| Vincent | Because the kitchen waste will get stinky and attract bugs if left overnight...Hey, why is it all wet around the **sink**? Why didn't you clean up the water around the sink and the floor after washing something? |
| | 因為廚餘放著過夜不但會發臭還會長蚊蟲…喂，水槽旁邊怎麼溼答答的呀？妳洗完東西怎麼不把水槽邊的水滴和地板擦乾淨！？ |
| Bella | You are really **exaggerating**! Well, it's just water, not stinky or attracting bugs. Why are you all freaking out? |
| | 你很誇張耶，這次就只是水而已，不會發臭也不會長蚊蟲，你大驚小怪甚麼？ |
| Vincent | The floor got wet, and you stepped on it with your indoor **slippers**. You will leave dirty marks on the white **tiles**. |
| | 地板濺濕了，妳又用妳的室內拖鞋來踩去，會在地上的白色磁磚留下髒污的。 |
| Bella | I would never expect to deal with so many rules for living with you. I'm off to bed now. |
| | 沒想到跟你住在一起規矩這麼多，我要去睡覺了啦。 |

Vincent　Hey, you just finished eating something.  You remember to brush the teeth and wash the face, and also change the dirty clothes before going to bed, otherwise you don't get in my bed.

Bella　I got it!  You're such a nagger!

喂，妳剛吃完東西，記得先去刷牙洗臉，順便把髒衣服換掉再去睡覺，否則妳別想上我的床。

知道了啦，真是囉嗦！

## ⭐ Some Words to Know

**❶ mysophobia** **n.** (U) 潔癖
It's not the fact that every Virgo has mysophobia.  It's just a stereotype.
並不是每一個處女座的人都有潔癖，那只是刻板印象。

**❷ ant** **n.** 螞蟻
Ants are very advanced insects with socialized behaviors.
螞蟻是一種非常厲害的昆蟲，具有社會化的生活習性。

**❸ microwave** **a.** 微波
A microwave can be used for heating up leftovers or milk.
微波爐可以加熱隔夜的飯菜或是溫熱牛奶。

**❹ waste** **n.** (U)(single) 廢棄物、廢料
Chinese people are used to feeding pigs with food waste.
中國人都將廚餘拿去餵養豬隻。

❺ garbage　n. (U) 垃圾

It was thrilling to see the little boy want to pick up the **garbage** on the street and bring home for the dumpster.

那個小男孩看到路旁的垃圾，竟然說要撿回家丟，真是令人感動。

❻ basement　n. 地下室

My dad asks me to grab some tools for fixing the car in the basement.

爸爸叫我到地下室幫他拿幾項修車工具。

❼ sink　n. 水槽

The kitchen sink seems clogged, and the water can't go down.

廚房的水槽好像堵住了，水下不去。

❽ exaggerating　a. 誇張、誇大

Some people always like exaggerating their own experiences to show off the abilities.

有些人總是喜歡誇大自己的經歷來凸顯自己的能力。

❾ slipper　n. 拖鞋

Some people get used to changing the indoor slippers once home, but some don't.

有些人習慣回到家要換上室內拖鞋，有些人則不用。

❿ tile　n. 磁磚、地磚

It's so easy to fall on the slippery ties in the bathroom, so I put on an anti-slip mat.

踩在浴室的地磚上很容易滑倒，因此我又鋪上了一層止滑墊。

## 30 秒會話教室

Get off my back. 少管閒事、別來煩我。這句話除了要某人別來煩你，也代表你認為自己沒有做錯事情的意思。

# 情境 3  與男方的朋友見面

 **Let's Talk in Love**

In an afternoon on a holiday, Chris brings his girlfriend Daisy to see a friend Hector, who is also the manager of the 333 Restaurant & Bar...

一個假日的午後，Chris 帶著女友 Daisy 去見一位朋友 Hector，他同時也是 333 Restaurant & Bar 的店經理…

| | | |
|---|---|---|
| Chris | This is the manager of 333 Restaurant & Bar, Hector.  He's also a friend of mine back in college.  Hector, this is my girlfriend, Daisy.  She's being a waitress in a restaurant now. | 這位是 333 Restaurant & Bar 的店經理，Hector，也是我大學時期的朋友。Hector，這是我的女朋友 Daisy，她現在在餐廳裡當女服務生。 |
| Daisy | Hi, nice to meet you. | 你好，很高興認識你。 |
| Hector | Nice to meet you too, Daisy.  Before, Chris came to my restaurant and brought me the reãpes you created so I could take a look.  I've had a great **impression** to your **originality** afterwards. | 我也很高興認識妳，Daisy。之前 Chris 到我店裡來，並拿了妳自己研發的食譜請我看看，我看了之後對妳的創意留下了非常深刻的印象。 |

| | |
|---|---|
| Daisy | Chris did mention this to me after he met you. Thank you, I think you overpraised me. Those are just some random ideas I **take down**. I didn't expect Chris brought them to you. |
| | Chris 事後有跟我提過這件事情。謝謝，你過獎了，那不過是隨手記錄下來的一些想法，沒想到 Chris 會把它拿給餐廳的經理看，真是丟臉。 |
| Hector | Not at all. I think you have some tremendous ideas for garnishing **desserts**. Chris told me you often make some at home for him. They are **entirely** different from the desserts **commercially** available. |
| | 不會呀，我覺得妳對於甜點裝飾這一塊非常有想法，Chris 也說妳經常在家裡做給他吃，跟一般市面上買的到的截然不同。 |
| Daisy | That was him exaggerating. I always feel I am not good enough. |
| | 那是他太誇張了啦，我總覺得還不夠好。 |
| Hector | You are too **modest**. Well, I got an idea. Are you willing to show me your skills on the spot? Use the materials and equipment we've got in the restaurant. |
| | 妳太謙虛了，不如這樣吧，妳願意現在為我現場展現一下手藝嗎？就用我們店裡的材料和設備吧。 |
| Daisy | Then I think I have no choice but to show you what I got. Let me see...There are some fresh berries and pudding. I think I'll sprinkle some powdered sugar and then make a creme brulee with fruit topping with a torch. Voila! Please have some. |
| | 那我就獻醜了。我看看…這裡有新鮮的莓果和布丁，我就再撒上一些糖，用瓦斯槍烤成焦糖水果布蕾吧。完成了，來，請用。 |

Hector　Wow.  Not only can you fast and well execute your cooking procedures, you also can make full use of the existing materials for making some dessert that **combines** both the appearance and flavor.  It's such a waste if we only let you be a waitress.  Recently we have a chef who is leaving us.  Today I'm thinking of talking to you about the possibility of you being willing to work in our restaurant as the pastry chef?

哇，妳的動作不但迅速俐落，還能充分利用現有的材料做出兼具外觀與口味的甜點，讓妳當服務生實在是太大才小用了。最近我們店裡有一位廚師要離職，今天找妳來就是想跟妳談談，不知道妳願不願意到我們餐廳來擔任甜點廚師呢？

Daisy　Oh, that would be my pleasure.  Thank you, Hector.  Thank you too for getting this opportunity for me, dear.

呵呵，這是我的榮幸，謝謝你，Hector，也謝謝你為我奔走，親愛的。

## ⭐ Some Words to Know

**❶ impression** n. 印象
The new teacher gives a very good first impression to the whole class.
新來的老師給全班同學留下了一個良好的印象。

**❷ originality** n. (U) 創意
His originality was highly praised by his boss.
他的創意受到上司的大力稱讚。

❸ take down **v.** **phr.** 寫下、記下
We need someone to take down the contents of the discussions in the meeting.
我們需要找人記下會議中的討論內容。

❹ dessert **n.** 甜點
Mom makes some pudding for dessert after the meal.
媽媽為我們準備了布丁當作飯後甜點。

❺ entirely **adv.** 完全地、徹底地
Despite the similarity of the appearances between spiders and crabs, they are entirely two different creatures.
蜘蛛和螃蟹長的很像，卻是完全不同的兩種生物。

❻ commercially **adv.** 商業上
He's plan is not commercially practical/viable.
他的計劃在商業上是不切實際的。

❼ modest **a.** 謙虛的
Chinese usually humbly respond to compliments.
中國人面對稱讚，通常習慣謙虛地回應。

❽ combine **v.** 兼備
Isn't it great if one can combine work with pleasure.
如果能結合工作與樂趣該有多好？

## ⭐ 30 秒會話教室

You overpraised me. 你過獎了。這是中國人謙虛的講法，若是外國朋友稱讚你，其實只要大方地說聲 Thanks. 就可以囉。

# 情境 4　與女方的朋友見面

## ⭐ Let's Talk in Love

Daisy just becomes a pastry chef in a restaurant as she always wanted. She is very exāted about sharing this good news with her **intimate friend**, Rebecca.  She also uses this opportunity to **introduce** her boyfriend, Chris, to her...

Daisy 剛如願當上餐廳的甜點廚師，興奮地約姊妹淘 Rebecca 出來分享這個好消息，也順便介紹自己的男友 Chris 給她認識…

Daisy　Rebecca, it's been a while.  You are still **slim** and gorgeous.  This is my boyfriend, Chris.  Chris, this is a very good friend of mine, Rebecca.

Rebecca，一陣子不見了，妳還是一樣苗條。這是我的男朋友 Chris，Chris，這是我的好朋友 Rebecca。

Chris　Hello, I'm so glad to see you.  Daisy has talked about you a lot.

妳好，很高興終於見到妳本人，Daisy 經常提起妳。

Rebecca　Likewise.  Daisy said it was all because of your effort that made it possible for her to become a chef. You really got something there!

彼此彼此，Daisy 說是因為有你的大力奔走才促使她成為廚師的，真是有你的耶！

Chris　Do not say that.  I just didn't want her to **hide** her **talents** in a napkin. I've heard that you **actively** wanted to help her?

別這麼說，我只是希望她的才能不要被埋沒。聽她說妳也很積極地想要幫她？

| Rebecca | Yes. I was so **amazed** with the dessert she made in the restaurant where she worked. I kept thinking that it's a **pity** that she only worked as a waitress. Unfortunately, I didn't know how to help her find a chef job. | 是啊，我在她工作的餐廳裡吃過她所做的甜點，當時真是驚為天人，一心想著她這麼厲害卻只能端盤子實在太可惜了。不過很遺憾的是，我不知道該如何幫她找到一份廚師的工作。 |
|---|---|---|
| Chris | My dear, didn't you say that restaurant didn't let you try to make some desert in the kitchen? | 親愛的，妳不是說那間餐廳不願意讓妳在廚房裡嘗試做甜點嗎？ |
| Daisy | Yes. I brought her the desert after I finished making it at home. Rebecca was originally just one of the customers I **served** in the restaurant. Her amazing appetite really surprised the hell out of me. Then we became acquainted. I found out she also knows much about food, so I began my own dessert for her to eat. | 是啊，我是在家裡做好帶去的啦。Rebecca 原本只是我在餐廳裡服務到的其中一位客人，她驚人的食量嚇了我一大跳，後來我們就越來越熟，她對美食也很有研究，於是我就試著開始拿自己做的甜點給她吃。 |
| Rebecca | I have brought home some of the dessert Daisy made to my boyfriend. Even a person like him who doesn't like too much seasoning thinks the dessert you make is very natural and **delicious**. | 我曾經把 Daisy 做的甜點帶回家給我男朋友吃，連不愛吃多餘調味料的他都覺得妳做的甜點很天然、很美味。 |

Daisy　Speaking of your boyfriend, I have always wanted to meet him. How about next time four of us find some time to meet each other? Dear, what do you think?

說到妳男朋友，我也一直很想見見他耶。不如下次我們四個人找時間一起出來見個面吧！親愛的你覺得如何？

Chris　Of course, no problem at all! If it works out for her boyfriend , then we can make it happen this weekend.

當然沒問題，如果 Rebecca 跟她男友方便的話，這個周末就可以成行囉。

## ⭐ Some Words to Know

❶ intimate friend **n.** **phr.** 至友、密友
Judy is my intimate friend. We've started hanging out since first grade.
Judy 是我的至友，我們從小學一年級就開始一起玩了。

❷ introduce **v.** 介紹
Can you introduce your friend to me?
你能介紹一下你的朋友給我認識嗎？

❸ slim **a.** 苗條的、纖細的
Every girl wants to have a slim body like a model does.
每個女生都希望能擁有像模特兒一樣苗條的身材。

❹ hide **v.** 隱藏、隱瞞
I never hide anything from my boyfriend.
我從不對男朋友隱瞞任何事情。

**❺ talent** [n.] 才能
Everybody praises me for my talent in languages.
大家都稱讚我有語言方面的才能。

**❻ actively** [adv.] 積極地、主動地
Being willing to actively take the initiative is the virtue the spoiled children are lack of.
願意積極主動地做事，是被寵壞的孩子所欠缺的美德。

**❼ amazed** [a.] 吃驚的、顯示出驚奇的
We're all amazed that dad went buying a smart phone as a gift for mom.
爸爸竟然會跑去買智慧型手機來送給媽媽，讓我們大感吃驚。

**❽ pity** [n.] 憐憫、同情
Everyone feels great pity on the little boy who just lost his parents and everything he could rely on.
大家都很同情那位剛失去父母、無依無靠的小男孩。

**❾ serve** [v.] 服務
That waitress kindly serves me a glass of water.
那位女服務生親切地為我端上一杯水。

**❿ delicious** [a.] 美味的
Grandma's homemade cooking is really delicious.
外婆做的家常菜真是美味。

 **30 秒會話教室**

It's a pity that you couldn't come. 你不能來真是太可惜了。也可以用 It's too bad.（真是太糟糕了）來表達惋惜。

## 情境 5　兩對情侶約會

 **Let's Talk in Love**

On one weekend holiday, a couple of good friends Daisy and Rebecca bring each of their boyfriends Chris and Joseph, for four people to meet up. They're ready for their first time **double** date...

周末假日，一對好朋友 Daisy 和 Rebecca 分別帶著自己的男朋友 Chris 與 Joseph，四人相約見面，準備來場初次的兩對約會…

| | | |
|---|---|---|
| Rebecca | We're sorry we come a little late. This is my boyfriend Joseph. This is Daisy Ross and her boyfriend Chris. | 抱歉我們稍微來晚了，這是我男朋友 Joseph。這位是 Daisy Ross 和她的男朋友 Chris。 |
| Joseph | Good morning, I am Joseph Anderson. Rebecca has told me about your last meeting. Congratulations to you for becoming a restaurant chef. | 你們早，我是 Joseph Anderson，Rebecca 有跟我提起你們上次的會面了，恭喜妳成為餐廳大廚。 |
| Daisy | Oh, thank you. I also want to thank Rebecca's **support** and **encouraging**. | 呵呵，謝謝你，我也要感謝 Rebecca 的支持以及鼓勵。 |
| Chris | I'm Chris Hamilton, very pleased to meet you. This restaurant wasn't very hard to find, was it? | 我是 Chris Hamilton，很高興能認識你。這家餐廳不難找吧？ |

**Joseph** I am so sorry.  We were thinking it was still early so we walked here **leisurely**.  It turned out Rebecca saw a hot dog **stand halfway** here and started eating.

真不好意思，我們想說時間還早，就悠閒地散步過來，結果 Rebecca 在半路看到賣熱狗的攤子 就吃了起來。

**Daisy** What?  We are going to have lunch at this restaurant, and still you got to eat something on the way here?

甚麼？我們已經約好要在這間餐廳吃午餐了，妳路上還吃啊？

**Rebecca** Because ...  I didn't want Chris to see my **shameful** performance when I binge on eating, but I was also afraid I couldn't get enough to eat, so I ate some first!

因為…我不想讓 Chris 看到我大吃特吃的醜態，又怕吃不飽難過，所以就想說先吃一些嘛！

**Chris** So you do not have to **scruple** so much.  No matter how much you eat, I will not be surprised.  You know usually the **thinner** people are, the more they can eat!

妳不必這麼顧忌啦，不管妳食量多大我都不會訝異的，因為通常都是越瘦的人越能吃啊！

**Joseph** You are so nice, but don't jump the gun so soon.  It could go crazy when she starts eating like a monster.

你人真好，不過話先不要說得太早，她狂吃起來真的很誇張。

Chris  How about let's **match**?  Let's have three versus Rebecca.

不然我們就來比賽吧,三個人對 Rebecca 一個人怎麼樣?

## ⭐ Some Words to Know

❶ double **a.** 雙倍的、成雙的
I'll pay you with double money, please sell me this last pair of shoes.
我付你雙倍的錢,請把最後這一雙鞋子賣給我。

❷ support **v.** 支持
Parents always support all the children's choices behind their backs.
做父母的總是默默支持著孩子的一切選擇。

❸ encourage **v.** 鼓勵、慫恿
His friends encouraged him to go chat with that pretty girl.
他的朋友慫恿他去和那位漂亮的女孩搭訕。

❹ leisurely **adv.** 從容不迫地、悠閒地
That old couple leisurely takes a walk in the park and looks very affectionate.
那對老夫妻從容不迫地逛著公園,看起來非常恩愛。

❺ stand **n.** 攤子、小販賣部
The stalls in the night markets in Taiwan sell all sorts of things, which have become the world famous culture.
台灣的夜市裡有販售各種東西的攤子,儼然成為一種世界知名的文化。

❻ halfway **adv.** 在中途、到一半
I told my boyfriend I would meet him about halfway to his house.
我跟男友約在我跟他家的中途見面。

**❼ shameful** **a.** 可恥的、丟臉的
She uploaded the pictures of bullying her classmates to the Internet.  This shameful act has made her bombarded by many Internet users.
她把霸凌同學的畫面上傳到網路上，這種可恥的行為已經讓她被眾多網友圍剿。

**❽ scruple** **vi.** 顧慮、顧忌
The robber didn't scruple to take the money from the old man.
那搶匪毫無顧忌地搶了那老人的錢。

**❾ thin** **a.** 瘦的
When my brother did his military service, he lost so much weight.
弟弟當了三個月的兵，整個人瘦了一圈。

**❿ match** **v.** 使較量、使比賽
He is so confident that he thinks no one can match him in skateboarding.
他很有自信的認為沒有人在溜滑板上可以跟他較量。

## ⭐ 30 秒會話教室

Don't jump the gun. 話不要說得太早。也就是要對方先等結果出來再行論斷的意思。

# 情境 6 一起帶寵物出門

 **Let's Talk in Love**

Stella takes her cat to a **pet** shop for **grooming**, **expected** after work to pick up , but the day with her boyfriend Gordon Stella just have an appointment to go shopping after work , so after reãeving the cat Stella directly accesses the appointment...

Stella 帶貓咪去寵物店美容，預計下班後去取，但這天 Stella 剛好也跟男友 Gordon 約好下班後一起去逛街，於是 Stella 領完貓咪後便直接前往赴約…

| | | |
|---|---|---|
| Stella | Dear, have you waited long? Sorry, I just went to the pet hospital to get Lucky. | 親愛的，等很久了嗎？抱歉，我剛去寵物醫院領 Lucky。 |
| Gordon | No, I just arrived. Pet hospital? Was Lucky ill? | 不會啊，我剛到不久。寵物醫院？lucky 生病了嗎？ |
| Stella | Not really. I haven't given him a bath for about two months because of the cold weather recently, so I took him to the pet hospital to let the **groomer** give him the full body grooming, and also let the **veterinarian** give him a checkup. | 沒有啦，是最近天氣冷，我大概兩個月沒幫牠洗澡了，所以帶牠去寵物醫院請美容師幫忙全身美容，也順便給獸醫檢查一下身體狀況。 |
| Gordon | Couldn't we wait till we finish our date and then go get him? | 不能等我們約會完再去領牠嗎？ |

| Stella | By the time we finish dinner, the pet hospital is about to close. I will feel very sorry to the groomers there. It would just a waste of time if I took him home first and came here. | 等我們吃完飯，人家寵物醫院可能也快打烊了，這樣對裡面的美容師很不好意思。要我先把牠帶回家再過來則是太浪費時間了。 |
|---|---|---|
| Gordon | That's true. In fact, I don't mind having this little third wheeler **accompany** us, but I'm afraid that whether he might feel frightened with the **strange surroundings**? | 也是，其實我並不介意有這位小電燈泡的陪伴，只是擔心牠會不會對外面的陌生環境感到害怕？ |
| Stella | Actually, on the way from the pet shop here, he felt a bit frightened, kept **growling**, and **crawled** in the corner which made it really hard for me to get him. | 其實我從寵物店一路走來，牠感覺上是有點受驚，一直發出低吼，也縮在籠子的一角讓我很不好拿。 |
| Gordon | He must have been scared all the time staying in the pet hospital. How about we just take out some dinner and eat at home? It is better to let him go home and rest soon. | 牠一整天待在寵物醫院也受驚了，不如我們把晚餐買回家吃吧！讓牠早點回家休息。 |
| Stella | Really? Are you really willing to cancel our dinner date for my pet, I am so touched! | 真的嗎？你願意為了我的寵物取消我們的晚餐約會，真是太感動了！ |
| Gordon | I didn't do it for you! I was doing that for Lucky! | 才不是為了妳呢！我是為了lucky！ |

## ✨ Some Words to Know

**❶ pet** `n.` 寵物
People who abandon pets in randomly are more detestable than those directly abuse animals.
任意遺棄寵物的人比直接虐待動物的人還要可惡。

**❷ grooming** `n.` (U) 打扮、修飾
The little girl is trying to do some grooming on her beloved pet by herself.
那個小女孩嘗試著自己動手幫心愛的寵物美容。

**❸ expect** `v.` 預計、預期
I expect that this work will be completed by the end of the month.
我預計這項工作會在月底完成。

**❹ groomer** `n.` 寵物美容師
There is a TV series about the competition of the pet groomers.
電視上正在播出一系列的寵物美容師比賽。

**❺ veterinarian** `n.` 獸醫
That veterinarian does good medical practice, and gives very good treatments to the animals.
那位獸醫的醫術非常高明，對待動物也很和善。

**❻ accompany** `v.` 伴隨、陪同
The little Boy wants his mother to accompany him to walk to school.
小男孩希望媽媽陪他走路去上學。

**❼ strange** `a.` 陌生的、不熟悉的
The new system the company has is all strange to me.
公司這套新的系統對我來說很陌生。

**❽ surroundings** `n.` (plural) 環境、周圍的事物
The kitten my brother brought back quickly becomes familiar with the surroundings at home.
哥哥帶回來的小貓很快就熟悉了家裡的環境。

**❾ growl** vi. （動物）叫

The dog keeps growling at that stange man.

那狗一直對著那陌生人叫。

**❿ crawl** vi. 爬行

The baby likes to crawl around the little sofa.

這寶寶喜歡繞著小沙發爬行。

## 30 秒會話教室

It's a waste of time. 這是在浪費時間。It's a waste of money. 這是在浪費錢。

# 情境 7　偶遇女友同事

 **Let's Talk in Love**

Phil receives a phone call from his girlfriend Tracy this day, asking him to pick her up after work at Tracy's company.  However, what Phil waits to see is his girlfriend held and helped walk out of the elevator by a colleague...

Phil 這天接到女友 Tracy 的電話，要他下班後到 Tracy 的公司接她下班。但 Phil 等到的卻是由同事攙扶步出電梯的女友…

| | | |
|---|---|---|
| Tracy | Honey, I'm sorry, I know you're busy but I still asked you to pick me up... | 親愛的，不好意思，明知道你在忙還要你來接我下班… |
| Phil | Don't **regard** me as an **outsider**.  What's wrong with you?  And this is... | 別這麼見外，倒是妳怎麼了？還有這位是… |
| Abby | Hello, I am her colleague, Abby.  Tracy's foot was hurt by the falling cabinet today while she was filing the documents.  Now she needs someone to support her when she walks. | 你好，我是她的同事，Abby。Tracy 今天在整理資料的時候被倒下來的檔案櫃壓傷了腳，現在走路需要人攙扶。 |
| Phil | How come that happened to her?  Why didn't you ask for leave instead of putting up with it till getting off work? | 怎麼會這樣？妳怎麼不請假去看醫生，硬要撐到下班呢？ |

| Tracy | My colleagues sent me to see a doctor right after it happened.  The doctor diagnosed that it was just some **flesh wounds** with **sprain**.  That's why I went back to work after I got the wound **dressed**. | 同事們第一時間就送我去看過醫生了，診斷後只是些皮肉傷跟扭傷而已，所以包紮好之後我就又回公司上班了。 |
| Abby | We also **persuaded** her to simply take a leave and go home to rest, but she insisted on not going home... | 我們也勸她乾脆請假回家休息，但她堅持不肯回去…。 |
| Tracy | That's because it's just foot injury and my upper body can still move!  I would cause trouble to my colleagues and work later if I didn't finish filing soon enough. | 因為只是腳受傷而已，上半身還是可以動啊！不盡快把資料整理好歸檔，會對其他同事以及後來的作業造成麻煩的。 |
| Phil | I know your personality is so responsible, but your limited mobility of the body in fact created a burden more to your colleagues.  You should ask for leave and take some rest once feeling any physical discomfort.  This is also team **chemistry**.  Abby, please say thank you to your colleagues for me and Tracy, and of course, thank you. | 我知道妳的個性就是這麼盡責，但妳拖著行動不方便的身體，其實更會對同事造成負擔，身體不適就應該要請假休息才是，這也是一種團隊默契。Abby，請代替我和 Tracy，跟妳的同事們道謝，也很謝謝妳。 |

Abby　Tracy, your boyfriend was right. Although we didn't think you as the **nuisance**, for the whole team's sake, we still hope you to come back to work after you recover from the foot injury.  After all, you need to be physically healthy in order to have better performance at work.

Tracy, 妳男朋友說的對, 雖然我們並不覺得受傷的妳是累贅, 但為了整個團隊好, 我們還是希望妳把腳傷養好再來上班, 畢竟身體健康才能有更好的工作表現啊。

Tracy　Well, I got it.  Then please help me to tell the supervisor.

好吧, 我知道了, 那就請妳幫我跟主管說一聲囉。

## 🌟 Some Words to Know

❶ regard **v.** …看作、把…認為
He treats the girl who works here temporarily as a maid.
他把來打工的女孩當作女傭一樣使喚。

❷ outsider **n.** 外人、局外人
Outsiders often have the difficulty to understand the real situation within a seemingly happy family.
外人通常很難理解一個看似幸福的家庭內實際的狀況。

❸ flesh **n.** (U) 肉、肉體
The spirit is willing but the flesh is weak.
力不從心。

❹ wound n. 創傷
The policeman got a gunshot wound on his leg calf.
那位警察的小腿上有一道槍傷。

❺ sprain n. 扭傷
According to the doctor, he's going to miss the rest of the season with that severe sprain in his right foot.
據醫生表示，因為他右腳嚴重的扭傷他將無法打完剩下的球季。

❻ dress v. 傷口敷藥、包紮
The mother helped the little boy who just fell dress the wound.
那位母親幫跌倒的小男孩包紮傷口。

❼ persuade v. 勸服
The clerk persuades customers to buy that expensive designer bag.
店員勸說客人買下那個昂貴的名牌包。

❽ chemistry n. (U) 化學作用
The basketball coach is trying to cultivate the teamwork chemistry between the players.
籃球教練努力地培養球員間的團隊默契。

❾ nuisance n. 累贅
Without giving any effort, someone who just wants to sit back and enjoy the success, is the team's nuisance.
一個不出力，只想坐享其成的人，是團隊裡的累贅。

**30 秒會話教室**

請假的說法要學起來喔。Ask for 3 day's leave.（請三天假。）Ask for sick leave.（請病假。）

# 情境 8 前男友來攪局

 **Let's Talk in Love**

When Gill is just about to further develop the relationship with Matt, her ex-boyfriend who cheated on her is constantly contacting her for getting her back. The situation is getting so out of hand that Gill can't hide it from Matt...

Gill 與先前認識的 Matt 才剛開始深交，她劈腿的前男友 Vincent 此時也為了挽回而頻頻與她連絡，搞得她無法繼續隱瞞 Matt 這件事⋯

| | |
|---|---|
| **Matt** What's the matter with you today? Your phone has been ringing since we came out eating. Is there a family **emergency**, or a flight duty? | 怎麼了？今天出來吃飯，妳的手機一直響，家裡有急事嗎？還是有勤務要飛？ |
| **Gill** No. Actually...my ex-boyfriend has been calling for getting back together. | 不是啦，其實是⋯我的前男友一直打電話想要復合。 |
| **Matt** Your ex-boyfriend? You mean that cheating **toxic bachelor**? I thought you didn't have any contact with him. | 前男友？妳說那個劈腿的負心漢嗎？我以為妳沒再跟他聯絡了。 |
| **Gill** Of course not. He took the initiative to call me, and also **unilaterally** disturbed my friends. He asked them to help out with saying something good about him. My friends are all getting so annoyed by him. | 當然沒有啊，是他主動打給我，又一直單方面打擾我朋友，請他們幫忙講好話，我的朋友都快被煩死了。 |

| Matt | This is indeed very troublesome. Perhaps you don't express your **stance** strongly enough so he thinks there is an **opportunity** to take **advantage** of. What do you think about this situation? Do you want to get back together with him? | 這樣的確挺麻煩的，或許是妳沒有強硬地表達妳的立場，才讓他覺得有機可乘的。妳自己的意思呢？想跟他復合嗎？ |
| --- | --- | --- |
| Gill | How in the world would I like that? I do not want to have anything **in common** with that **arrogant** narãssistic man. Besides that, I've already met you... | 怎麼可能？我才不想再跟那個狂妄自戀的男人有任何交集，而且，我也已經認識你了啊…。 |
| Matt | Oh, I have a good idea that should be able to let him **retreat**. | 呵呵，其實我有個好方法，應該可以讓他知難而退。 |
| Gill | What's that good idea? | 甚麼好方法？ |
| Matt | Next time if he calls again, you let me answer that phone. I will tell him, "Is there anything you need to talk to my girlfriend?" What do you think? | 下次他再打來，妳就把手機拿給我接，我會跟他說『找我女朋友有事嗎？』妳覺得如何？ |
| Gill | Haha, I didn't expect to find this idea. Maybe in fact he is doing me a big favor by giving me all the trouble! | 呵呵，沒想到會聽到這種方法，或許他來攪局其實反而是幫了我大忙呢！ |

## ☆ Some Words to Know

**❶ emergency** **n.** (U) 緊急情況
In case of emergency, please call 119.
如果遇到緊急情況，請撥打 119。

**❷ toxic** **a.** 有毒的
That small black bottle in the physics/chemistry classroom says "Highly toxic: Do not eat!"
理化教室裡那個黑色的小瓶子上面寫著「有毒的，請勿誤食」。

**❸ bachelor** **n.** 單身漢、鰥夫
He's a confirmed bachelor.
他打定主意一輩子單身。

**❹ unilateral** **a.** 單方面的
Blindly to accuse each other is just to vent out unilateral emotions; one should have a good talk to solve the problem.
一味的指責對方只是單方面的情緒發洩，應該要好好談才能解決問題。

**❺ stance** **n.** 立場、態度
Regarding the request from the parents who wanted that teacher to get expelled from school, the school took a strong stance to oppose it.
對於家長希望學校開除那位老師一事，校方採取強硬的反對態度。

**❻ opportunity** **n.** 機會、良機
Tomorrow you may have the opportunity to replace the physical discomfort actress to appear on stage.
明天妳或許有機會代替身體不適的女主角上台演出。

**❼ advantage** **n.** 利益、好處
What is your advantage in this?
從中你有獲得甚麼好處？

**❽ in common** **prep.** **phr.** 共同的、共有的
Humans and mice have much in common genetically.
人類和老鼠在基因上有許多共同之處。

**❾ arrogant　a.** 驕傲的、自大的

Her personality is very arrogant, and does not allow anyone to criticize her for anything.

她的個性非常驕傲自大，不容許任何人批評她的不是。

**❿ retreat　vi.** 撤退、退縮

After ten months of fierce fighting, the siege of the enemy finally retreated.

在經過長達十個月的激烈戰況，攻城的敵人終於撤退了。

## ⭐ 30 秒會話教室

I want you back. 我希望你回來。這句簡單的話也就是「希望你能回到我身邊」、想挽回感情的意思。

## 情境 9　健身教練的話如同聖旨

 **Let's Talk in Love**

Every time Ivan wants to ask his girlfriend Jessica to have night **snack** together, or lie on the couch watching TV after dinner, Jessica always rejects him by quoting the fitness coach's words.  He doesn't much **relish** the situation...

每當 Ivan 想找女朋友 Jessica 去吃宵夜，或是吃完飯後想叫女友跟他一起躺在沙發上看電視時，Jessica 都會搬出健身教練的話來拒絕他，讓他覺得很不是滋味…

| | |
|---|---|
| **Ivan** | My dear, leave the dishes in the sink and wash them later.  Come watch TV with me first. |
| | 親愛的，碗放著等一下再洗就好了啦，先過來陪我看電視。 |
| **Jessica** | No, Nathan said your **hips** will get bigger if you sit right after getting stuffed. |
| | 不要啦，Nathan 說一吃飽就坐著臀部會變大的。 |
| **Ivan** | Nathan ... is that the **annoying** fitness trainer?  You already leave the **gym**.  Why do you still keep repeating his words? |
| | Nathan…又是那個討厭的健身教練，妳都離開健身房了，還把他的話掛在嘴邊做甚麼？ |

| | | |
|---|---|---|
| Jessica | Oh, doing **physical training** is something you do anytime and anywhere.  It's not just something you only do in the gym.  Isn't that like doing you a great favor if you can do housework and keep your body in shape at the same time? | 哎呀，鍛鍊身體是隨時隨地的事情啊，又不只限於健身房內。順便把家事做一做還能維持身材，不是幫了你大忙嗎？ |
| Ivan | Your body figure has been good enough.  When you walk on the street, many guys are checking you out.  That makes me feel proud, but also worried on the one hand... You're finally finished...Can you now sit down and be a good company? | 妳的身材已經夠好了，走在路上都會有好多男人回頭看，這讓我一方面感到很驕傲一方面又很擔心…。妳終於忙完了…現在可以坐下陪我了吧？ |
| Jessica | No!  I want to hold the sofa and **stretch** out my body. | 不要，我還要扶著沙發伸展一下身體。 |
| Ivan | Since you don't want to sit down, how about you take a walk with me to buy some night snacks back? | 既然妳這麼不想坐下，不然妳陪我散步去買宵夜回來吃吧！ |
| Jessica | No way!  Nathan said, If I have night snacks at night, the next day I need to do 30 minutes more of exerāse. | 不行啦，Nathan 說我晚上要是吃宵夜，隔天就要多做 30 分鐘的鍛鍊。 |

| | |
|---|---|
| Ivan | Alright, alright, forget about it! I do not want you to have any **unnecessary** contact with him. |
| Jessica | Actually I can do some more exerāse while going with you, but I'm afraid I cannot resist the **temptation** of food. If you want to eat something, go on your own. |

好好好，那算了！我才不希望妳跟他有多餘的接觸時間。

其實陪你去買是可以順便運動，但是我怕我抵擋不了食物的誘惑，所以你要吃的話就自己去吧。

## ⭐ Some Words to Know

**❶ snack** **n.** 小吃、點心
He randomly ate some snacks and then later continued working.
他隨手吃了一些小點心之後又繼續工作。

**❷ relish** **v.** 喜好、愛好
She doesn't relish the idea that some people are favored by the boss by brown nosing only without doing much around.
一想到平常不做事、只會拍馬屁的人特別得到上司的寵愛，她就覺得心裡不是滋味。

**❸ hip** **n.** 臀部
The mother standing in the doorway with her hands on her hips looks very angry.
媽媽兩手插腰站在門口的樣子看起來非常生氣。

**❹ annoying** **a.** 討厭的、惱人的
It was really annoying that there were mosquitoes flying around my ears last night while I was sleeping.
昨晚睡覺時有蚊子在我耳旁飛來飛去，真是討厭。

**❺ gym** **n.** 健身房、體育館
The boy goes to the gym every day, hoping that his body becomes stronger.
那個男孩每天都到健身房裡運動，希望能讓身材變壯。

**❻ physical** **a.** 身體的、肉體的
Doing housework is also a way to do physical exercise.
做家事也是鍛鍊身體的一種方式。

**❼ training** **n.** (U) 訓練、鍛鍊
The Police all undergo professional training at police academy.
警察都在警察學校受過專業的訓練。

**❽ stretch** **v.** 伸展
The wild cat on the roof sluggishly stretches the body after a midday nap.
野貓在屋頂上睡完午覺後慵懶地伸展了身體。

**❾ unnecessary** **a.** 額外的、多餘的
A smart housewife knows how to avoid unnecessary expenses.
聰明的家庭主婦會避免額外的開支。

**❿ temptation** **n.** 引誘、誘惑
Married people don't give in to temptation.
已婚的人千萬不要敗給了誘惑。

## ⭐ 30 秒會話教室

My mother <u>keep saying</u> the same thing <u>over and over</u>. 我媽媽總是把那件事情掛在嘴邊。

# 情境 10 房東不允許其他房客的出現

##  Let's Talk in Love

Trevor is going to go abroad to pursue his own dreams, so he first returns the house that he **rents**, and temporarily move into Zoe's place in the same building.  Zoe is the girls he has been flirting with.  Zoe's **landlady** hears about it so she comes show some **consideration** for her concerns...
Trevor 即將出國追尋自己的夢想，因此他先將租來的房子退租，並暫時住在同一棟樓的曖昧對象 Zoe 家，很快地，Zoe 的房東也聽到風聲而過來關切…

| | |
|---|---|
| Zoe  Ah, it's you, my landlady.  What brings you up here?  It's not the time for the rent yet. | 啊，是房東太太啊，您怎麼跑來了？收房租的時間應該還沒到啊？ |
| Mrs. Lin  I've heard that you let a man move in to stay with you.  I didn't believe it at first...Now I have to after I saw several pairs of men's shoes on the shoe cabinet at the door. | 我聽說妳讓一個男人搬進來住，本來還不太相信…剛才看到門口鞋櫃上好幾雙的男鞋後就不得不信了。 |
| Zoe  I'm so sorry about that.  In fact, he is also the tenant in this building.  He's soon going to go abroad, so he first returnes his place and comes stay here for a few days. | 真是不好意思，其實他也是這棟大樓的住戶，只是過不久就要出國了，所以先把房子退掉，暫時在這邊住幾天…。 |

| | |
|---|---|
| **Mrs. Lin** | Except our **lease** clearly states that you are the only female tenant allowed to live here. Now there's one more man, who should I ask for the compensation if there's **furniture** or decoration got damaged? Besides, the utility bill will also be increasing. |

可是我們的租約上清清楚楚寫著只限妳一個女孩子住啊，現在多了一個人，要是他把我的家具或裝潢弄壞了要找誰賠呢？而且水電費也會增加的。

| | |
|---|---|
| **Zoe** | He won't break anything, and he really just needs to stay for a few days ...let me tell you what, I'll pay for the **utility** bills this month. Please accommodation the situation for us, my landlady. Ah, Trevor, you are awake? |

他不會弄壞任何東西的，況且他真的只是借住幾天…不然這樣好了，這個月的水電費由我來付，請房東太太通融一下。啊，Trevor，你醒啦？

| | |
|---|---|
| **Trevor** | Hello, ma'am. I just overheard your conversations while I was in there. I would like to apologize for all the inconvenience that I have caused, but I really just need to stay for a few days until I go abroad. I will try to compensate you as much as we can. |

房東太太您好，我剛才在裡面聽到妳們的對話了，給您造成麻煩真的很抱歉，不過我只是要借住幾天直到我出國為止，錢的部分我們會盡量補貼給您的。

| | |
|---|---|
| **Mrs. Lin** | Oh, I know you! We've met in this building many times. Once you saw me carrying bags of **groceries**, you took the initiative to come help me. It was you, Trevor! |

喔，我認得你啊！我們在這棟大樓裡面遇過不少次，有一次你看我提著大包小包的雜貨，還主動過來幫我，原來你就是 Trevor 啊。

| Trevor | Yah, I didn't know that your were Zoe's landlady. | 是啊，我當時也不知道您就是 Zoe 的房東。 |

| Mrs. Lin | Sigh.  Well, I'll **pretend** I didn't see that judging by the fact that you two are so polite at all times!  But you'll still need to pay for the utility bill this month. | 哀，好吧，看在你們兩個年輕人平常都這麼有禮貌的份上，我就睜一隻眼閉一隻眼啦！不過這個月的水電費還是要給妳付喔！ |

| Zoe | No problem, thank you, my landlady. | 沒問題，謝謝您，房東太太。 |

## ⭐ Some Words to Know

**❶ rent** [v.] 租
We rent a car for an overnight trip to Taitung.
我們租了一台車準備進行兩天一夜的旅行。

**❷ landlady** [n.] 女房東
My landlady is very generous to me, and often invites me to her house for dinner.
我的女房東對我非常慷慨，經常請我去她家吃晚餐。

**❸ consideration** [n.] (U) 考慮、關心
He showed no consideration for his children.
他從不關心他的孩子們。

❹ lease **n.** 租約
That well-known diner's lease will be expired at the end of the month. The female owner is going to move to somewhere with a cheaper rent.
那間知名小吃店的租約月底就到期了，老闆娘準備搬到租金更便宜的地方去。

❺ furniture **n.** (U) 家具
Fancy antique furniture is filled in that rich woman's house.
那位貴婦家中擺滿了高級的古董家具。

❻ utility **n.** 公用事業
I forgot to pay for the utility bills.
我忘記繳水電費了。

❼ groceries **n.** (plural) 食品雜貨
That elderly woman carrying a large bag of groceries looked very struggling.
那位老奶奶提著一大包食品雜貨，看起來非常吃力。

❽ pretend **v.** 佯裝、假裝
That thief pretended to be a plumber and entered the victim's house for burglary.
那個小偷佯裝是水電工人，進入被害者家中行竊。

## ⭐ 30 秒會話教室

I'll pretend I didn't see that. 我會假裝我沒有看到。也就是「我會睜一隻眼閉一隻眼」的意思。

# 情境 11 參加男友上司的聚會

 **Let's Talk in Love**

Rebecca dresses up nicely tonight and put on her cocktail dress that she **seldom** wears, because her boyfriend Joseph is going to take her to **attend** a business gathering hosted by his **supervisor**...

Rebecca 今晚精心打扮並穿上她很少穿的晚宴服，因為男友 Joseph 要帶她去出席一場由上司所舉辦的商界聚會⋯

| | | |
|---|---|---|
| Joseph | This is our company's general manager, Bruce Wang. Manager Wang, this is my girlfriend, Rebecca Lewis. | 這是我們公司的總經理，Bruce Wang，總經理，這是我的女朋友 Rebecca Lewis。 |
| Rebecca | Hello, Mr. Wang. Thank you for looking after Joseph all the time. | Mr. Wang 您好，感謝您平日對 Joseph 的照顧。 |
| Mr. Wang | You are Joseph's that beautiful girlfriend? No wonder he has been working so hard to build up his **career**. It is all because he has found a beautiful and magnificent girlfriend like you so he wants to **settle down**. | 妳就是 Joseph 的漂亮女朋友啊？難怪他會這麼努力拚事業，就是因為找到這麼美麗大方的好對象，所以想安頓下來了吧。 |

| Rebecca | You have overpraised me. Joseph also often mentioned me about your deãsiveness and great **vision** at work. He says he can learn a lot of things from you by working with you. | 您過獎了，Joseph 也經常向我提起您在工作上的果斷與過人的遠見，他說跟在您身邊能學習到很多東西。 |
| --- | --- | --- |
| Mr. Wang | Joseph, where did you find such a witty girlfriend? You surely know where to look for! Come on in, let's catch up more inside. | Joseph，你是到哪裡找到這麼會說話的女朋友的啊？你的眼光真是不錯！來來來，我們進去再聊。 |
| Joseph | Where's your wife? I've heard that your wife is the best of the **better half**. I would like Rebecca to learn something from your wife. | 夫人呢？其實夫人才是最厲害的賢內助，我還希望能讓 Rebecca 多跟夫人學習呢。 |
| Mr. Wang | She is helping me host some of the guests over there! Come over here, there's some cocktail and refreshments. You two have something to eat first, then come find me. I will introduce the "**somebody**" in our business. It will be very helpful with your sales promotion. | 她在那邊幫我招待客人呢！來，這裡有些雞尾酒和小餐點，你們先填飽肚子，之後再過來找我，我介紹一些商場上有頭有臉的大客戶給你認識，對你跑業務會非常有幫助的。 |
| Rebecca | I will leave you to do your business. Would you mind If I walked around the house by myself? | 那我就不跟過去打擾你們談生意囉，您介意我自己四處逛逛嗎？ |

| Mr. Wang | Don't worry. We have expected that the ladies who attend the party might feel bored, so you can go to beauty **salon** on the second floor. My wife will be right up. She has prepared a tryout for some **cosmetics** there. | 別擔心，我們早就預料到參加這場晚宴的女伴們會感到無聊，所以妳可以到二樓的會客室去，我太太待會就上去，她在那邊準備了彩妝試用會呢！ |
| --- | --- | --- |
| Rebecca | That's great! Thank you, Manager Wang. | 那太好了！謝謝總經理！ |

## ⭐ Some Words to Know

**❶ seldom** `adv.` 很少的（地）、難得的（地）
My serious father seldom reveals his feelings.
嚴肅的父親很少表露出他的感情。

**❷ attend** `v.` 出席
The chairman of the board did not attend the meeting today again. I wonder if he is sick.
董事長今天又沒有出席會議，不知道是不是病了？

**❸ supervisor** `n.` 上司
That middle-aged man in black suit is my supervisor.
那位穿黑西裝的中年男子是我的上司。

**❹ career** `n.` 事業
People are worried that she is building up her life career based on that dead-end job.
她把那份毫無前途的工作當成終身事業在經營，旁人看了都為她擔心。

**❺ settle down** `v.` `phr.` 安頓下來
I want to get married and settle down before 30.
我想在 30 歲以前結婚安頓下來。

**❻ vision** `n.` 遠見、眼光、洞察力
That businessman can create his own business empire step by step owing to his great vision.
那位商人就是因為有遠見，才能一步步打造屬於自己的事業王國。

**❼ better half** `n.` `phr.` 配偶、夥伴
Many people haven't really thanked their better halves for their years of devotion in their marriages.
很多人都不曾感謝過另一半在婚姻中長年的付出。

**❽ somebody** `n.` 重要人物
She has become an important figure in the fashion industry as a result of her creativity.
她憑著創意打出名號，現在已經是時尚界的重要人物了。

**❾ salon** `n.` 會客室、交誼廳、沙龍
She went to a beauty salons to get her hair done for going on a date.
她到美容院做完頭髮，準備去約會。

**❿ cosmetics** `n.` (U) 化妝品、美容品
Cosmetics has been the sector that female consumers spend the most money in.
化妝品一直是女性消費者花費最多錢的區塊。

### ⭐ 30 秒會話教室

I've heard a lot about you. 我已經聽過不少關於你的事。這句話也可引申為「久仰了」。

# 情境 12 與保險業務的往來

 **Let's Talk in Love**

Tracy works in the business intelligence department for the government. Although her work content doesn't involve any danger, the department has **insured** the employees with some basic insurance.  Still she follows her boyfriend Phil's advice, and wants to buy more insurance for protection.

Tracy 在政府的商業情報單位工作，雖然工作內容並不危險，且單位已為員工投保了基本的保險，但她仍聽從男友 Phil 的勸，想再多買一份保障更多的保險…

| | | |
|---|---|---|
| Phil | This is my insurance **agent**, Joseph Anderson.  I've started purchasing insurance from him since I got my first job.  This is my girlfriend, Tracy Spark. | 這位是我的保險業務 Joseph Anderson，從我出社會第一次為自己買保險開始，都是跟他接洽的。這位是我的女朋友 Tracy Spark。 |
| Tracy | Hello, Mr. Anderson. | Mr. Anderson 你好。 |
| Joseph | You can just call me Joseph.  Phil and I are old friends.  I sold my first insurance **policy** to him. | 叫我 Joseph 就可以了，我跟 Phil 也可以算是老朋友了，我的第一張保單就是賣給他的。 |
| Phil | You were all nervous and **stammering** back then when you explained the insurance policy.  Now you're a sales **expert** who can handle the business all by yourself! | 那時候看你說明保單內容還會緊張到結巴，現在已經是一位獨當一面的業務高手了呢！ |

| | |
|---|---|
| Joseph | Oh, do not say that.  Today it's Tracy who wants to buy insurance, right?  Do you mind telling me your profession? | 唉，別這麼說。今天是 Tracy 想要買保險對吧？方便請問一下妳的職業是甚麼呢？ |
| Tracy | About this ...I'd rather not say. | 這個…有點不方便說。 |
| Joseph | How **mysterious**!  Normally we will require people who purchase life insurance to provide information of health check records and career, but recently because of the heated competition between all the insurance companies, so the regulations aren't so strict anymore.  Plus, you are Phil's girlfriend, I won't make you to tell me. | 這麼神秘呀！通常我們投保壽險都會要求檢查投保者的健康檢查紀錄和職業，不過最近因為各家保險業者競爭激烈，所以規定也就沒那麼嚴格了，再加上妳是 Phil 的女朋友，我就不強迫妳說了。 |
| Phil | It's not like something secretive about what she's doing.  She just needs to keep some **secrets** at work.  I'd like to ask you to find the right insurance policy for her based on your expertise, but I don't want you to be **unable** to explain to your boss. | 她做的不是甚麼見不得人的職業啦，只是需要保密，所以就麻煩你依你的專業看看有沒有適合她的保單，不要害你不好跟公司交代。 |

Tracy　That's right.  In fact, the company has provided me life insurance and personal acãdent policy.  I'm actually more interested in some **investment** policy that I can claim it all back after the policy expires.

是啊，其實壽險和意外險方面公司已經為我保了，我對投資型的保單比較有興趣，最好是期滿可以領回的那種。

Joseph　Well, that should be no problem.  I happen to have some packages with me.  Let me give you more introduction to each one of them.

那這好辦，我手邊剛好有這幾種商品，我來一一為妳說明。

## ⭐ Some Words to Know

❶ insure **v.** 為…投保
They insured themselves before they traveled.
他們出國旅遊之前已經先為自己投保了旅遊平安險。

❷ agent **n.** 代理人、仲介人
The boss assigns the manager to be his agent while he's overseas.
老闆出國期間請總經理擔任他的代理人。

❸ policy **n.** 保險單、保險
He bought himself a new personal accident policy for his new car.
他為自己的新車買了一份意外險。

❹ stammer **v.** 結結巴巴地說
When he was called up by the teacher to answer a question, he was stammering and too nervous to answer the question.
他一被老師叫起來回答問題就會因緊張而結結巴巴地回答不出來。

**❺ expert n. 專家、熟手**
Now there are even experts in playing online games.
現在連玩線上遊戲都有專家了呢。

**❻ mysterious a. 神秘的、不可思議的**
Our universe is so mysterious and beautiful!
我們的宇宙是多麼神秘又美麗的呀!

**❼ secret n. 秘密**
I never told anyone the secret about that old house.
我從沒告訴過任何人關於那棟老房子的秘密。

**❽ unable a. 沒有辦法的、不能的**
That father was unable to afford a whole set of toys, but he still bought a small model car for his son.
那位父親買不起整套的玩具,但他還是買了一輛小汽車送給他的兒子。

**❾ investment n. 投資、投資額**
The company has invested high investment and manpower onto this new product.
公司對這個新產品投入了高額的投資和人力。

## ⭐ 30 秒會話教室

Please keep it a secret. 請幫我保密。Please keep it dark about my new job.
請幫我的新工作保密。

# 情境 13 幫忙照顧弟妹

 **Let's Talk in Love**

Stella, who has finished school and worked for years, has a twin siblings ten years younger than she is. This weekend her parents **entrust** the siblings to her while they are traveling to somewhere far...

早已出社會工作的 Stella 底下還有小她十歲的一對雙胞胎弟妹,這個周末假日 Stella 的父母要出遠門,於是將弟妹託給 Stella 照顧…

| | | |
|---|---|---|
| Stella's sister | Sis, is this the place you rent in the **downtown** area? Wow, this is nice, I want to move out too soon. | 姊,這就是妳在市中心租的房子啊?好棒喔,我也想趕快搬到外面住。 |
| Stella | Not after you go to a nice college. If you go to a private school, Mom and Dad will not have enough money to **provide** you. | 先等妳考上好大學再說,如果考上私立的,爸跟媽可是沒錢供妳學費喔。 |
| Stella's brother | Sis, how come there's some guy's staff all over your room? Did you **stealthily** bring men to stay overnight here? | 姊,妳的房間怎麼到處都看的到男生的東西啊,妳偷偷地帶男人回來過夜嗎? |
| Stella | That's my boyfriend who comes here stay with me sometimes. I've mentioned this to Mom, but haven't to Dad, so you two don't speak out of turn once you go back. | 我男朋友有時候會過來一起住啦!我已經跟媽說過這件事了,但是爸還不知道,所以你們回去以後不要多嘴喔。 |

| Stella's brother | What are you going to give us the **hush** money?  Dad will be so furious once he finds out and asks you to move back **wrathfully**. | 那妳要拿甚麼來當我們的封口費呢？爸爸知道以後一定會非常生氣地叫妳搬回家去！ |
| Stella | I knew you the **cunning** boy would say that, so I bring my boyfriend over to take you guys out having fun in the city all day long, what do you say? | 早就知道你這賊小子會這麼說了，所以我今天特別找我男朋友過來，待會帶你們去城裡面吃喝玩樂一整天，好不好？ |
| Gordon | I'm coming in, Stella!  Hi, I'm Gordon, you two surely look **similar**!  Tell me all the places you want to go today, I'll bring you there. | Stella，我進來囉！嗨，你們好，我是 Gordon，你們倆長的還真像呀！你們今天想去甚麼地方玩都儘管說，不用跟我客氣喔！ |
| Stella's sister | Yah, that's super great!  Can you take me to the record store in the department store?  I want to buy the new **album** my idol just lanched. | 耶！太棒了！那可以帶我去百貨公司跟唱片行嗎？我想買偶像的新專輯。 |
| Stella's brother | I want to go see the movies, and eat all the junk food Mom never lets us eat.  She always says, "It's all junk food!" | 我想去看電影，還想吃一堆平時媽媽都說是不准我們吃的東西，她都說是「垃圾食物」！ |
| Stella | Okay, okay, you two are still so **immature** even being at high school, and you haven't said Hello to Gordon. | 好，都高中生了還這麼幼稚，而且你們好像也還沒跟 Gordon 打招呼耶！！ |

## ☆ Some Words to Know

**❶ entrust** **v.** 委託、託管

I entrust my four cats to my neighbor when I travel to somewhere far.

我出遠門時都會把四隻貓咪託給鄰居照顧。

**❷ downtown** **a.** 城市商業區

Most of the downtown restaurants have later opening hours than the ones in the suburban area.

城市裡的餐廳大多營業得比郊區的餐廳還要晚。

**❸ provide** **v.** 提供

The community center in the neighborhood provides some free karaoke equipment for the residents.

社區活動中心提供免費的卡拉 OK 設備供居民使用。

**❹ stealthily** **adv.** 暗地裡、偷偷摸摸地

The burglar stealthily sneaked to the door and prepared to break the lock, but got busted at the scene by the police.

竊賊偷偷摸摸地來到屋主的門前準備撬開門鎖，卻當場被警察逮個正著。

**❺ wrathfully** **adv.** 憤怒地

The family of the victim wrathfully shouted to the murderer.

受害者的家屬憤怒地對殺人犯咆嘯。

**❻ cunning** **a.** 狡猾的、奸詐的

She comes up a cunning plan to get rid of the competition in her relationship.

她想出了一個狡猾的計畫以除掉情敵。

**❼ similar** **a.** 相像的、類似的

The last customer who came here for getting a loan has very similar questions to yours.

上一位來貸款的客戶遇到的問題跟你的非常類似。

❽ album　**n.** 唱片、相簿

It's a pity that some real good singers have only one album coming out and then disappear.

有些很有實力的歌手只出一張唱片就銷聲匿跡了，真是可惜。

❾ immature　**a.** 幼稚的、不成熟的

It's such an immature and dangerous behavior to put pushpins on the chairs of the classmates.

在同學的椅子上放圖釘真是一種很幼稚又危險的行為。

## 30 秒會話教室

speak out of turn 有「不按順序說話」的意思，因此也可引伸為「說了不該說的話」，例：Did I speak out of turn?（我是否多嘴了？）

# 情境 14　探望爺爺奶奶

 **Let's Talk in Love**

Daisy hasn't visited her grandparents who live in the **country** for a long time.　Chris happens to have some vacation days, so Chris is being very considerate to drive Daisy to go to where her grandparents live, also make it like a small trip for two of them...

Daisy 很久沒有回去探望住在鄉下的爺爺奶奶了，剛好男友 Chris 也有假期，於是 Chris 貼心地開車載 Daisy 返鄉，順便當作兩人的小旅行…

| | | |
|---|---|---|
| Daisy | Grandpa, It has been a long time.　I am Daisy, can you still recognize? | 爺爺，好久不見了，我是 Daisy，還認得我嗎。 |
| Daisy's grandfather | Of course we recognize you! My lovely granddaughter! How come you come visit us without letting us know first? | 當然認得啊！我可愛的孫女，怎麼沒說一聲就跑來了呢？ |
| Daisy | I want to give you a **surprise**! Where's grandma?　I'd like to introduce my boyfriend to you. | 我想給你們一個驚喜嘛！奶奶呢？我想介紹我的男朋友給你們認識。 |
| Chris | Hi, grandpa, I am Chris Hamilton. | 爺爺好，我是 Chris Hamilton。 |

| Daisy's grandmother | Is that Daisy over there? How come you didn't tell me she's here, Dear? Daisy **finally** brings her boyfriend to meet us. | 是 Daisy 來啦？老伴你怎麼不趕快叫我呢！？Daisy 終於帶男朋友來給我們看了，來，快進來坐。 |
|---|---|---|
| Daisy | Grandpa, grandma, I've brought you some **handmade** pudding. I've only put **less** than half sugar in it, but it's still **tasty**. Come have some. | 爺爺、奶奶，我帶了自己做的手工布丁來給你們吃喔，糖分我特別為爺爺奶奶減量了，吃起來還是很順口，你們嚐嚐看。 |
| Daisy's grandmother | It has been a while that we had some of the dessert you made, We've really missed it. You used to make something with me in the kitchen. I've heard your mom say that now you're a **chef** in a restaurant. | 好久沒吃到妳做的甜點了，好懷念呀！從前妳總是跟著奶奶在廚房做東西，聽妳媽說現在妳已經在餐廳當主廚啦？ |
| Daisy | I'm not the main chef, I'm just a pastry chef in charge of making dessert. I have to thank Chris for making all this happen though. He helped me introduce to the manager in the restaurant. | 不是主廚啦，只是負責做甜點的師傅而已，不過這都是托 Chris 的福喔，是他幫我引薦的。 |
| Daisy's grandfather | Hmm, such a fine young man, just like I used to be. | 嗯，真是個好男人，跟我當年一樣！ |

Chris　Uh-uh, how can I **compare** with Grandpa?　I was hoping I could have some opportunities to learn how a husband can **cherish** his wife.

呵呵呵，我怎麼能跟爺爺比呢，希望有機會能多跟爺爺學習怎麼樣當個疼老婆的好男人。

## ⭐ Some Words to Know

**❶ country** n. 鄉下、郊外
Before he moved to the city, he had lived in the country for a while.
他在搬到城市以前，曾在鄉下住過一段時間。

**❷ surprise** v. 驚喜、讓人驚訝的事
That the singer announced to drop out of the signing business is a big surprise.
那位歌手宣布退出歌壇的消息使大家大吃一驚。

**❸ finally** adv. 最後、終於
My sister finally gets the doll she has been dreaming of on Christmas.
妹妹終於在聖誕節收到她夢寐以求的洋娃娃。

**❹ handmade** a. 手工的
Hand-made things are now much more expensive.
現在手工物品昂貴多了。

**❺ less** a. 較少的
The amount of water left in the reservoir is less than one month storage. If it doesn't rain soon, there might be some water shortage this year.
水庫裡的水量剩不到 1 個月份，若再不下雨，今年就有可能會缺水了。

**6** tasty **a.** 美味的、可口的

I've never eaten such tasty steak, how did you cook it?

我從沒吃過這麼美味的牛排,妳是怎麼烹調的呢?

**7** chef **n.** 主廚、廚師

Tonight's dinner is tremendously delicious, please help me to pay my tribute to the chef.

今晚的晚餐實在太美味了,請幫我向主廚致意。

**8** compare **v.** 比較、匹敵

Comparing with that world champion, those kids skateboarding in the streets can only be regarded as amateurs.

跟那位世界冠軍相比,那些在街頭玩滑板的孩子只能算是業餘的。

**9** cherish **v.** 珍愛、愛護

That old couple loves this stray dog as their child.

那對老夫妻把這隻流浪狗當成自己的孩子一樣愛護。

## ⭐ 30 秒會話教室

Long time no see. It has been a long time. It has been a while. 以上三句都是「好久不見」的口語用法。(第一句雖然仍在英美學術界有些爭議,但民眾並不排斥,仍可使用無虞。)

# 情境 15　見男友的妹妹

 ## Let's Talk in Love

Matt wants to introduce his new girlfriend to his sister, Grace, but he doesn't tell her **beforehand** and just asks her out.  As a result, Grace feels slightly **embarrassed** that she finds out her brother brings his girlfriend ...

Matt 想介紹剛交往的女友 Gill 給妹妹 Grace 認識，但他沒有先跟 Grace 說一聲就直接約她出來，害 Grace 到了現場才發現哥哥帶了女朋友，有點尷尬…

| | | |
|---|---|---|
| Grace | Uh...hi, excuse me...who is this? | 呃…嗨，請問…這位是誰呀？ |
| Matt | Grace, we've been waiting for you for quite a while.  This is my girlfriend, Gill.  Gill, this is my sister, Grace. | Grace，我們等妳很久了呢，這是我的女朋友，Gill。Gill，這是我妹妹 Grace。 |
| Gill | Hi, Grace, I've heard a lot about you, it's very nice to meet you. | Grace 妳好，久仰大名，很高興認識妳。 |
| Matt | Why don't you say something?  Are you getting hungry?  Come sit down first, order whatever you'd like. We've already placed our orders. | 妳怎麼不說話呢，是肚子餓了嗎？來，先坐下吧，想吃甚麼儘管點，我們已經先點好餐了。 |
| Gill | I see your face being all **pale**, are you sick?  Let me take a look. | 我看妳臉色發白，是不是身體不舒服，我幫幫妳看看。 |

| | | |
|---|---|---|
| Grace | Don't **worry about** it.  Brother, I think I'd better go home first.  Enjoy your dinner, bye! | 不用妳操心，哥，我看我還是先回去好了，你們慢慢吃吧，再見。 |
| Matt | Grace, how come you **behaved** so **unusually** today?  Hey, wait up, wait! Gill, let me go get her and check on her, please wait me here. | Grace，妳今天怎麼表現的這麼不尋常？喂，等等我啊！Gill，我跟過去看看她怎麼了，妳先在這裡等我。 |
| Gill | Hmm, okay. | 嗯，好。 |
| Matt | I'm sorry for keeping you waiting long.  Sigh, it has been so long since that drama took place.  I thought we could just keep regular brother-sister relation, but I didn't expect that she still has feelings... | 對不起，讓妳久等了。唉，那件事情都過那麼久了，我以為我們可以恢復正常的兄妹關係，沒想到她還對我…。 |
| Gill | The relation between you two seems very **complicated** to me.  Can you tell me **exactly** what **happened**?  Or I will have a **knot** in my heart. | 你們之間的關係好像很複雜耶，可以請你一五一十地說清楚嗎？不然我對這段感情會有疙瘩的。 |

## ⭐ Some Words to Know

**❶ beforehand** `adv.` 預先、事先
Grandpa likes to be prepared for anything beforehand, and he never shows any signs of panicking.
爺爺要做任何事情都會預先準備好，從來沒有表現的慌慌張張過。

**❷ embarrassed** `a.` 窘的、尷尬的
All day I feel so embarrassed that there's a hole in my skirt.
我的裙子破了一個洞，一整天我都尷尬極了。

**❸ pale** `a.` 蒼白的、灰白的
A little girl got so scared of a cockroach that her face is all pale.
小女孩被一隻蟑螂嚇得臉色發白。

**❹ worry about** `v.` `phr.` 擔心、焦慮
Grandmother wants everyone not to worry about her illness.  Such speech makes many of the relatives feel sorry and their hearts ache for her.
祖母要大家不用擔心她的病，這番話讓眾多親戚更是感到心疼不捨。

**❺ behave** `v.` 行為舉止、表現
The new young guard who encounters unexpected situations has very alert performance.
那位新來的年輕警衛遇到突發狀況時表現的非常機警。

**❻ unusually** `adv.` 不尋常、非常
That antique vase is painted with unusually beautiful patterns.
那個骨董花瓶上面繪著不尋常的美麗圖案。

**❼ complicated** `a.` 複雜的、難懂的
The operation of that operating system is way too complicated for me.
那套作業系統的用法對我來說太複雜了。

**❽ exactly** `adv.` 確切地、完全地
Could you please tell me where you are exactly located?  I will send someone to drive there and pick you up.
請告訴我您的確切位置，我會派人開車過去接您。

**❾ happen** vi. （偶然）發生

Something funny happened while I was waiting for the train on the platform at the station today.

我今天在車站月台上等車時發生了一件好笑的事情。

**❿ knot** n. 難題、疙瘩

They don't know how to cut the Gordian knot which is namely to solve their love triangle problems.

他們不知道該如何解決眼前這段三角戀的難題。

## ⭐ 30 秒會話教室

I have been looking forward to seeing you. 我一直很期待能見到你。也就是「久仰大名」的意思。

# 情境 16 誰在電話的那一頭陪你？

 **Let's Talk in Love**

Trevor has **arrived** in Paris for a week. After the **international** call he made to report his safety, this is the first time he contacts Zoe who is waiting for his calls in New York after Trevor settles down everything...

Trevor 已經抵達巴黎一個星期了，繼剛下飛機報平安的那通國際電話，這是他安頓好後第一次和人在紐約等他消息的 Zoe 聯絡…

| | |
|---|---|
| Trevor | Hi, Zoe, it's me, Trevor. Did I **wake** you **up**? |
| Zoe | No, you didn't. It's only 10 pm here. What about in Paris? Is it still morning there? |
| Trevor | It's 4 pm here. People are still having the afternoon tea at the outdoor cafés. In a **twinkle** of an eye, there is a 6-hour time **difference** between us being apart from each other. |
| Zoe | Yes, but now it is not the time to be sentimental. Are you all getting situated yet? |

Zoe，是我，Trevor，我吵到妳睡覺了嗎？

沒有啊，現在這裡才晚上 10 點，巴黎呢？還是早上嗎？

現在這裡是下午四點，街上的人都還坐在咖啡廳喝下午茶呢。才一轉眼，我們就已經相距了 6 小時時差的距離了。

是啊，可是現在還不是感傷的時候，你在那邊的生活都安頓好了嗎？

Trevor　Hum, I have found a place to stay, and also paid a visit to the master I'm going to study painting with. I also find a nice part-time job opportunity! There should be no problem to **hold** the **minimum quality** of life.

嗯，我已經找好住的地方了，也到要進修學畫的大師那邊拜訪過了，我還找到一份不錯的打工機會呢！維持最低限度的生活品質應該是不成問題。

Zoe　Hmm, it is good. If you have any difficulties there, there is always a way I can thinking of helping you... Hey, how come I keep hearing a girl calling "Trevor, Trevor?" Do you already get a French girlfriend there?

嗯，那就好，如果有甚麼困難要跟我說喔，我會盡量想辦法的…咦，我怎麼聽到有女生一直在叫「Trevor、Trevor」，你該不會在那邊交了法國的女朋友吧？

Trevor　No, I don't. That was the sound of my students Clara. Come, Clara, say hi to Miss Zoe in English.

沒有啦，那是我的學生 Clara 的聲音啦。來，Clara，跟 Zoe 小姐用英文問聲好。

Clara　Good afternoon, Miss Zoe, I'm Clara Petit. I am 10 years old this year.

下午好，Miss Zoe，我是 Clara Petit，今年十歲…。

Zoe　10 years old...?

十歲…？

Trevor　Do you hear that? Her English is pretty good, right!? Clara is the landlord's daughter , and she wants to learn English, so the landlady asks me to teach her. She will not only pay me some **tuition**, but also invite me to have meals with them! She really helps me a lot.

聽到了嗎？她的英文還標準吧！？Clara 是房東的女兒，她想學英文，因此房東太太拜託我教她，不但會付我學費，平常還會招待我跟她們一起吃三餐呢！真是幫了我大忙。

## ⭐ Some Words to Know

**❶ arrive** **vi.** 抵達
That Hollywood superstar arrived in London last night, ready for a new three-day film promotion for the new movie.
那位好萊塢巨星昨晚抵達倫敦，準備為新戲進行為期 3 天的宣傳。

**❷ international** **a.** 國際性的、國際間的
As long as one has a ranking in an international competition, a person can get further education with very little problem.
只要在國際性的比賽得過名次，要升學幾乎是無往不利。

**❸ wake up** **v.** **phr.** 使醒來、使起床
Go get your sister to wake up, or you'll be late for school.
快去叫妹妹起床，不然上學就要遲到了喔。

**❹ twinkle** **n.** 瞬間、一剎那
In a twinkle of an eye, the kitten swiftly disappeared.
才一眨眼，那隻小貓就一溜煙地不見了。

**❺ difference** **n.** 差異、差距
Can you tell me the difference between baboons and monkeys?
你能告訴我沸沸和猴子之間的差異嗎？

**❻ hold** **v.** 持續、保持
We all hope that this good weather will hold till the Christmas holiday.
大家都希望這樣的好天氣持續到聖誕假期。

**❼ minimum** **n.** (U) 最低限度、最小量
The Department of Health recommends that the minimum daily requirement of physical activity is 30 minutes a day for every person in order to achieve the effects of exercise.
衛生署建議，每人每天最少必須運動 30 分鐘，才能達到鍛鍊身體的效果。

**❽ quality** **n.** 質、品質
Cars made in Germany have the top qualities in the world.
德國製的汽車品質擁有世界頂尖的水準。

**❾ tuition** **n.** (U) 學費

I have signed up a total eight courses for the Ukulele lessons. The tuition is only four thousand NT dollars.

我報名的烏克麗麗課程共有 8 堂課，學費只要四千元台幣。

## ☆ 30 秒會話教室

There's more than one way to skin a cat. 想剝貓皮的方式不只有一種。看起來有點殘忍的句子，其實是「山不轉，路轉；路不轉，人轉」的意思。

# 情境 17　父母急著抱孫

 **Let's Talk in Love**

Wesley and Olivia have been married for about a year.  They still haven't gotten the good news of the wife being **pregnant**.  It makes the elderly family members very worried, espeãally Wesley's mother, has tried to push these two once she gets a chance...

Wesley 和 Olivia 結婚近一年，夫妻倆一直沒有傳出懷孕的消息，讓急著抱孫子的長輩非常擔心，尤其是 Wesley 的媽媽，只要找到機會就不停催促兩人…

| | | |
|---|---|---|
| Olivia | Mom, what are you doing here?  We were just thinking about going to visit you and Dad a few days later. | 媽，您怎麼來了？我們才在想過幾天要到鄉下去看看您和爸的。 |
| Wesley's mother | I happen to be around in this neighborhood, so I **drop by** and pay a visit to you.  Where's my son? | 我剛好到附近辦事情，就順道過來看看你們。我兒子呢？ |
| Olivia | He's in the room.  Let me go get him.  Please come on in and have a seat. | 他在房裡，我去叫他。您先進來坐吧。 |
| Wesley | Mom, what brings you here today? Where's Dad? | 媽，妳怎麼跑來啦？爸呢？ |

| Wesley's mother | Ah, I didn't tell your dad about coming here. I've heard there's some Chinese **herbal** mediãne for getting pregnant. I come here all the way only for buying and bringing this. If your dad finds out about his, he will say I have blind faith in a **folk prescription**. | 哎呀，我是瞞著你爸跑來的。我聽說有一種對生小孩很有幫助的中藥方，所以我就專程跑去買來給你們吃，要是被你爸知道了，一定會說我迷信偏方的！ |

| Wesley | Mom, didn't we agree that we should let nature take its course? Olivia and I will have so much **pressure** if you keep mentioning this to us. | 是啊，媽。我們不是說好生小孩這件事情順其自然就好了嗎？妳不要整天把這件事掛在嘴上好不好，這樣我跟 Olivia 會有壓力的。 |

| Wesley's mother | (Sigh) I don't have much time left for becoming a grandmother. Can't you two try to **accomplish** my wish by letting me have my grandchildren? | 哀，我也沒剩多少日子可以當祖母了，你們夫妻倆就不能完成我想抱孫子的願望嗎？ |

| Wesley | Mom, you are really exaggerating! We will get on that after another couple of years. Now we both have to work, I really don't want to get up in the middle of the night changing the diapers or making milk. | 媽，妳太誇張了啦！頂多再讓妳等一、兩年我們就會積極做人了，現在我們倆都要上班，我實在不想半夜還要起來幫小孩換尿布、泡奶粉的。 |

Olivia   Yes, mom. It's not like we can't have babies, it's just that we are not yet finanãally ready for welcoming a new member to the family, so we want to work hard for another few years.

是啊，媽，不是我們生不出小孩，只是我們的經濟狀況還沒有準備好迎接新生命的到來，所以想再拚個幾年看看。

Wesley's mother   Why didn't you say so? This is no problem for me. I won't selfishly ask my daughter in law to **quit** her job to take care of the baby at home. As long as you're willing to have a baby, I will **unconditionally** help you babysit. Isn't that a nice **offer**? Don't keep me waiting long.

哎呀，早說嘛！這個問題簡單，我不會自私地叫媳婦辭掉工作在家帶小孩的，只要你們肯生，媽一定會無條件幫你們帶孩子的。這個提議不錯吧！？不要再讓我等太久囉。

## ⭐ Some Words to Know

**❶ pregnant** **a.** 懷孕的、懷胎的
The passengers on the bus all yield the seat to that pregnant woman.
公車上的乘客紛紛讓座給那位孕婦。

**❷ drop by** **v.** 順道拜訪
I will drop by and visit the teacher once I get the chance.
只要有機會我一定順道去拜訪老師。

**❸ herbal** **a.** 草本的
The Chinese herbal medicine is milder than regular medicine, which can be used for keeping the body in a good shape. However, it's still better to see a doctor at a hospital if a person is having immediate illness.
中藥比起西藥溫和，可以用來養身，但若有急病還是到大醫院找醫生看診會比較好。

**❹ folk** **a.** 民間的、通俗的

Healing burn injury with rice wine is a common long-believed folk remedy, but it has no affect when it puts it perspective of science.

米酒是民間流傳已久治療燒燙傷的偏方，但以科學來看完全沒有效果。

**❺ prescription** **n.** 處方、藥方

This is the medicine that requires a doctor's prescription.

這是需要有醫生開立的處方才能拿到的藥。

**❻ pressure** **n.** (U) 壓力

Some people cannot give any good performance as usual when they are under pressure.

有些人在有壓力的情況下便無法發揮平常的水準。

**❼ accomplish** **v.** 完成、實現、達到

The bonus will be gone if we don't accomplish the sales goal the department has set for us this month.

若沒有達到部門預設的業績目標，這個月的績效獎金就沒有著落了。

**❽ quit** **v.** 辭職、離開

That new secretary quit not even a week after she started the job.

那位新來的秘書工作不到一周就辭職了。

**❾ unconditionally** **adv.** 無條件地

The wife of that rich man is willing to get divorced unconditionally because she has put up too much with his bad temper.

那位富商的妻子願意無條件地離婚，因為她實在受夠了他的壞脾氣。

**❿ offer** **n.** 提議

I must say the offer of a whole week in Vienna is quite tempting.

我必須說待在維也納一個禮拜的提議真的很誘惑人。

 **30 秒會話教室**

I won't worry about it anymore. I'll let nature take its course.（我不會再煩惱那件事了，我會順其自然）。

# 情境 18 小孩的保母

 **Let's Talk in Love**

Raymond and Helen have a one-year-old child.  Now the couple finally feels more comfortable that every time they want to go out, they don't have bring their kid with them all the time, instead, they can ask a babysitter to take care of the baby at home...

Raymond 和 Helen 的小孩已經滿周歲了，夫妻倆也終於比較放心，現在他們要出門時不必再把孩子帶來帶去，而是請保姆來家裡照顧小孩⋯

| | | |
|---|---|---|
| Helen | Honey, are you ready yet?  We're running late.  The nanny has already arrived. | 親愛的，你準備了嗎？我們快遲到了，保姆也已經到了喔。 |
| Raymond | Okay, let me **shave** first.  I'll be right out. | 好，我刮個鬍子就來。 |
| Nina | Mr. And Mrs. Stewart, are you going to the movies today again?  That's nice. | Mr. and Mrs. Stewart，你們今天又要去看電影啊？真好。 |
| Helen | Nah, we are going to attend a dinner party organized by Raymond's colleagues tonight, where some men will smoke.  We don't think it's appropriate to go there with a little baby, so...  I am sorry we have to bother you again. | 不是啦，我們今晚要去參加 Raymond 同事所舉辦的餐會，那裏的男士有的會抽菸，我們覺得不太適合帶小 baby 去，所以⋯不好意思又要麻煩妳囉。 |

| Nina | Not at all, Mrs. Stewart. I like to look after a little baby, plus little Ray doesn't cry a lot. It's not trouble at all taking care of him. | Mrs. Stewart 妳別這麼說，我很喜歡照顧小 baby，而且妳們家的小 Ray 不愛哭，照顧起來一點都不麻煩。 |
| --- | --- | --- |
| Helen | Really? I'm so relieved to hear you say that. He just had a **slight fever** for the past few days although we took him to see a doctor already. It's nothing serious now, but I'd still like you to pay attention on his conditions. Please remember to feed him the mediāne after you feed him some milk. | 真的嗎？聽妳這麼說我真是太高興了。不過 Ray 他這幾天有點發燒，雖然已經看過醫生、沒有大礙，但還是要注意一下，待會妳餵他喝完牛奶記得也要餵他吃藥喔。 |
| Nina | Okay. Is there anything else? | 好的，還有其他吩咐嗎？ |
| Helen | Please make sure to put more warm clothes on him after giving him a bath tonight, also check on the **diapers** more often to see if they are needed to be changed. He has slight **diarrhea** too. Everything is at its regular place. if you have any questions, feel free to call me. | 今晚幫他洗完澡時更要穿暖一點，尿布可能也要常注意一下是否需要更換，他有點腹瀉。東西都放在老地方，如果有甚麼問題隨時打電話給我。 |

Raymond　Honey, I'm ready, we can go now. Nina, thank you every time for helping take care of Ray. Helen and I were just thinking that if we gave you enough hourly rate? After all, you come help us take care of the baby after school and often have to stay late.

親愛的，我好了，可以出門了。Nina，謝謝妳每次都來幫忙照顧 Ray。我跟 Helen 還在討論給妳的時薪會不會太少了？畢竟妳可是利用放學後的時間，幫我們照顧到七晚八晚。

Nina　Mr. Stewart, the **hourly** rate you offer me you has been much higher than the average in the market! While no one would **complain** about having too much salary, but I still feel a bit sorry. We can wait till you come back and have more discussion! Aren't you running late for the party?

Mr. Stewart，你們給我的時薪已經比行情高出許多了！雖然沒有人會嫌薪水太高，但我有點過意不去，還是等你們回來再說吧！你們不是快遲到了嗎？

 ## Some Words to Know

❶ shave　**v.** 刮（鬍子）
My boyfriend does not feel confident enough to go out as long as one day he doesn't shave.
我的男朋友只要一天不刮鬍子就覺得沒有自信出門。

❷ look after **v.** **phr.** 照顧
Many children from double-income families are looked after by their grandparents in Taiwan.
台灣有許多雙薪家庭都由祖父母照顧小孩。

❸ slight **a.** 輕微的、微小的
The new thermometer is so accurate that slight temperature differences can be shown.
那支新型溫度計非常精準，連微小的溫度差異都顯示得出來。

❹ fever **n.** 發燒、熱度
When I got up this morning, I found myself having a little fever. I called the company and asked for sick leave for that reason.
今天早上起床我發現自己有點發燒，於是向公司請了病假。

❺ diaper **n.** 尿布
Honey, can you help me change the baby's diaper?
親愛的，你可以幫我換一下孩子的尿布嗎？

❻ diarrhea **n.** (U) 腹瀉
Women usually have slight diarrhea during their menstrual periods, which is a normal phenomenon.
女生的生理期間會伴隨著輕微的腹瀉，這是正常現象。

❼ complain **v.** 抱怨、發牢騷
This suite is cheap in rent and so close to the station. I have nothing to complain about.
這間套房租金便宜，離車站又近，我已經沒有甚麼可抱怨的了。

## ⭐30 秒會話教室

What would the hourly rate/salary/wage be? 請問時薪是多少？國外一般都是試做之後才討論薪資問題，可別先問失禮喔。

# 夢想熱血在我心

# 情境 1 來經營民宿吧！

 **Let's Talk in Love**

Linda has helped her father manage the ranching business after she graduated from the college.  Being young and ambitious, she wants to utilize what she has learned at school to transform the family business into running a BNB.  While she's doing the **preparatory** work, she receives a phone call from her ex-boyfriend, John...

Linda 大學畢業後就回到家中幫忙父親管理牧場，年輕有衝勁的她想利用自己在大學所學的專業將家中的牧場轉型為民宿，正在進行籌備工作之際接到了前男友 John 的電話⋯

| | | |
|---|---|---|
| John | Hello, is this Linda?  I haven't seen you for months, can you still recognize my voice? | 喂，是 Linda 嗎？幾個月不見了，還認得我的聲音嗎？ |
| Linda | Of course I can, it's not like I have very bad memory.  How's everything **lately**, John? | 當然囉，我的記性又沒有那麼差。John，最近還好嗎？ |
| John | I'm calling to check on your **recent** situation.  What are you up to lately? | 我也是打來想關心妳的近況，妳最近在忙些甚麼呢？ |
| Linda | Do you remember my dad has a small ranch?  I've been trying to **convince** my dad to build a BNB on the vacant property. | 你還記得我父親的小牧場吧？我說服爸爸，想利用空地蓋一間民宿。 |

| John | BNB! That **sounds** like a **tremendous** work! Can you handle that all by yourself? | 民宿呀！聽起來是一件浩大的工程耶！妳一個人忙得過來嗎？ |
|---|---|---|
| Linda | My dad has saved up some money after all these years of hard working, I think there should be no problem we pay for a construction company to build the BNB. The real challenge is how I am going to **promote** this place located in the remote area in the countryside. That's what I'm really working on now. | 爸爸這些年工作下來也存了一筆錢，利用那筆錢請人蓋民宿是不成問題，不過蓋好之後要如何將這個鄉下小地方推廣出去，才是我現在正在努力的地方。 |
| John | **Marketing** is your major at college. I believe you can make it happen for sure. | 行銷可是妳大學的主修呢！我相信妳一定沒問題的。 |
| Linda | Well. The reason I chose Marketing as my major was to help the ranching business for my family back in college, little did I know that I could really apply it in the real life. | 呵呵，我當初選這門主修就是為了幫忙改善家裡牧場的經營狀況，沒想到如今真的能派上用場！ |
| John | If you need someone to help you with building up a website, I'll be the first one in line. Actually I haven't had much to do around since I helped my cousin setting up the website of his surfing store. You know I'm not **lack** of money, I'm doing this only because... | 如果妳有需要人幫忙架設網站，我一定義不容辭！其實我幫我堂哥架設完衝浪店的網站之後，就一直找不到事情做了。不過我可不是因為缺錢喔，我是因為…。 |

Linda    Hey, I know you're only doing this for the sake of our past relationship.  Well, I won't hesitate about seeking your help.  Let's **keep** in touch for more discussions on the website, okay?

呵呵，我知道你是念在我們的舊情上，那我就不客氣了。架設網站的事我們再保持聯絡吧！

## ⭐ Some Words to Know

**❶ preparatory** a. 預備的、籌備的
The PE(Physical Education) teacher asks the students to do some preparatory exercise every time before the class.
體育老師每次要上課前都會要學生們做準備運動。

**❷ lately** adv. 最近、近來
"Have I Told You Lately?" is a very wonder song.
「我最近告訴過你我愛你嗎？」這首歌非常好聽。

**❸ recent** a. 最近的、近來的
That is a recent photo of my baby.
那是我寶寶最近的照片。

**❹ convince** v. 說服、使信服
I convinced my mom to let me go to a party with my boyfriend.
我說服我媽媽讓我跟男同學去參加舞會。

**❺ sound** v. 聽起來
This singer's voice sounds very pleasant to the ear.
這位歌手的聲音聽起來非常悅耳。

**❻ tremendous** **a.** 巨大的、極大的
The news reports that the government spends a tremendous amount of money to support the diplomatic country.
新聞報導說政府花了極大的一筆錢幫助邦交國。

**❼ promote** **v.** 宣傳、推銷
This new cosmetics brand is intensively promoted on TV.
電視上正在強力推銷這一個新的化妝品品牌。

**❽ marketing** **n.** (U) 行銷學、交易、銷售
I have studied marketing at school.  But I got failed for skipping classes too often.
我曾經修過行銷學，但最後因為太常翹課而被當了。

**❾ lack** **n.** 欠缺、不足
Some desert regions are severely lack of water resources.
沙漠地區嚴重缺乏水資源。

**❿ keep** **v.** 保持、保有
I have kept the gold necklace my grandmother gave me.
我一直保存著祖母送我的金項鍊。

---

## ⭐ 30 秒會話教室

What are you up to lately?（你最近在忙些甚麼呢？）What have you been doing lately?（你最近過的怎麼樣呢？）以上這兩句都是問候對方的話喔。

# 情境 2　鏡頭下的世界

## ⭐ Let's Talk in Love

Chris is a **photographer** shooting **catalogs** for companies.　After work, he actually likes to **capture** the beautiful **scenery** and portraits everywhere. His girlfriend, Daisy, also highly admires his passion...

Chris 的工作是幫廠商拍攝商品型錄的攝影師，但他私底下喜歡用相機捕捉各處美麗的風景和人像，女友 Daisy 也很欣賞他的興趣…

Daisy　It's always you taking pictures of me. How about let me take some of you once in a while, okay?

出來玩你老是都在幫我拍照，偶爾我也幫你拍一張照片留念吧！？

Chris　That won't be necessary.　I've had the best memories by taking all the pictures of the beautiful scenery and people on the trips.

不用了啦，拍下旅途中的見聞和美麗的風景、人物，對我來說就是最好的回憶了。

Daisy　I have so many personal **photos** that my friends thank I'm being a model for outdoor shooting.　Let's ask someone to a picture of us.

我的個人照已經多到朋友都以為我在當外拍模特兒了，不然我們請人幫我們拍張合照吧。

Chris　Okay, but there aren't many people around.　Let me take more **close-up** photos of the fallen leaves and flowers, and wait for someone coming.

好啊，可是這附近沒甚麼人，我再拍幾張落葉和花卉的特寫，等到有人來再說吧。

| Daisy | Okay. You must have **accumulated** a large **mass** of albums of the scenery and portraits you've taken. Are you planning on publishing them? | 嗯。你至今拍下的風景照和人像已經累積成數十本相簿了吧，你有打算公開它們嗎？ |
|---|---|---|
| Chris | That idea does come across my mind! So far I just upload the pictures to share with some afiãonados on the blogs. Some have asked me if I want to have an exhibition. | 我的確有這麼想過耶！我目前都是把照片上傳到部落格跟同好交流，是有一些人問我怎麼不辦個展覽？ |
| Daisy | An exhibition? Can we make some money out of it? Are there people spend lots of money buying your photos? | 展覽！？可以賺到錢嗎？會不會有人出大錢買你的照片？ |
| Chris | I think chances are we have to spend our own money on hosting the exhibition, not to mention making money. People don't spend much money on buying photos nowadays, more likely oil paintings I would say. | 我想不但賺不了錢，連展覽都還要自掏腰包辦呢！而且這年頭應該不會有人想要花大錢買照片，油畫或許還有可能。 |
| Daisy | Even so, I will still give you my full **support** if you want to have your own exhibition for once. You've always been so supportive to my work after all. | 即使如此，若你想辦一次個展，我一定會支持你的。畢竟你支持我的工作也是不遺餘力。 |
| Chris | Thank you! I'm much appreãated and happy hearing you say that. | 謝謝妳！有妳這麼說我就心滿意足了。 |

## ⭐ Some Words to Know

**❶ photographer** 🟦n. 攝影師

One should first have some basic knowledge to photography and also some aesthetics if s/he wants to become a photographer.

想成為攝影師首先要對攝影有基本的認識，還要具備美感。

**❷ catalog** 🟦n. （商品、圖書等）目錄

Every time I look at the catalog of that furniture store, I can't help to have the impulse of making my house look just like that being gorgeous and splendid.

每次欣賞那間家飾用品店的型錄就會忍不住想要將家裡打造的同樣美輪美奐。

**❸ capture** 🟦v. （用照片等）紀錄、拍攝

The beautiful figure of that old lady being young was all captured in the pictures.

那位老奶奶年輕時候的倩影都被記錄在照片中。

**❹ scenery** 🟦n. (U) 風景、景色

The scenery of the Yellow Stone National Park is very marvelous.

黃石國家公園的景色非常壯麗。

**❺ photo** 🟦n. 照片

The photos in black and white hanged all over on the wall bring people the nostalgic atmosphere in that coffee shop.

那間咖啡廳的牆上掛滿黑白的照片，很有懷舊的氣息。

**❻ close-up** 🟦n. （電視、電影等）特寫

The close-up shots of the actress in a sexy cocktail dress have repeatedly appeared on TV.

電視上不停出現那位身著性感晚禮服的女星的特寫鏡頭。

**❼ accumulate** 🟦v. 累積、積聚

After the flood is gone, there are many giant rocks and garbage accumulated in the downstream area.

一陣洪水過後，河川下游累積了大量的垃圾和巨石。

**❽ mass** **n.** 大量、眾多

I have a mass of files waiting for me to process after the New Year holiday.

休了一個年假，辦公桌上有大量的文件等著我處理。

**❾ supportive** **a.** 支持的

Children with supportive parents are often healthier and happier.

有父母陪同支持的小孩常常會比較健康也比較快樂。

 **30 秒會話教室**

Can I take a picture with you? 我可以跟你拍一張合照嗎？Excuse me, would you kindly take our picture? 不好意思，可以麻煩你好心幫我們拍張照嗎？

# 情境 3  麻辣教師 GTO

 **Let's Talk in Love**

Gill who has a new boyfriend has already put the past behind her when she sees the recent posts of her ex-boyfriend, Owen.  She takes the initiative to say hello to Owen, and Owen quickly **responds** to her...

Gill 在臉書上看到前男友 Owen 的近況，已有新男友的她對過去早已釋懷，於是主動向 Owen 打招呼，Owen 也很快地就有回應…

Gill  It's been a while, how's it going with everything?

好久不見了，最近好嗎？

Owen  It's really been a long time, espeãally since what happened before...

真的好久不見了，自從那件事情之後…。

Gill  Well, let **bygones** be bygones, I've already put the past behind me. Although I did feel surprised about your updates when I saw your pictures. Are you a school teacher now?

呵呵，過去的事就讓它過去吧，我早就不放在心上了。倒是你讓我嚇了一跳，我看到你的照片，你現在在學校當老師？

Owen  That's right!  Wasn't I still in the Normal University when where we were still dating?  After that I had done my internship at a school, and now I'm **officially** a school teacher at a high school.

對呀！跟妳交往那段時間我不是還在念師範大學嗎？後來我到學校實習，現在已經正式在高中擔任老師了。

**Gill** It's really hard to **imagine** you being a teacher...

你當老師，真的有點難以想像…。

**Owen** You mean my sexual orientation? I didn't tell the school and the students about that 'coz I think it's something personal and there's no need to report it. On the other hand, I'm actually pretty **popular** among the students because of my sexual orientation.

妳是說我的性向一事吧？這件事我沒有告訴校方和學生，因為我覺得這是個人的私事，不需要報備。但也反而因為我的性向，讓我在學生之間挺受歡迎的。

**Gill** Oh, that sounds nice, although I don't quite understand why...Can you make a few **examples** for me?

喔，這是好事啊，不過我不太明白其中原因…你可以實際舉幾個例子給我聽嗎？

**Owen** One thing is I can understand what the girls think very well, so a lot of female students come talk to me whenever they've got something in their minds. As for the male students, they also think I'm not that **stuffy** as they expected. They actually think I dress fashionably in style.

像我非常能夠了解女孩子的想法，所以女學生都覺得有任何煩惱都可以找我傾訴。至於男學生這方面，也覺得我不是想像中那些嚴肅古板的老師，反而覺得我的打扮很時尚、很有型。

**Gill** Uh-uh, this is indeed your strong point. I might have been **attracted** by your **distinguishing characteristic** before when we were dating.

呵呵，這的確是你的優點。我當初可能也是被你的這些特點吸引的吧？

Owen  I'm sorry I didn't lay you out the truth. That's why I keep reminding myself of being careful with what I say and do as a teacher. I know you've forgiven me but I still want to say sorry to you.

當初騙了妳是我的錯，這也讓我不斷提醒自己，為人師表一定要謹言慎行。我知道妳已經原諒我了，但我還是想對妳說聲對不起。

## ⭐ Some Words to Know

**❶ respond** **v.** 作答、回答
The telecommunications company hasn't responded to me about the unusual problems on the line.
關於線路異常的問題，電信公司到至今還沒有給我回覆。

**❷ bygones** **n.** (plural) 往事、過去恩怨
Grandpa has never been able to forget the bygones on the battlefield.
爺爺始終無法忘懷當年在戰場上的往事。

**❸ officially** **adv.** 官方地、正式地
That department store officially opened last month.
那間百貨公司上個月正式營業。

**❹ imagine** **v.** 想像、猜想
I can imagine how surprised they will be when I tell my parents I want to donate my organs.
我可以想像當我告訴父母我要捐贈器官時，他們會有多驚訝。

**❺ popular** **a.** 受歡迎的
South Korean artist PSY's gangnam style dance is hugely popular in the world.
韓國藝人 PSY 的騎馬舞在全球受到熱烈的歡迎。

**❻ example** **n.** 例子、樣品

The teacher gives two examples to explain this grammar in English.

老師舉了兩個例子來說明這個英文文法。

**❼ stuffy** **a.** 古板的、保守的

That stuffy principal always puts students into sound sleep every time he gives a speech.

那位古板的校長每次演講台下都會有許多學生呼呼大睡。

**❽ attract** **v.** 吸引、引起⋯的注意

The Taipei 101 building has attracted many foreign tourists to come here and take a trip.

台北 101 大樓吸引了許多國外觀光客前來遊玩。

**❾ distinguishing** **a.** 有區別的

Can you tell the distinguishing features of the dragons in the myth?

你能說出神話中龍的特徵嗎？

**❿ characteristic** **n.** 特性、特徵

The bushy hair is her greatest characteristic.

一頭濃密的秀髮是她最大的特徵。

## ⭐30 秒會話教室

過去的事就讓它過去吧、既往不咎。

Let bygones be bygones.

# 情境 4　環遊世界 80 天

## ⭐ Let's Talk in Love

While studying painting in Paris, Trevor go look for the beautiful scenery for painting everywhere in Paris whenever he has some free time.  After a while, he begins to fall in love with this free lifestyle, and wants to expand his horizons...

人在巴黎學畫的 Trevor 只要有空，便會帶著畫具在巴黎的大街小巷內尋找適合寫生的美景，一陣子之後，他也開始愛上這種自由自在的生活方式，開始想拓展他的足跡…

Zoe　Hey, slow down.  I've heard you talk nonstop once I pick up the phone.  What's all the exātement about?

呵呵，說慢一點，電話一接起來就聽到你劈哩啪啦講個不停，甚麼事情這麼興奮呀？

Trevor　I said, yesterday I finally went painting on the famous riverside of Seine River where I felt so alive.  I strongly feel that coming to Paris to study painting is really a right deāsion.

我剛才說，我昨天終於到著名的塞納河畔寫生了，在那裏我真的有種充實的感覺，我深深覺得來巴黎學畫真是個正確的決定！

Zoe　It is a right deāsion indeed!  I really want to go along after hearing you say that.  Unfortunately, I have no **specialty** that I can make a **living** there.

本來就是啊！聽你這麼形容，害我也好想跟著去喔。可惜我在那邊沒有一技之長可以謀生。

| | | |
|---|---|---|
| Trevor | If I had money, I could get you here and live together.  Before that, however, I still want to achieve a naive dream. | 如果我有錢，就可以把妳接過來一起生活了。可是在那之前，我還有一個任性的夢想想要實現。 |
| Zoe | A naive dream...?  What's that? | 任性的夢想…？那是甚麼？ |
| Trevor | I want to **travel** round the world! More **precisely**, I want to start with traveling the **continent** of Europe. | 我想要環遊世界！更精準地來說，是先環遍歐洲大陸！ |
| Zoe | This ...  This should be everyone's dream, right?  But with your current situation, how are you going to achieve it? | 這…這應該是每個人的夢想吧？但是以你現在的狀況，要怎麼實現呢？ |
| Trevor | I have asked the teacher who I study painting with, and he was very much in favor of me to go out and see the world while I am still young.  I can carry my painting tools and simple belongs, so I can travel and draw people for a living at the same time. Not only can I earn travel **passage**, I can also refine my painting **skills**.  It's like killing two birds with one stone. | 我已經問過學畫的老師了，他很贊成我趁年輕多出外走走看看，我可以背著畫具和簡單的行囊，邊走邊幫人畫畫維生。不但可以賺到繼續往前走的旅費，還能磨練畫技，這樣不是一舉兩得嗎？ |

Zoe    That sounds very **desirable**, but certainly it's not so simple as matter of fact.  What if you don't earn enough travel passage to eat?  How about overnight **accommodations**?  Where are you going to stay on the trip?  What about the landlady?

這樣聽起來很理想，可是實際上一定沒有這麼簡單，萬一賺不到旅費，沒錢吃飯怎麼辦？還有住宿的問題呢？你沿途要住哪裡？房東太太那邊又怎麼辦？

Trevor    I realized how **reckless** I was after hearing you say that.  Although in any case, I still want to fulfill this dream.  I guess I have to save a little more money for the journey and then hit the road.

聽妳這麼說，我才想到自己有多麼魯莽。不過無論如何我還是想實現這個夢想，等我存到多一點盤纏再上路吧！

## ⭐ Some Words to Know

**❶ specialty** n. 專長、專業
His specialty is playing the violin.
他的專長是小提琴彈奏。

**❷ living** n. 生計
That old man shines shoes for a living on the street.
那位老伯伯在路邊靠幫人擦鞋維生。

**❸ travel** v. 旅行
We plan on traveling to Japan during the Chinese New Year.
我們安排農曆過年期間到日本旅行。

❹ precisely **adv.** 準確地

Please tell me precisely the location of the fire, I will send a fire truck to put out the fire.

請準確地告訴我火災發生的位置，我將派消防車過去滅火。

❺ continent **n.** 大陸、陸地

I always wonder how it feels to discover a new continent.

我一直很好奇發現新大陸是怎樣的感覺。

❻ passage **n.** 旅費、旅行

His travel passage and identification were all stolen by the thief.

他的旅費和身分證件全被小偷扒走了。

❼ skill **n.** 技能、技術

English listening and speaking are two different skills.

英文的聽力和口說是兩種不同的技能。

❽ desirable **a.** 值得嚮往的、令人滿意的

The realtor takes the couple to see their desirable mansion.

房屋仲介帶那對夫妻去看他們嚮往的夢幻豪宅。

❾ accommodation **n.** 住宿、膳處

He has found a very cheap accommodation on the Internet. Finally he can feel worry-free taking a working holiday in Australia.

他在網路上找到了非常便宜的住宿處，終於可以放心前往澳洲遊學打工。

❿ reckless **a.** 魯莽的、不顧後果的

Riding a scooter passing the busy crossroads is a very reckless behavior.

騎機車闖過車水馬龍的十字路口是非常魯莽的行為。

---

 **30 秒會話教室**

英文也有這樣的諺語來形容一次做好兩件事，例：Kill two birds with one stone.（一石二鳥。）也可換個說法為：Get two jobs done at once.（事半功倍。）

# 情境 5  喵星人地球總部

 **Let's Talk in Love**

Whenever Stella, a cat-lover, sees stray cats on the street, she always stops to see if she can help them.  She hopes inside her heart that every stray cat and dog can find a home...

超愛貓咪的 Stella 每當看到街頭的流浪貓都會停下腳步看能否幫助牠們，她的心中更希望所有的流浪貓狗都能找到一個家…

| | | |
|---|---|---|
| Stella | Remember I always want to establish a "Kitty's Garden" to keep all the little poor stray cats? | 記得我一直希望能成立一個「貓園」，收留所有可憐的流浪貓嗎？ |
| Gordon | Of course.  But only when we win the **lottery**, or where else can we get enough fund and keep running it? | 當然記得啊，只是若沒有中樂透，哪來的經費去實踐、甚至是營運下去呢？ |
| Stella | That's what I thought.  But yesterday when I talked to my parents on the phone, they told me that they are interested in a 1323 square meter land in a mountain outside the āty.  It comes with a little house.  They want to have it for **retirement**.  They asked me about my ideas with the use of the large land. | 我原本也是這麼覺得，不過昨天打電話回家，我爸媽竟然說他們看中了外縣市山上一塊占地 400 坪，附一棟小屋的地，想要買來養老，並問我剩下那麼大一塊空地，有沒有想到甚麼用途？ |

| | |
|---|---|
| **Gordon** | If so, we have solved the major problem: **location**.  So how did you tell them? |
| **Stella** | My dad heard about my plan to build the Kitty Garden and he was interested then.  So he might bear this in mind when they think about buying a land. |
| **Gordon** | Your dad is so nice!  But even if we have the land, how can we get the money for the enormous feeding from after keeping the cats around? |
| **Stella** | I've got that all well planned.  I'll save the money little by little, build the **enclosure brick** by brick; then adapt the little cottage to a coffee house, making it a pet restaurant of style.  This way it will get cat-lovers coming and **self-sufficiency**. |
| **Gordon** | Indeed, many people who keep stray animals have to **raise** money endlessly for lack of the fund.  In fact, self-effiâency is the right model for **sustainable management**. |

如果是真的，那麼最重要的地點問題就解決了耶，那妳怎麼回答？

我爸爸也曾經聽我提過成立貓園的計畫，當時他也有興趣，這次想買地可能也有順便幫我圓夢的意思。

你爸爸人真好呢！不過即便有了地，等到開始收留流浪貓以後，龐大的飼料費要從哪裡來呢？

我早就計畫好了，我會慢慢地存錢，一磚一瓦的由圍牆開始蓋起，然後再將那塊地上原先的小屋改建成咖啡屋，打造成一間有特色的寵物餐廳，這樣一來就可以吸引同樣愛貓的客人上門，才能自給自足。

的確，有許多憑藉著愛心收留流動動物的人，都因為缺乏經費必須不停向大家募款，其實自己自足才真的是能永續經營的模式呢！

Stella　Right. I will make an announcement to tell all the guests that the coffee house's **income** will be used on the stray cats and we take donations as well. So more 'Meowians' on planet Earth will be taken care of.

沒錯，我會公告所有上門的客人，咖啡屋的收入都將用於照顧流浪貓身上，同時也接受捐款，這樣就能照顧到更多地球上的喵星人了。

Gordon　If your dream of having a coffee house is realized, even you will sell things a bit more expensive there, cat-lovers will understand that.

如果妳的咖啡屋真的實現了，就算裡面的東西賣貴一點，我想愛貓人士們也會諒解的。

## ⭐ Some Words to Know

**❶ lottery** [n.] 彩券、彩票
I would go travelling around the world if I won the lottery.
如果我中了樂透頭獎，我就要去環遊世界。

**❷ retirement** [n.] (U) 退休生活
He moved to a lakeside cottage with fresh air and lived a carefree life after his retirement.
他退休後就搬到空氣好的湖邊小屋，過著自在的生活。

**❸ location** [n.] 地點、位置
The company officials are looking for a new location for their office.
公司高層正在物色新辦公室的立地位置。

**❹ enclosure** [n.] 圍牆、圍欄
Playing hide-and-seek with her dad, the little girl used books to make an enclosure and hid behind.
小女孩用書本圍成了一道圍牆，躲在後面跟爸爸玩捉迷藏。

**❺ brick** **n.** 磚塊
Accidentally kicking the brick when playing in the garden, that kid felt so hurt and cried.
那孩子在花園玩時不慎踢到磚塊，痛得他哇哇大哭。

**❻ self-sufficiency** **n.** (U) 自給自足
Since the agriculture era, human beings have leaded a lifestyle of self-sufficiency.
自的農業時代以來，人們的生活型態都是自給自足的。

**❼ raise** **v.** 募（款）、招（兵）
The volunteers are raising fund for the victims of the tsunami in southern Asia.
義工們正在街頭為了南亞海嘯的災民募款。

**❽ sustainable** **a.** 能保持的、能維持的
I think the government should greatly support solar energy for its being sustainable.
我認為政府應該大力支持太陽能這項能永續利用的能源。

**❾ management** **n.** (U) 經營、管理
The colleagues have become more united since the company changed its way of management.
自從公司改變了管理方法之後，同事們就更有向心力了。

**❿ income** **n.** 收入、所得
It causes debt when the expense is over the income.
當支出大於收入就會造成負債。

## ★ 30 秒會話教室

要如何表達自己是愛貓人士或愛狗人士呢？可以用片語 cat-lover、dog-lover，或是 I'm a cat person.（我是傾向於喜歡貓的人。）

# 情境 6　I love Rock'n Roll

## ⭐ Let's Talk in Love

Since Matt started playing rock music as a teenager, he has fallen in love with it like crazy.  Since then he taught himself to play bass, and formed an **underground** band with some rock **aficionados** at college.  Today he asks his sister Grace to pay a visit to the basement he usually **rehearses** in...

Matt 自從少年時期接觸搖滾樂之後就瘋狂愛上無法自拔，之後憑著自學學會彈奏貝斯，大學時期更和搖滾樂同好組成了一支地下樂團。今天他約妹妹 Grace 到他平常練團的地下室⋯

| | | |
|---|---|---|
| Matt | Last time I asked you to eat out, you turned around and leave without even sitting down.  I couldn't catch you afterwards, so I want to really talk to you today. | 上次找妳出來吃飯，妳都還沒坐下轉身就跑，事後我也追不上妳，所以今天想找妳出來談談。 |
| Grace | You don't have to mention what happened last time.  I got what it means since you bring your girlfriend to show me. | 上次的事就不要再提了，你都特地帶女朋友給我看了，我很明白這是甚麼意思。 |
| Matt | I didn't try to hurt your feelings.  I've treated you like my sister since what happened before, and I hope you can do the same and get along with me like I'm your brother, okay?  I even write a song for you to let you know you're my **irreplaceable** family. | 我並沒有要傷害妳的意思，自從那件事情之後，我就一直都把妳當成妹妹看待，希望妳也能像對待哥哥般跟我相處，好嗎？我還為妳寫了一首歌，讓妳知道妳永遠都是我無可取代的親人。 |

**Grace**　Huh, aren't there other band members coming for practice?

咦，今天沒有其他團員一起過來練習嗎？

**Matt**　The **drummer** can't make it today so we cancel the rehearsal.  I ask you to come here today so you can hear me **solo** sing the song for you.

鼓手今天有事，於是我們乾脆取消了練習。所以我就約妳過來，想讓妳聽聽我只為妳一個人獻唱的獨奏。

**Grace**　I've thinking a lot since then.  I know it's **unhelpful** no matter how much I can't accept it.  I might as well play my role as your sister so I can stay with you forever.

其實我在那之後想過很多了，也知道再怎麼不肯接受也無濟於事，倒不如稱職地扮演好妹妹的角色，這樣也能永遠在你身邊啊。

**Matt**　As long as you can leave this behind you.  Like our first time we enrolled the Ho-hai-yah Rock Festival, we got rejected.  We all had very **pessimistic** attitude towards it.  But this year we finally successfully get selected, so now we are delightfully **compose** a new song, and we practice together whenever we have some free time.

妳能想開就好，像我們樂團第一次報名參加海洋音樂祭的時候被拒於門外，大家對此也很看不開。不過今年我們終於成功入選了，現在大家都興高采烈地創作新歌，一有空就聚在一起練習。

**Grace**　Really?  My brother is going perform on the stage as a bass player!  I feel so exāted about that.

真的嗎！？我的哥哥要以貝斯手的身分上台表演搖滾樂，我覺得好興奮喔！

Matt　Really really!  Please make sure you come enjoy our hard-working creation by then.

這是真的，到時候請妳務必一定要在台下欣賞我們團員嘔心瀝血的創作！

Grace　I will cheer for you with your girlfriend in the audience!

我會跟你的女朋友，一起在台下為你歡呼的！

## ⭐ Some Words to Know

**❶ underground** a. 地下的、祕密的
That criminal organization dedicates to underground transactions to tax evasion.
那個不法組織專門進行地下交易，藉此逃漏稅。

**❷ aficionado** n. ⋯迷、⋯狂
He is an aficionado of online games.  Every day he stays up all night in front of the computer playing games.
他是個線上遊戲狂熱者，每天都熬夜在電腦前玩遊戲。

**❸ rehearse** v. 排練、練習
The students are rehearsing for the school drama performance.
學生們正在為學校的話劇表演進行排練。

**❹ irreplaceable** a. 不能調換的、無可取代的
That puppy is an irreplaceable member in that family.
那隻小狗對那個家庭來說是無可取代的一分子。

**❺ drummer** n. 鼓手
That singer was a drummer of a band before he started his singing career.
那位歌手在出道前曾是一個樂團的鼓手。

**❻ solo** **n.** 獨奏、單獨表演

She isn't used to performing solo.  She feels more comfortable when she plays with other musicians.

她不習慣單獨表演，要有其他樂手在旁伴奏才比較自在。

**❼ unhelpful** **a.** 無益的、無用的

It's unhelpful that you have been worried about your condition.  You might as well change your eating habits, do exercise, and maybe you'll get well just by doing so.

妳一直擔心自己的病情也於事無補，不如改變飲食習慣、多做運動，說不定自然就好起來了。

**❽ pessimistic** **a.** 悲觀的

One shouldn't deal things with a pessimistic attitude so she/he can perceive the beauty of life.

對待任何事情都不應該用悲觀的態度，才能察覺到生命中的美好。

**❾ compose** **v.** 作（詩、曲等）

The teacher wants us to practice composing a poem about praising our great mothers.

老師要我們練習作一首詩，主題是歌頌母親的偉大。

## ⭐ 30 秒會話教室

「想不開」便是把事情放在心上的意思，因此可說：Don't take such small things to heart. 別為了一點小事想不開。

# 情境 7 急診室的春天

## Let's Talk in Love

Phil is the doctor in the emergency ward where doctors face many patients in accidents every day. He has a very busy life, but full of meaning. Today, he gets delayed with the working hours because of an emergency case before he gets off work...

Phil 是急診室裡的醫生，每天都要面對許多因意外而送醫的病患，生活過的非常忙碌但充滿意義。今天他也因為快下班前的一件急診而延誤了下班時間…

| | |
|---|---|
| **Phil** I'm sorry, dear, I just saw your missed calls. I was dealing with patients so I missed them. | 親愛的對不起，我現在才看到妳打來的未接來電。我剛剛在處理病患，漏接了。 |
| **Tracy** I'm okay as long as you reply me. I was worried that whether you were in some kind of acãdent on the way back since it was long after your working hours were over. | 妳有回我就好，都超過下班時間那麼久了，我還在擔心你會不會在下班途中發生意外了呢？ |
| **Phil** Don't you worry about that. I work in a hospital, and if there is any acãdent, I will be sent back to the hospital, so you can definitely fine me here. | 不會的啦，我自己就在醫院工作了，若是有什麼意外一定會被送回醫院的，在醫院一定找的到我。 |
| **Tracy** how can you **curse** yourself like that? Even doctors have to get off work. You can't get back to sleep again today, right? | 你怎麼這樣詛咒自己呢？就算是醫生也該有下班時間啊，你今天也不能回來睡覺了吧？ |

| Phil | Yeah right. A patient who got hit by a drunk driving driver was just sent in. He had no sign of life at first. After our first **aid**, he is currently in the ICU (**intensive** care unit) for further observation. So by the time I get home, it should be early morning. You should go sleep soon. | 對啊，剛剛臨時送來一位被酒後駕車駕駛撞上的傷患，一度沒有了生命跡象，經過我們的急救後，目前還在加護病房觀察中。等我回到家應該是凌晨了，妳先睡吧。 |

| Tracy | In order to save the patient's lives, doctors need to give it all out! You do **sacrifice** at a **noble** cost, but for the **long-term** I am still very worried about your health. | 醫生們為了拯救病患的性命，可說是拿自己的生命在拼呢！你所做的犧牲雖然崇高，但長期下來我還是很為你的身體健康擔心。 |

| Phil | Saving people's lives is the doctor's **duty**. Although we also want to go home from work at normal hours, get up and go to bed early, but we can't see people's lives are in critical condition without doing something to help them, espeãally when we see patients are about to die and carried in on the **stretchers**. | 救人是醫生的職責，雖然我們也很想正常下班回家、過著早睡早起的生活，但是看到被擔架抬進來的命危傷患，實在無法見死不救。 |

| Tracy | (Sigh) I understand. But some family members forget doctors are also human beings. They are only supposed to cure diseases, if they don't, it's like they are guilty of committing some heinous crime. | 哀，我懂。但就是有些家屬會忘了醫生也是人，治的好病是應該的，治不好就像犯了滔天大罪似的人人喊打。 |

Phil　Well, I guess there's nothing we can do about it. When the family is in grief, they first certainly want to blame the **attending physician**. That's something a doctor must bear and face. Because of the illness and death I see every day, I have more profoundly feelings to the impermanence of life and cherish everything around me. I'm proud of my career.

這沒辦法呀，家屬在悲痛的心情之下，主治醫生一定是首當其衝的，這也是當醫生必須要面對的事情。也是因為每天看盡生老病死，讓我更加感嘆生命的無常，並懂得珍惜身邊的一切，我以我的職業為傲。

Tracy　I'm also proud of you. Okay, let's cut it short, you should go back take care of your patients.

我也以你為傲。好了，不跟你多說了，快回去照顧你的病患吧。

## ⭐ Some Words to Know

**❶ curse** **v.** 詛咒、咒罵
The two women kept cursing each other, which seemed like they had a long feud.
那兩位婦人不停咒罵對方，好像已經結仇許久了。

**❷ aid** **n.** 幫助、救援
All the pedestrians who come and go can see the old man fall to the ground, but no one wants to come to his aid.
來來往往的路人都看到老先生倒在地上，卻沒有人要幫助他。

**❸ intensive** **a.** 特別護理的、密集的
The hospital gives some intensive care to that premature infant.
醫院對那位早產的新生兒進行特別的照顧。

**❹ sacrifice v. 犧牲**
Parents always sacrifice much of their money and time for their children.
父母總是為孩子犧牲許多金錢和時間。

**❺ noble a. 崇高的**
That great man's noble ideas still affect many people nowadays.
那位偉人崇高的思想至今仍然影響著許多人。

**❻ long-term a. 長期的**
So long as a little extra fat is intaken every day, it will accumulate excess fat for the long-term.
只要一天攝取一點多餘的脂肪，長期下來便會累積成多餘的贅肉。

**❼ duty n. 職責、義務、本分**
Her duty is to take good care of the preschool children until their parents get off work.
她的職責是照顧好學齡前的孩童直到他們的父母下班。

**❽ stretcher n. 擔架**
That football player who was seriously injured in the field was carried away immediately on the stretcher by the EMT (emergency medical technician) from the stadium.
那位足球員在場上受了重傷，馬上被醫護人員用擔架抬離球場。

**❾ attending a. 主治的**
Grandpa's attending doctor is very optimistic about his condition and asks the family not to worry.
爺爺的主治醫生對他的病情非常樂觀，要家屬不必擔心。

**❿ physician n. 醫生、治療者**
The doctor asked him to come back for a subsequent visit three days later.
那位醫生要他三天後再來複診。

 **30 秒會話教室**

I'm proud of myself.（我以我自己為傲。）I'm proud of you.（我以你為傲。）這兩句話要經常對自己和深愛的家人說喔。

## 情境 8　親上火線的救火英雄

 **Let's Talk in Love**

Ivan passed the rigorous examination and interview, and eventually became a full-time **fireman** belonged to the government department.  His girlfriend, Jessica, feels very worried every time she thinks that he might go fire **fighting** on the frontline...

Ivan 通過了嚴格的考試和面試，終於成為隸屬於公家機關的專職消防隊員，女友 Jessica 一想到他之後就有可能親上火線救火，感到非常擔心…

| | | |
|---|---|---|
| Ivan | Baby, look, this is my picture I took after I reported to the fire department today.  Do I just look great once I put on my fire-entry suit standing in front of the fire **engine**? | 寶貝妳看，這是我今天到消防隊報到後所拍的照片，我穿上消防服站在消防車前面的樣子很帥吧！ |
| Jessica | It looks just like the heroes you've always wanted to be, but...Are you really sure you want to be a firefighter? | 看起來就像你一直嚮往的英雄一樣，但…你真的確定要當消防員嗎？ |
| Ivan | Why not?  Didn't you still support me when I prepared for the exam? | 為什麼不呢？我在準備考試的時候妳不是還很支持我嗎？ |
| Jessica | That's because I was not sure if you'd get admitted...now you do, it makes me feel really uneasy. | 那是因為當時還不確定你會錄取…現在真的實現了，反而讓我感到不安。 |

| Ivan | What's wrong? Don't you believe in my ability? Don't you believe that I can do this job well that requires courage? | 怎麼了？妳不相信我的能力嗎？不相信我能做好這份需要膽識的工作？ |
| Jessica | No! I just feel putting out fire is too dangerous! Why do you risk your life to enter the fire scene? The house may **collapse** down to suppress you, or you may be **choked** by the heavy smoke, get **burned**, just for saving some **complete** strangers...? | 不是的！我是覺得救火太危險了！冒著生命危險進入熊熊燃燒的火場，房子還有可能倒塌下來壓住你，或是被濃煙嗆傷、被火燒傷，就為了救素未謀面的陌生人…！？ |
| Ivan | I understand your **concern**, but if everyone thinks like that, who is going to put out fire? | 我明白妳的擔憂，但如果每個人都這麼想，那又要由誰去救火呢？ |
| Jessica | I...I know it's selfish, but no one would want their loved ones to die. | 我…我知道這麼想很自私，但誰都會希望不是自己的親人呀。 |
| Ivan | I can assure you that we all have received professional training, as well as good teammates and advanced equipment, even if I really die in the fire, I do it for saving lives. Would you still love me if I were a **coward**? | 妳放心，我們受過專業的訓練、還有優秀的隊友和先進的裝備，就算我真的命喪火場，也是為了拯救生命，如果我是個懦夫，妳還會如此愛我嗎？ |

Ivan　I understand your **determination**, but I still sincerely hope we do not have to face the day we will be apart by death.

我明白你的決心了，但我還是衷心期盼我們都不必面對生離死別到來的那一天。

## ⭐ Some Words to Know

**❶ fireman** n. 消防員、救火員
The work of a firefighter is dangerous and could get one killed.
消防員的工作非常危險，還有可能送命。

**❷ fighting** n. (U) 戰鬥、搏鬥
He lost his best battle mate in that fighting.
他在那場戰鬥中失去了最要好的戰友。

**❸ engine** n. 引擎、消防車、救火車
There are a few fire engines roaring by. I wonder where the fire is.
有好幾輛消防車呼嘯而過，不知道是哪裡發生了火災？

**❹ collapse** vi. 倒塌
A large earthquake made many houses collapsed, and caused a great number of casualties.
大地震使許多房子倒塌，並造成多起傷亡。

**❺ choke** v. 使窒息、梗住
The child was choked by jelly stuck in his gullet, and he was almost suffocated.
那個小孩被果凍梗住食道，幾乎快要窒息了。

**❻ burn** **v.** 燒毀、燒傷

The entire factory was burnt and destroyed by the flames, leaving only ashes behind.

整棟工廠都被火舌給燒毀了，徒留灰燼。

**❼ complete** **a.** 完全的、徹底的

He completely forgot about our agreement.

他把我們的約定忘的一乾二淨。

**❽ concern** **n.** 擔心、關心的事

The president expressed his concern to the victims and promised to give the maximum assistance.

總統對災民表達了關切，並承諾會給予最大的協助。

**❾ coward** **n.** 懦夫、膽怯者

Because he did not dare to catch the frog with his bare hands, he was being laughed at as a coward by the classmates for the whole semester.

他因為不敢徒手抓青蛙，被同學嘲笑是懦夫整整一個學期。

**❿ determination** **n.** 決心

He had the determination to overcome all the difficulties until he became the state governor.

他下定決心要排除一切困難，直到當上州長為止。

## ⭐ 30 秒會話教室

要表達事不關己，可用以下兩句，如：That's no concern of mine. 那不是我該操心的。It's none of my business. 那不關我的事。

## 情境 9　我要當總統！

 **Let's Talk in Love**

Gordon was born in a political family that his grandfather is a senior government official, his father is the **mayor**, and his brother is a **senator**. Now with his family's support, Gordon has decided to run for the next senate election...

出生於政治世家的 Gordon，爺爺是政府高官、父親是市長、哥哥是議員，如今在家人的支持下，Gordon 也決定參選下一屆的議員…

Gordon　My dear, can you help me review my listed views in politics see if they are too exaggerating?

親愛的，妳幫我看看我所列出的參選政見草稿，這樣會不會太過浮誇呢？

Stella　Let me see...your political views are very consistent with **current affairs**, I think there should be no problem, but...

我看看…你的這些政見很符合時事，我想應該沒問題。不過…

Gordon　But what?　Are they still too **naive**?

不過甚麼？果然還是太天真了嗎？

Stella　You seem to have too little description to your experiences though.　Espeãally if you are a new face, people won't be able to know where you are from as a **candidate**.

不過你對自己的經歷的描述，好像少了一點，尤其你又是新面孔，大家會不知道你是打哪裡來的候選人？

| | | |
|---|---|---|
| Gordon | Isn't that enough showing my father's name? I was worried that if my work experience was only being my brother's assistant, would it look too inadequate? | 光報上我父親的名號還是不夠嗎？我是擔心如果說出我的工作經歷是擔任哥哥的助理，不知道會不會太遜了一點？ |
| Stella | Your family from generation to generation is in politics. Your background should be no problem solely based on that. I think you can also mention that you were graduated from the department of political sãence, so it makes you look more qualified. | 你們家代代都是從政的，光就這一點，你的背景算是沒問題。我想你可以順道提一下你是政治系畢業的，這樣就更不像是半路出家的了。 |
| Gordon | Let's do what you said. If now I tell the voters that my long-term goal is to run for the **president**, is my **ambition** being too big? | 就照妳說的做。那如果現在就告訴選民我的長遠目標是參選總統，野心會不會太大了？ |
| Stella | It's okay to show such ambition, but are you sure you really want to run for the president? | 有這樣的野心說出來是無妨。不過你是真的想參選總統呀？ |

Gordon  Actually, I always have this idea in my mind, and now I'm running for the senator, it makes me feel I'm getting closer to my goal. I will continue to go into this direction. Regardless of the final outcome, I will get up to a higher and higher position. It is beyond the doubt.

其實我心裡一直都有這麼想，現在真的要參選議員了，讓我覺得這條路彷彿離我越來越近，我會持續往這個目標邁進的，無論最終結果如何，我都會越爬越高，這是無庸置疑的。

Stella  Oh, after you are **elected** as the senator, you must help me launch the TNR bill that can completely solve the problem of stray animals.

呵呵，等你真的選上了議員，一定要幫我推動能夠徹底解決流浪動物問題的 TNR 法案唷。

## ✦ Some Words to Know

❶ mayor  **n.**  市長、鎮長
The Mayor is invited to attend the ribbon-cutting ceremony for the opening of a new elementary school
市長受邀出席新小學的開幕剪綵儀式。

❷ senator  **n.**  參議員
Over the majority of senators agreen passing this bill.
有過半數的參議員同意通過這一項法案。

❸ current  當前的、現時的
We are too short-sighted about our current energy policy today; instead we should actively develop alternative energy.
我們當今的能源政策太過短淺了，應該積極開發替代能源才是。

**❹ affair** n. 事件、事務

All you need to do is to concentrate on the important affairs in the company and leave the rest to the heads of the departments.

你只要專心處理公司裡的重要事務即可，其他就交給各部門的主管吧。

**❺ naive** a. 天真的、幼稚的

Being so naive even as a father, aren't you afraid the kids might laugh at you?

都已經當爸爸了還這麼幼稚，不怕小孩笑你嗎？

**❻ candidate** n. 候選人

The past of the candidate will be all exposed in the media.

候選人的過去全都會被媒體挖出來攤在陽光下。

**❼ president** n. 總統

Barack Obama is the first African American president of the U.S., which has changed the position of the African Americans in history.

歐巴馬是美國第一位黑人總統，改寫了歷史對黑人的定位。

**❽ ambition** n. 野心、雄心、抱負

The young man has the ambition to be the leader of the tribe.

那個年輕人一心想成為族人的首領。

**❾ elect** v. 選舉、當選

The classmates elected that lively witty boy to serve as the chief of recreation.

班上同學推舉那位活潑風趣的男孩擔任康樂股長。

## ⭐30 秒會話教室

It is no doubt that no creature can live forever. 沒有任何生物能長生不老，這是無庸置疑的。

# 情境 10　業務員的堅持

 **Let's Talk in Love**

Joseph, the insurance salesman cultivates a group of loyal customer base with his friendly and **meticulously** sales service that makes his work done impressively...

保險業務員 Joseph 憑著親切的服務及無微不至的售後服務，培養出一群死忠的顧客群，將業務工作做得有聲有色…

| | | |
|---|---|---|
| Rebecca | Honey, I watch the TV commerãal and it says your company has introduced a new policy.  The scope of its protection seems very broad.  How come you don't sell it to your friends and family like you usually do? | 親愛的，我看電視廣告說，你們公司推出了一種新的保單，保障的涵蓋範圍好像很廣耶，怎麼沒看你像往常一樣跟親朋好友推銷呢？ |
| Joseph | (Sigh) It is because there are some **unequal** treaties hidden inside the new policy.  The company has deliberately makes the text on the printed manual very small, and particularly asks the salesmen to deliberately use **quibble** words.  I do not want to promote this insurance policy. | 哀，那是因為新保單裡面隱藏著一些不平等的條例，公司又故意把說明書上的文字印的很小，也特別交代我們這些業務員故意講的模稜兩可，所以我就不想推廣那份保單。 |

| Rebecca | This is why, I see!  No one would have any **pointless** expense if all the insurance salesmen in the whole world were just like you having so much consãence. | 原來是這樣啊！如果全天下的保險業務員都像你這麼有良心，就不會有人花冤枉錢了。 |
| Joseph | But if everyone were just like me, the **insurers** wouldn't make any money!  They still need to have a salesman who is willing to promote the product.  As for me, I'll make peace with my mind by giving them the chance to make money. | 可是如果大家都像我這樣，保險公司就不會賺錢啦！所以還是需要有願意推廣的業務員存在，至於我，還是把賺錢的機會讓給他們比較心安。 |
| Rebecca | That is to say that if you could sell more poliães like this, you sales **achievement** would get sky high. | 也就是說，如果你能昧著良心多賣一些這樣的保單，業績就會扶搖直上囉。 |
| Joseph | That's true indeed, but my usual sales performance is enough, so I feel there's no need to do that.  Do you think I don't have enough ambition? | 的確是這樣子的，但我平常的業績也夠了，所以覺得沒有必要這麼做，妳說我這樣是不是很沒有上進心呢？ |
| Rebecca | Not at all.  I think there are both advantages and disadvantages.  Each salesman has to feed their own families, so that doesn't make them a bad person for selling those poliães.  They just make money out of the **loopholes** caused by the customers' negligence to the policy details. | 不會呀，我覺得各有利弊，每個業務員都有自己的家庭要養，他們賣出那些保單也不見得就是壞人，只是利用客戶自己沒有注意到那些條例的漏洞來賺錢。 |

Joseph You are exactly right. If every **policyholder** could be just like you knowing the importance of reading the **declarations** pages carefully, I would not have so much conflict or dilemma at work.

妳說的也是，如果每個投保人都能像妳一樣，知道要好好詳閱保險說明頁，也就不會有讓我天人交戰的情形發生了。

Rebecca You can still actively promote the poliães that do not have the problem, so you can receive additional performance bonuses, can't you?

但你還是可以積極推廣那些沒有問題的保單呀，這樣就可以領到更多業績獎金了不是嗎？

Joseph If you want to receive more money, then I will have less time I can spend with you, are you sure about this?

如果想領到更多獎金，那我可以陪妳的時間就會減少囉，妳確定嗎？

## ☆ Some Words to Know

❶ meticulously **adv.** 一絲不苟地、極細心地
The craftsmen meticulously create vehicles that are considered the best sports car in the world.
工匠一絲不苟地打造出一輛輛世界上最頂級的跑車。

❷ unequal **a.** 不平等的、不公正的
She could not bear the unequal treatment in her workplace so she angrily filed a complaint to the Bureau of Labor Insurance.
她無法忍受在職場中的不平等對待，憤而向勞保局投訴。

❸ quibble **n.** 說模稜兩可的話、詭辯

Her quibble words did not get anyone's agreement when we could all distinguish the rights from the wrongs as we heard it.

她那番詭辯的話並沒有得逞，大家一聽就知道孰是孰非。

❹ pointless **a.** 無意義的

Explaining to the people who don't believe you is pointless.

跟已經不相信你的人解釋再多都是毫無意義的。

❺ insurer **n.** 保險業者、保險公司

The insurance policy she has sold in the insurer has higher stacked up than the books we have read.

她在保險公司賣出的保單疊起來比我們讀過的書還要厚。

❻ achievement **n.** 成就、成績

The achievement that Neil Armstrong reached has become the legacy in the present and the future.

阿姆斯壯當年所達成的成就足以留芳後世。

❼ loophole **n.** （法律等的）漏洞

The criminals find a loophole in the law to avoid sentences.

歹徒利用法律的漏洞來逃避刑責。

❽ policyholder **n.** 投保人、被保險人

The policyholder is the person actually needs to pay for the insurance.

投保人，即為實際上要繳付保險費的人。

❾ declaration **n.** 宣告、聲明

That country's move is equivalent to a declaration of war to our country.

那個國家的舉動等同於向我國宣戰。

##  30 秒會話教室

It cuts both ways. 各有利弊。There are both advantages and disadvantages.

這件事情各有優劣。

# 情境 11　我要飛上青天

## Let's Talk in Love

Gill is a **cabin attendant** who has a slim and beautiful figure.  The life style of traveling to many countries from time to time meets her personality that likes changes and challenges.  She finally has found a good man, and no longer had to worry about her frequent flight duties would attract her attention on maintaining a relationship...

Gill 是一位身段窈窕的美麗空姐，時常來往許多國家的生活滿足了她喜歡變化與挑戰的個性，而她也終於找到好男人，再也不必擔心頻繁的出勤會使她無暇經營感情了…

| | |
|---|---|
| Gill | Last time I was cheering for you together with your sister Grace in the audience, we also talked a lot.  I feel she no longer has hostility to me and begins to open up her heart to me. | 上次跟你妹妹 Grace 一起在台下為你加油時，我們聊了好多，感覺她不再敵視我，也開始對我敞開心房了。 |
| Matt | Yeah, she told me afterwards too.  After she finds out your occupation is flight attendant, she has more **favorable** impression on you. | 對呀，她事後也跟我說，聽到妳的職業是空姐之後，她對妳就更有好感了。 |
| Gill | Why?  I thought only men **fancy** of flight attendants. | 為什麼呢？不是只有男生才對空姐有遐想嗎？ |

| | |
|---|---|
| **Matt** Nah, she said she was longing for the life style, espeãally being able to travel around, and also having romantic encounters in different countries. | 不是啦，她說她很嚮往空姐的生活，尤其是能到處旅遊，還能在不同國家有豔遇。 |
| **Gill** She was all thinking of the **bright** side of this career as a flight attendant. Maybe she'd immediately **surrender** once she knew the dark side. | 她說的都是空姐這個職業的光明面，若是知道了黑暗面，說不定她馬上就舉手投降了。 |
| **Matt** Oh, what's the dark side? Like flirting with the **captain**? | 喔，有哪些黑暗面呢？比如說跟機長搞曖昧嗎？ |
| **Gill** Oh, this should be regarded as the bright side of it. There are things like all day long dealing with the unreasonable guests, often having air **turbulences**, and always staying in the hotel alone after landing, also worrying about if the boyfriend back home would use this opportunity to have an affair.. | 呵呵，這應該算是光明面吧。像是成天遇到蠻不講理的客人、經常在空中遇到亂流，還有落地之後老是孤零零地住在旅社裡，還要擔心家鄉的男友會不會趁機搞外遇…。 |
| **Matt** Why do I feel you're making **oblique accusations**? | 我怎麼有一種妳在指桑罵槐的感覺。 |

Gill    Anyway, if Grace really wants to be a flight attendant, then I'll ask her out and have more conversations about it. I will tell her everything I know about this industry and share my experiences with her.

反正如果 Grace 真的有心想當空姐的話，就再約她出來聊聊吧，我把這個行業所知道的一切資訊和經驗全都傳授給她。

Matt    You're the best!  By the way, I won't have an affair while you go abroad. You're the only one for me.

妳最好了！對了，我絕對不會趁妳出國搞外遇的，妳就是我的唯一。

## ⭐ Some Words to Know

**❶ cabin** **n.** （飛機等）客艙、駕駛艙
Being a cabin attendant is a dream job for many women.
空服員是許多女性嚮往的夢幻職業。

**❷ attendant** **n.** 服務員、侍者、隨從
The attendants of the Arabic oil prince's visit are as many as 50 people.
阿拉伯石油王子的出訪隨從多達 50 人。

**❸ favorable** **a.** 贊同的、討人喜歡的
This movie has received a favorable review right after it came out.
這部電影一推出後就獲得廣大的好評。

**❹ fancy** **v.** 愛好、迷戀
He has found he is fancying of his classmate.
他發現自己愛上了同班的同學。

**❺ bright** **a.** 明亮的、前途光明的
Her bright smile has captured the hearts of many boys.
她燦爛的笑容迷倒了不少男生。

**❻ surrender** **v.** 投降、放棄
After two days of fierce fighting, the enemy quickly surrendered.
在經過 2 天的激戰之後，敵軍很快地就投降了。

**❼ captain** **n.** 機長、艦長、船長
The captain ordered to launch a torpedo to sink the goal.
艦長下令發射魚雷擊沉目標。

**❽ turbulence** **n.** 亂流、動亂、騷亂
All the passengers were all panicked when the aircraft met the turbulence.
飛機遇上了亂流，所有乘客全都驚慌失措。

**❾ oblique** **a.** 拐彎抹角的、不直接了當的
He spoke in an obligue way in order to conceal the fact that he was married.
他講話拐彎抹角的，就是為了隱瞞自己已婚的事實。

**❿ accusation** **n.** 指責、指控
He made the accusation that a government official privately accepted his bribes for up to three years.
他指控某位政府官員私下收受他的賄賂長達 3 年之久。

## ⭐ 30 秒會話教室

He surrendered/gave up his dream of becoming a teacher. 他放棄了當老師的夢想。以上兩種說法都有放棄的意思。

# 情境 12　愛的麵包魂

 ## Let's Talk in Love

Zoe, who likes **baking** some pastries and gives them to her neighbors, has been well known for her **gourmet** cooking skills.  With everyone's encouragement, she has decided to use the living room of her own apartment as the baking classrooms, and begin to teach everyone to do baking...

平時就喜歡動手烘焙糕點分送鄰居的 Zoe，好手藝當然是聲名遠播。在大家的鼓舞之下，她決定利用自己的公寓客廳充當烘焙教室，開始教大家做烘焙…

Trevor　What's going on there?  How come you picked up the phone after it rang so long?  I always call you 10 pm sharp at your local time every Friday.

妳怎麼了，這次怎麼讓電話響了這麼久才接，我都每周五準時在妳那邊晚上 10 點的時候打過去呀。

Zoe　I'm sorry.  I was preparing the ingredients in the kitchen, and there was **flour** my hands.  I had to wash it off before I picked up the phone.

抱歉，我剛剛在廚房準備食材，手上沾滿了麵粉，趕緊洗掉才過來接起電話。

Trevor　As long as you're fine.  Why are you still working in the kitchen at this late hour?  Have you eaten dinner yet?

妳沒事就好，這麼晚還在廚房，晚餐還沒吃嗎？

**Zoe**  That's because there'll be some mothers come to my place and learn how to make bagels. I was making the **dough** so it has enough time to rise. That will save me some time tomorrow in class.

是這樣的，明天有一些媽媽們要到家裡來跟我學做貝果，我剛剛正在揉麵團，想先發酵好，明天上課會比較節省時間。

**Trevor**  Class? How come you suddenly become a teacher?

上課？妳怎麼突然開始當起烘焙老師了呀？

**Zoe**  You know I usually make some **croissants** and bagels and give them to everyone. After they have some, everyone keeps asking if I could teach them. I happens to need to make more money, so I say yes to them and give them a class every Saturday.

你也知道我平常總是會拿一些牛角麵包和可頌分送給大家吃，她們一直吵著想學做法，剛好我也想多賺一些錢，所以就答應在每個周六為她們上一次課。

**Trevor**  I was worried about whether you just got yourself into more trouble. Since you **charge** them for tuition, I think that's fine with me. I **guess** you want to make more money for giving me finanãal **assistance** to my dream of traveling around the world, I feel I'm such a loser. I'm sorry.

我本來還擔心妳義務教她們只是多為自己找麻煩，不過既然有收學費，我也就不反對了。我猜妳想多賺錢是為了資助我環遊世界的旅費，我這麼沒用，真是對不起妳。

**Zoe**  Don't **reproach** yourself!  I'm doing this because I see you working so hard fulfilling your dream, I feel I have to keep up with you, make myself shine in the professional field that I love.

你別自責，我是看你那麼積極地在為自己的夢想努力，覺得自己也不能輸給你，我也要在自己鍾愛的領域有所發揮才行。

**Trevor**  If you really save up enough money by baking, don't **finance** me, use the money and come to Paris first.  I miss you so much.

如果妳真的靠烘焙存到錢了，不要資助我了，用那些錢先過來巴黎吧，我好想妳。

**Zoe**  Me too...I think I can also go tour around the bakeries in France and learn some delicate skills from the French bakers by then.

我也是…。到時候我就可以順便去逛法國的麵包店，學習法國麵包師父的巧思了。

## ☆ Some Words to Know

❶ baking  **n.** (U) 烘焙、烘烤
The oven for baking is toasting some delicious white bread.
烤爐裡面正烤著香噴噴的白吐司。

❷ gourmet  **a.** （食物）高品質的
The gourmet restaurant is highly recommended on the Internet.
這家超美味餐廳在網路上被大大的推薦。

❸ flour  **n.** (U) 麵粉
There was nothing she could do to blow the tennis balls out of the bowl filled with flour.
她怎麼樣也無法把乒乓球吹離開裝滿麵粉的碗。

**④ dough** n. (U) 生麵糰

Father is making a home cooking dough for the beef noodles.

爸爸正在揉麵準備做家鄉的牛肉麵。

**⑤ croissant** n. （法）新月型麵包

I like the freshly baked croissants the most from that bakery.

我最喜歡那家麵包店剛出爐的牛角麵包。

**⑥ charge** v. 索價、收費

That owner of the scooter store helped me pump the tires and didn't charge me.

那間機車行的老闆幫我為輪胎打氣，而且不跟我收費。

**⑦ guess** v. 猜測、推測

Can you guess the age of that young woman?

妳能猜出那位少婦今年幾歲嗎？

**⑧ assistance** n. (U) 援助、幫助

I've really appreciated for your assistance to this research project.

感謝您對於此研究計畫的援助。

**⑨ reproach** v. 責備、斥責

The father reproached the mother being so clumsy that she couldn't even hold a cup well.

父親責怪母親笨手笨腳地，連個杯子都端不好。

**⑩ finance** v. 提供資金給

The entrepreneur has financed the artist for years.

該企業家贊助這名藝術家好幾年了。

---

**30 秒會話教室**

Don't make self-accusation. 你不需要自責。Don't blame yourself. 不要責怪自己。以上兩句都是勸人的方法喔。

# 情境 13　我也是「禽」聖

 **Let's Talk in Love**

Working in the **municipal** zoo as a **zookeeper**, Jessica spends time with animals every day.　Being good looking and having a hot body, she is the best **description** of "being pretty inside out." In addition to the lovely animals, she is the most beautiful **focus**...

在市立動物園擔任管理員的 Jessica 每天都與動物們為伍，容貌姣好身材又火辣的她正是「人美心也美」的最佳寫照，除了可愛的動物們以外，她就是最美的焦點…

Ivan　What's the matter with you?　Why are you giggling while looking at the computer screen?

妳怎麼了？一直看著電腦螢幕傻笑？

Jessica　Come take a look, this is the email sent by the kids having a field trip to the zoo.　It's also attached with a few photos.

你過來看看，這是上個禮拜到動物園進行校外教學的孩子寄給我的 email，裡面還附著幾張照片。

Ivan　Are they all high school students? How do they get your email address?

這些不是高中生嗎？他們怎麼會有妳的 email？

Jessica　I gave it to them because they took so many pictures of me and they were going to send those pictures to me.

是我告訴他們的呀，因為他們幫我拍了好多張照片，說要寄給我。

| | | |
|---|---|---|
| Ivan | Didn't they come see the animals? How come they all took pictures of you?  The animals are just in **contrast** with you. | 他們不是去看動物的嗎？怎麼都拍起妳來了呀？動物們簡直就像妳的陪襯一樣。 |
| Jessica | Actually, I think they didn't do this on purpose!  Almost every day when I **feed** the animals in the cages, there are tourists taking pictures.  One reason might be it's fun to see it during the feeding time, and secondly...Gosh, am I being too shameless saying myself? | 其實他們也不是刻意的啦！幾乎每天我在籠子裡面餵食動物的時候都會有遊客順便拍照。一來可能是覺得剛好遇到餵食時間很新鮮，二來…唉唷，這個我自己講會不會太不要臉了？ |
| Ivan | I know what you mean without you saying it.  It must be because they have never seen such a beautiful zoo keeper like you!  I didn't expect even high school students would be so enchanted by you. | 妳不用說我也知道，一定是因為沒看過像妳這麼漂亮的動物園管理員！真沒想到妳的異性緣好到連高中生都被迷住。 |
| Jessica | See what this kid write in the email, "I've never seen such a hot gorgeous zookeeper who gently treats the animals and puts the needs of the animals in the first place..." I think they just wanted to take pictures while I interacted with the animals.  It's not like what you think! | 你看這個孩子 email 裡寫的，『我從沒看過這麼溫柔對待動物、把動物的需求擺在第一位，而且還長的超漂亮的動物管理員…』，我想他們只是在我跟動物互動時順手拍了下來，才不是你想的那樣！ |

Ivan   Who could've thought that you would be a **spokesperson** for animals who treated animals better to your own **species**?

當初在夜店認識妳的時候，誰想的到妳會是一位對待動物比對同類還好的動物發言人呢？

Jessica   Animals have feelings too, but they just can't speak.  As long as one day I am in the zoo, I'll do my best to protect them, take care for them until they die a natural **death**.

動物也有感情，只是不會說話而已，只要有我在動物園裡的一天，我就會盡全力保護牠們、照顧牠們直到終老。

## ⭐ Some Words to Know

**❶ municipal  a. 市立的、市的**
He decided to let the children go to the municipal high school more far away, rather than the neighboring private school.
他決定讓孩子去就讀較遠的市立中學，而非家附近的私立學校。

**❷ zookeeper  n. 動物園管理員**
The zookeeper is sweeping the area where the polar bears live.
動物管理員正在清掃北極熊住的區域。

**❸ description  n. (U) 形容、描述**
She is the best description of being a good teacher.
她是一位好老師的最佳寫照。

**❹ focus  n. 中心、 集中點、 重點**
The focus of the whole event is on that star couple who has publicized their breakup.
全場的焦點都在於那對鬧不合的銀色夫妻身上。

**❺ contrast** **n.** 對比、懸殊差別、反差

Her beautiful appearance with the deep voice became a great contrast.

她美麗的外表跟低沉的聲音成了極大的反差。

**❻ feed** **v.** 餵食、飼養

They feed the crocodile in the pond on some raw meat.

他們用生肉餵食池子裡的鱷魚。

**❼ interact** **vi.** 互動

That class couple never interacts in the classroom in class after they broke up, and the scene is very awkward.

那對分手後的班對在課堂上從不互動，場面非常尷尬。

**❽ spokesperson** **n.** 發言人

The spokesperson in the presidential hall organizes a press conference declaiming that the death of the vice president is completely misinformation.

總統府發言人開記者會聲明副總統身亡一事完全是訛傳。

**❾ species** **n.** 物種、種類

The giant pandas in China are an endangered species.

中國的大熊貓是瀕臨絕種的動物。

**❿ death** **n.** 死亡

The death of that religious spiritual leader has shocked the entire Western world.

那位宗教界精神領袖的死震驚了整個西方世界。

**30 秒會話教室**

They <u>feed</u> sheep <u>on grass</u>.（他們餵羊吃草。）I have a <u>large family to feed</u>.（我有一個大家庭要撫養。）用甚麼食料來餵養的介係詞是用 on 喔。

# 情境 14 來看我的畫展吧

 ## Let's Talk in Love

Helen is a novice **artist**. She has accumulated a lot of **engraving** and paintings and is preparing to open a solo exhibition for building **reputation** in the art world...

Helen 是一位初出茅廬的藝術家，她已累積了不少的版畫和油畫作品，正準備開一場個展，好在藝術界打響名聲⋯

Helen　Honey, can you help me move my paintings in the studio to the car? I am ready to take them to the **gallery**.

親愛的，你可以幫我把我的工作室裡的畫都搬上車嗎？我準備要把它們運到畫廊去囉。

Raymond　No problem. Isn't the exhibition started next week? How come we should move them over there now?

沒問題。不過展出時間不是下禮拜嗎？怎麼現在就要移動過去了？

Helen　It's because the theme of each **piece** of my paintings is not the same, even the **frames** are not the same size. I was worried bout not knowing how to display them on the scene, so I discussed with the gallery owner first.

因為我的每幅作品主題都不一樣，連畫框的大小也不盡相同，我正愁不知道現場該怎麼擺設呢！於是就找藝廊的老闆商量。

| | | |
|---|---|---|
| Raymond | He's willing to let you move the paintings to the scene first and look how it goes, right? | 他願意讓妳先搬到現場擺放看看，對不對？ |
| Helen | Yes! I really have to thank the owner who not only offers me the place, he also often says my work is a **masterpiece**. I feel so embarrassed hearing him say that. | 對呀！真的很感謝那位老闆，不但提供我場地，也經常稱讚我的作品是傑作，害我聽了都感到害臊了！ |
| Raymond | No need to feel embarrassed. You always insist on your aesthetics, which shows you're born to be an artist. The best proof of it is you can organize this exhibition. | 不用害臊呀，妳對美感很有堅持，是個天生的藝術家，妳這次能舉辦畫展就是最好的證明啦！ |
| Helen | Thank you for your support. Even though I have not found a buyer for my paintings, you never complain about me from engaging in this work without salary. | 謝謝你這麼支持我，即使我的畫還沒有找到買主，你也從不埋怨我從事這門沒有月薪的工作。 |
| Raymond | I know that this is your interest, rather than work to feed the family. As long as my income is steady, I'll continue to support your dream. Moreover, what a cool thing it is to host an exhibition. I want to go around showing off. | 因為我知道這是妳的興趣，而不是養家餬口的工作。只要我的收入還穩定，我就會繼續支持妳追夢的。再說，開畫展是多麼酷的一件事呀，我要到處去炫耀！ |

Helen　Oh, hold it first. I only hope that those **critics' comments** won't be too **harsh**, and also hope to get everyone's recognition.

呵呵，先別急，我現在只希望那些評論家的評語不要太過苛刻。還有希望能獲得大家的肯定。

Raymond　Everybody look at art from different perspectives, don't worry too much. Let's go move the paintings!

每個人欣賞藝術的眼光不同，妳就別擔心了，我們快去搬畫吧！

## ⭐ Some Words to Know

**❶ artist n. 藝術家、美術家、畫家**
The artist's work was not taken seriously during his lifetime. His work became famous after his death.
那位畫家生前的作品並不受到重視，是等他死後才開始有名氣。

**❷ engraving n. (U) 版畫、雕版印刷品**
The finished work of engraving is the opposite to the contents of the prints.
版畫的成品跟在雕刻時的內容是左右相反的。

**❸ reputation n. 名譽、名聲**
The reputation of that restaurant was ruined when the guest found a piece of nail in the meal.
客人在餐點裡吃到一片指甲，就毀了那間餐廳的名聲。

**❹ gallery n. 畫廊、美術館**
That gallery is renovated to a restaurant where still retains a deep sense of art in the interior.
那間畫廊重新改建成餐廳，內部仍舊保有濃濃的藝術氣息。

**❺ piece** n. 作品、曲、篇

I can recognize which piece of Mozart's work when he casually hum tune.

他隨口哼了一句，我就聽出來是莫札特的哪一首曲子了。

**❻ frame** n. 框架、框子

The fireplace at home is filled with a lot of frames, in which there are family photos.

家中的壁爐上擺滿了許多相框，裡面都是家人的照片。

**❼ masterpiece** n. 傑作、名作

That master's masterpiece has sold over hundreds of millions dollars.

那位大師的名作光是一幅就已經賣到上億。

**❽ critic** a. 評論家

In addition to writing, I also work as an amateur movie critic.

除了寫作，我平常還從事業餘的電影評論工作。

**❾ comment** n. 批評、意見

The teacher had no comments on her insights and directly asked her to sit down.

老師對她提出的見解沒有做出任何評論，直接示意她坐下。

**❿ harsh** n. 嚴厲的

The judges use very harsh reviews that make the contestants feel very wronged.

評審使用了非常嚴厲的評語，使參賽者覺得受了委屈。

## 30 秒會話教室

You're born to be an artist. 你天生就是要來當藝術家的。I was meant to do this. 我註定就是要吃這一行飯的。

# 好書報報

Best Publishing

## 要說出流利的英文，就是需要常常開口說英文!

國外打工兼旅遊很流行，如何找尋機會? 訣竅方法在這裡。

情境式基礎對話讓你快速上手，獨自出國打工，一點都不怕!

不同國家、領域要知道哪些common sense?!

出門在外，保險、健康的考量更要注意，各國制度大不同?!

貼心的職場補給站，全部告訴你!

作者：Claire Chang & Melanie Venecamp
定價：新台幣469元
規格：560頁 / 18K / 雙色印刷

## 心理學研究顯示，一個習慣的養成，至少必須重複21次!

全書內容規劃為30天的學習進度，讓讀者搭配進度表，
在一個月內，不知不覺中養成了英語學習的好習慣!

- ■圖解學習英文文法，三效合一!
  - →刺激大腦記憶 + 快速掌握學習大綱 + 快速「複習」
- ■英文文法學習元素一次到位：
  - →20個必懂觀念 30個必學句型 40個必閃陷阱
- ■流行有趣的英語不再只出現在會話書了!
  - →「那裡有正妹!」、「今天我們去看變形金剛3吧!」

作者：朱懿婷
定價：新台幣349元
規格：336頁 / 18K / 雙色印刷

## 用Mind Mapping來戰勝E-mail寫作

12大主題，各種情境的範例解說，
遇到各種問題都能輕鬆應對，迅速有效率!

情 ◎心智圖 + 寫作技巧錦囊
境 ◎單字、片語、實用例句
單 ◎英文範例 + 段落大意 + 中文翻譯
元 ◎換個對象寫寫看
介 ◎文法解析實用句型
紹 ◎心智圖動動腦 + 練習範例分享

作者：陳瑾珮
定價：新台幣349元
規格：320頁 / 18K / 雙色印刷

# 好書報報

Best Publishing

**好學易上手的 Hotel 英語會話**
Simply Learning Simply Best

旅館的客人有各行各業，也有為數不少來自不同國家，
因而操持著流利的旅館英語，是旅館人員不可或缺的利器，更是必備的工具！
本書內容精心安排 **6** 大主題 **30** 個情境 **120** 組超實用對話內容
☆以中英對照的方式呈現對話內容，閱讀更舒適！
☆精選好學易懂的key word：生字＋音標＋詞性，學習更札實！
Part I  Front Desk 櫃檯
Part II  Reservations 預約
Part III  Housekeeping Department 房務部
Part IV  Amenities 設備
Part V  Banquets 宴會
Part VI  Crisis Management 經營管理危機
作者：Claire Chang & Mark Venekamp
定價：新台幣469元
規格：504頁 / 18K / 雙色印刷 / MP3

**餐飲英語 easy 說**
Conversational English For Restaurant Workers

從不會說到說得跟老外一樣好，循序漸進做練習，職場英語一日千里！
身處餐飲英語職場環境，懂得用英語對話一一接招、讓英語交談字字精準！
老外服務生的餐飲致勝話術，國際化餐飲時代不可不學！

★**基礎應對**→訂位、帶位、包場、特殊節日訂位、公司行號預訂尾牙或酒會等大型活動
★**餐廳前場與後場管理**→擺設學問、服務生Must Know、主廚推薦、食物管理與內部清潔
★**人事管理**→客人生氣了、客人不滿意、遇到刁鑽的客人、部落客評論
120個餐廳工作情境 + 100%英語人士的對話用語！
擁有這一本，餐廳工作無往不利，即刻通向世界各地！

作者：Claire Chang & Mark Venekamp
定價：新台幣369元
規格：336頁 / 18K / 雙色印刷 / MP3

**航空英語會話 Live Show**
GET TO KNOW THE AIRLINE INDUSTRY

THE TOP & THE ONLY ONE

人氣「Steve飛行筆記」部落客小夫 大力推薦

這是第一本以航空業為背景，強調實務，從職員角度出發的航空英語會話工具書
從職員vs 同事、職員 vs 客戶兩大角度
　　呈現出100%原汁原味的航空職場情境
從前台到後台所發生的精采對話實錄
　　猶如身歷其境更能學以致用，達到全方位的學習目標

特別規劃：
★**職業補給站**→提供許多航空界的專業知識
★**英語實習Role-play**→以Q&A的方式，介紹各種可能面臨到的情況
像是免稅品服務該留意什麼、旅客出境的SOP、
違禁品的相關規定、迎賓服務的幾個步驟與重點、
飛機健檢大作戰有哪些...，為你的職場實力再加分。
作者：Claire Chang & Mark Venekamp
定價：新台幣369元
規格：352頁 / 18K / 雙色印刷 / MP3

Learn Smart! 017

# 跟著偶像劇的腳步學生活英語會話

作　　者／伍羚芝
英　　譯／倍斯特編輯部、吳悠嘉
封面設計／高鐘琪
內頁構成／菩薩蠻有限公司

---

發 行 人／周瑞德
企劃編輯／倍斯特編輯部
印　　製／世和印製企業有限公司
初　　版／2013 年 8 月
定　　價／新台幣 349 元

出　　版／倍斯特出版事業有限公司
電　　話／（02）2351-2007
傳　　真／（02）2351-0887
地　　址／100 台北市中正區福州街1號10 樓之 2
Ｅｍａｉｌ／best.books.service@gmail.com

總 經 銷／商流文化事業有限公司
地　　址／新北市中和區中正路752號7樓
電　　話／（02）2228-8841
傳　　真／（02）2228-6939

國家圖書館出版品預行編目(CIP)資料

跟著偶像劇的腳步學生活英語會話 / 伍羚芝 ；
　倍斯特編輯部, 吳悠嘉譯. — 初版. — 臺北
市：倍斯特, 2013. 08
　　面； 公分
　SBN 978-986-89739-1-6(平裝)

1. 英語 2. 會話

805.188　　　　　　　　　　102015319

Simply Learning, Simply Best!

Simply Learning, Simply Best!